Pr

"*Absolutely loved this book about healing, forgiveness, and that we all have secrets. Highly recommend to anyone over the age of 12. Comatose woman serves as confessor to friends and family and thereby comes to understand herself and their perspectives on situations from her past.*" - Emily C.

"*Twelve Hearings is about the choices for future. The title is also so apt because Emma finds her healing through hearing what her loved ones have to say. The book is a pleasure, again. It's a book about letting go of our past burdens and embracing what the future has to offer. It's about forgiveness, to ourselves and others. It's about how at the end of the day, we all need to go back home. As already said, it's a beautiful book about the value of family and grace.*" - Kabir

"*Twelve Hearings*" *is a unique and witty tale. I have read uncountable books in past few months and have not come across a storyline as powerful and unique as this one. The book is a long read but it will entertain the readers throughout the story. The wise talk between Emma's soul and the man in the garden, the confession of Emma's friends and family members are entertainer. The cover is eye catchy and relatable. The title is amusing. Story is fast paced and language is for voracious readers. Looking forward to read the next part which is yet to be released.*" - Pratibha M.

"*A very unique plot and heart-wrenching as well.*" - Farha K.

BOOK TWO

TWELVE

HEARINGS

A NOVEL

LAURA GAISIE

Also by Laura Gaisie

TWELVE HEARINGS

BOOK 2

Laura Gaisie

Purple Pearls
PUBLISHING

ISBN Paperback 978-1-7325269-3-8
ISBN Paperback 978-1-7325269-5-2
ISBN Ebook 978-1-7325269-4-5

Library of Congress Control # 2019912628

Purple Pearls Publishing

Purple Pearls
PUBLISHING

In loving memory of my mother-in-law

Noble Evelyn Gaisie

WEEK ONE

A WOMAN WITH a heavy southern voice whispers from behind the door.

"Miss San Romun, Miss San Romun," she says. "How long you planning to stay like this?"

When there's no response, she begins to hum; low at first then rising higher as I continue listening. On the other side of the door, I lie in a coma. When I turn the doorknob, I'll regain consciousness——but I'm not sure I want to live.

The day my Mercedes hit the wall, I wanted to die. Instead, I awoke on the other side of death, to a peculiar, playful light that led me into this hallway——the corridor——with majestic walls and a golden floor. My eyes scale the length of the pristine walls, and the spotless, solid door. I like that it's shut tight——no one enters, and no one leaves; except by turning the worn, wobbly doorknob, which I refuse. I make eye contact with the Gentleman who is leaning against the wall, waiting for my decision.

"You know I can't leave yet," I say, before looking away. "I need more time with her."

Rising from my seat, I peer out to the courtyard from the chair I had been napping in. My daughter Suniva was on my lap when I fell asleep, and now she is gone.

I was going to have a baby, my second to be exact, though no other living person knew this. Twelve Mondays was a goal I set while in my second trimester of pregnancy. It was a simple plan; attend a twelve-step class every Monday night, for three months, and get sober. On the fourth Monday, my plan fell apart.

Nothing made sense the morning of my accident. The news reporter gave an update on a tragic case; a small child, Suniva Venable had died from a common childhood illness. Now I would never be able to make amends. There was no time to call for a driver, that's why I drove. I needed someone to listen to a story I'd hidden since leaving Sebec Lake nine years ago. The fact that I had been drinking, and was a terrible driver never crossed my mind.

I didn't mean to hit the wall, the weather made it difficult for me to see; but there he was, my fiancé, standing in the rain. My best friend, Tamar, was in his face, and Victoria exchanged inflammatory words with her. After the altercation ended, he stayed with her—my enemy. I knew she wanted to destroy me, and I wasn't sure if I blamed her. In my inebriated state, it was hard to gauge the distance between them and my car.

I now realize that perhaps I may have overreacted. Orion could've gathered them together to discuss a surprise baby shower for me; a

2

plausible theory had Victoria not been there. From our first meeting at the age of five, she despised me, and I've grown to have the same feelings toward her.

When Victoria appeared at the same dance audition as me, seventeen years later, I knew a plan for revenge had been carefully crafted. The days and weeks after our happenstance encounter left me unnerved. Still, murder wasn't on my mind when I pressed down on the accelerator and lurched forward. I was a terrible driver, always had been.

The Gentleman with the kind eyes came to me at first like a vision after I hit the wall. Reaching out to me with an extended hand, He guided me to this door that opened, and then shut after I'm safely inside. I believe He is an angel, though He may be Jesus himself. Once I was safe inside, He left me standing in the Corridor.

To my delight, the beautiful girl who came to me after I was left alone is my first-born child, Suniva; though it was after the Gentleman returned that I learned of her identity. The last time I saw her was as a newborn baby. My friend, Shelly, stood holding her after our shady adoption deal in the middle of Central Park. I ran from them both, refusing to turn back. How could I leave her a second time?

I'm not sure how long it took for me to realize that as I now sit here in a beautiful garden at the farthest end of the Corridor, I also lie clinging to life in a hospital bed. The light that initially rose and fell before me turned out to be one of the multiple eye exams testing my responsiveness.

* * * * * *

For a moment I am present in my body. Though my eyes

3

are closed, I can feel the fluorescent lights from the hospital room warming my skin. I hear the surgeon talking, and other staff members surrounding me. Then I wonder if a forced attempt to awake will be of any use. Deciding against the effort, I rest instead.

* * * * * *

When I am asleep in the hospital bed, I resume my perpetual merriment with Suniva in the garden. Having been clothed in her immortal garments at the age of four, she keeps busy with hopping, skipping, and a game of tag. She enjoys running from one end of the garden to the other, as I had done many years ago on the front lawn of my childhood home. When we sit, her multifarious questions fill the air.

"Why is your hair long and mine is short?" she asks.

I think to tell her it is because she was four, and I am 26, but before I could answer.

"I'm lighter than you, why are you darker?" Her head turns upward with curiosity.

"Because my parents are Black and Cuban, and your father is European," I say.

"My eyes are lighter too, is that why?"

When I first saw her in the Corridor, I believed she had gray eyes like my Fathers were, but now in the sunlight, I see a mixture of light greenish-yellow flecks in her eyes. Suniva leans in to rest her head on my breast, that's when I notice my flattened stomach.

The Gentleman mentioned earlier that my second child had been delivered via cesarean section after the accident. For a moment, I

4

daydream about the color of my newborn's eyes, what features does she have?

"Your eyes are beautiful," I say, stroking Suniva's eyebrows, twirling a curly strand of her hair around my fingers. It's not long before she tugs at my arm, signaling for me to stand.

Running behind her, the wind is sweet, smelling of lavender and jasmine; reminding me of my father and Grandma Rose. They are here too, though they have already come and said their goodbyes. I imagine them standing far away and watching as I make peace with my past. After all, this is the reason for my layover beyond the wall. The Gentleman has already informed me—when I am ready to return, my respite will end.

Movement is best, it keeps me here longer in my celestial body; resting initiates teleportation to that uncompromising hospital bed. Soon as I'm standing, Suniva takes off in a sprint, her excited expression begging for a game of chase.

"Tag, you're it!" I laugh with her when I catch up.

After rounding the perimeter of the garden for the third time, Suniva tumbles to the ground in glee. Lying with our backs against the ground we blow kisses, imagining them like bubbles carried away in the wind. Reveling at the moment, I close my eyes.

The sound of my heart beating alerts me of my error. It was two seconds of resting, but a second is enough to initiate my return to the other side of the door.

*   *   *   *   *   *

Before my eyes can open, I am arrested again,

detained by this rigid hospital bed. Straining to listen, I can hear what sounds like aquatic voices somewhere beyond my eclipsed vision. Past being able to hear, there is no other sensation for me. No taste, sight, touch, or smell—it's just the darkness and my hearing. I try to raise an arm or kick either of my legs, but nothing moves. This is why I'd rather not be here. For me, this body is death. I must get back to the garden. Suniva needs me, and I need her.

Just as I'm about to lose my mind, a peculiar thing happens—I began to levitate. Not my physical body, that one remains immobile, but my soul rises. I am looking down on a woman with a puffy face and swollen shut eyes. There's an endotracheal tube in her mouth and bandaging about her head. Refusing to believe this woman is me, I look her over for distinguishing marks. Her stomach is flat, mine would be seven months pregnant.

Ah, yes, I remember—the Gentleman said my baby was delivered by cesarean section. This is me, the damage done by my own hands. And the ugly voice that once screamed has been silenced. Scanning the room, I hope for a glimpse of Orion holding our newborn baby. If not my fiancé, someone should be here.

Instead, there are machines, tubes, and other sterile gadgets strategically placed around the bed to sustain my life. In this room, there is a less formidable sized door than the one leading to the Corridor with the golden floor.

I want to see my baby, who is probably in the

neonatal intensive care unit. Looking back to the woman lying alone in her hospital bed, I decide to stay. Leaving my body poses many risks. I am her soul, and she is my portal. Without it, how will I find my way back to the garden, and to Suniva? If she were here with me, then I would be free to leave. We could play another game of chase to see who found our baby first.

As I contemplate my next move, a man dressed in dark pants and a white shirt enters my hospital room. Behind him are two others dressed in scrubs. I watch as they approach my body, murmuring words I don't understand. Then all of a sudden, the hospital bed uncoils its tentacles— it reaches out and pulls me forward. As soon as my soul reenters my body, the bed constricts me into its darkness again.

"Worst case scenario for this patient is she will never regain consciousness," says the man dressed in slacks.

I hear the pen of one, and the movement of the other, who I imagine goes about the room checking and adjusting the monitor and tubes. Between their discussion, I hear another voice—a woman praying.

"Father God, I believe she will recover and be in good health…" she says.

"Best outcome, she'll regain consciousness although there is a likelihood of severe permanent physical and cognitive limitations," says the physician. "Have her prepped for surgery first thing in the morning."

"She shall live and not die…" says the praying woman.

This is my friend Naomi's voice, though she hadn't been in the room. Somehow, I can hear her praying for my recovery. I try to ignore the medical prognosis pronounced over my body, but they continue talking as if I'm not in the room. The intubation tube will be removed in a day and replaced with a tracheostomy. Otherwise, my vitals were stable. The sound of the machine keeping time of my internal organs is a distraction from their conversation.

beep…beep… The machine cues in perfect pitch.

Lub-dub, lub-dub, lub-dub… My heartbeat follows in the key of C minor.

Beep…beep…Lub-dub, lub-dub, lub-dub…

The orchestra plays accomplice to the bed holding me captive.

"Wait until you see our baby, she's perfect."

Between the cadence, I hear Orion at my bedside. Then in a strained voice, he says, "Emma, you can't leave me now. What will I do without you?"

"The incision will be about here, which will be the least of her concerns should she pull through," says the surgeon.

Beep…beep…Lub-dub, lub-dub, lub-dub…

The rhythmic beat of my heart quickens along with the machine until Naomi's prayer breaks through the noise.

"I believe in your healing power!"

The machines go silent, and all conversations cease.

* * * * * *

The jasmine-scented air lets me know I'm no longer in the hospital bed. Opening my eyes, I'm relieved to see Suniva here. After making ripples in the pond, she flicks a few drops of water in my direction. When I reach for her, she crawls onto my lap.

"I want to tell you a story. It's about a woman who made a sacrifice out of love," I say.

Suniva makes no attempt to interrupt, so I continue.

"The woman I want to tell you about is me, and the sacrifice I made was for you. I didn't know it then, but I loved you very much. If I could change the past...well, a lot would be different now," I pause only for a quick breath. "I gave you to a friend who needed love in her life. Mommy-Shelly, do you remember her? Mommy-Shelly took care of you while I was trying to get better," I say and peer over the full head of curls resting against my breast.

"Mommy-Shelly will get better too, they won't hurt her," Suniva adds.

I want to ask if she knew where Shelly was, did she know she'd been arrested? I wait until Suniva's ready to speak. When the silence grows, I continue with my story.

"I left you with mommy-Shelly because it was quiet and safe there. I thought she'd teach you things I couldn't, like eating healthy and being free," I mumble.

"That's why the people took mommy-Shelly away, she made the medicine that got me sick," says Suniva.

A chill passes over me as she speaks. Suniva had come down with influenza, and with a lack of traditional medical care or vaccinations, had succumbed to untreated symptoms.

"I'm sorry I wasn't there for you, I won't leave again," I say, but stop short of promising because it's not in my power to do.

Whenever we rest in the garden, the hospital bed summons for me. Sometimes it's a voice, other times, sitting or lying in the grass causes my soul to drift back. Each time, I feel as though I'm leaving her all over again.

* * * * * *

One of the days when I am present in my body, the machines are quiet, but I still hear the faint 'lub-dub' echoes of my pulse. The air is vile here, not sweet like in the garden. I listen once again to another round of instructions about my care, and what medical science predicts my outcome will be. When I try to flinch, the hospital bed taunts my effort.

The medical professional postulates my aftercare; if or when I regain consciousness physical therapy is necessary. Some basic motor skills were of concern, like the ability to hold objects, standing or even walking. Life without being able to jog through Central Park, or dancing, would be unbearable for me.

I recall the days as a young girl in Castle Rock when fleeing from my first altercation with Victoria, I learned that movement plus speed equals distance. Running faster than I thought capable, the wind stripped away layers of fear and humiliation. Like a sheet left out on a clothesline during a storm, my troubles were carried away into a wind-funnel. This experience has taught me that no matter how fast—or how far I could run—the situation I'm trying to escape must be dealt with when my legs grow weary. I'll never run far enough away from the sex-trafficking ring in Breaux Bridge. Reba will always be my mother, and I will still have problems that demand some form of retribution.

If this bed of darkness emancipates me, I plan to forgive my mother for her part in my kidnapping. Now that I know more about her addiction, it's easier for me to forgive; especially after having my own struggles with alcohol abuse.

Sometimes we find ourselves in bad circumstances, other times we're the ones causing pain. Trapped in this hospital bed, my delusions about life are quickly crumbling away. Where guilt and shame once built a home, anger and rage left ruins. Now I must lay a new foundation built-up on hope.

* * * * * *

I have fallen asleep in the hospital bed, and when I awake, Suniva's bright eyes smile at me. She aligns a handful of lavender buds, the same way I used to count pinecones as a child.

"You'll remember this place after you've gone," she says.

"I'm not going anywhere, my little angel," I answer.

Lifting her into my arms, I reach into the pond with a free hand. After dipping my fingers in the water, I drizzle a few droplets over her head; observing how her curls glisten, then slicken from the weight of the moisture. Using my shirt, I wipe a wet spot from her temple. "This is what it feels like here," says Suniva. Then reaching her arms around my neck, she gives me a long, gentle squeeze. After the hug, she plants a kiss on the side of my face. "It feels like this, but all the time," she says.

"That feels nice, you must be happy here?" I ask.

She is smiling, then stretching her arms wide like the wings of a bird, or a butterfly she pretends to fly.

"I can play with you here until you get better. Then you can be happy too," she answers.

"I'm happy being here with you. We're together, and I can take care of you now."

But her response leaves me with another clue; my being here isn't a choice of life or death. Our encounters in the garden have more to do with repairing a fracture in my soul, created the night of my high school graduation. In an attempt to conceal the incident, I've managed to alienate the closest people in my life. Despite having thousands of people around me, living by myself in Manhattan is lonely. The only times I've felt free to open up is when talking to strangers on a park bench—I love talking to strangers. They're usually the ones that let me babble long enough to clear my mind.

At first, drinking and partying seemed to fill a void. But before I knew what was happening, I drank to numb my feelings, and to drown out the chaos in my head. These are the reasons—if I had to decide between living and dying—I'd choose to stay here in the garden. Suniva lays down in the grass and continues counting her lavender stems. I watch her until my eyelids grow heavy.

12

＊　　＊　　＊　　＊　　＊　　＊

When I awake, my wounded body constricts, as the darkness greets me in the hospital bed. The orchestra of my pulse and the machines have quieted; but the beeps continue, now sounding more like an annoying alarm clock.

DURING THE SECOND week of my hospitalization, something wonderful occurs; I feel a sensation on the tip of my left pointer finger. This miracle happens once, but it's enough to give me hope. Listening to footsteps at my bedside, I await another grim report from the attending physician.

"How about that, can you feel anything?" says Tamar.

Despite our recent troubles, hearing her voice is like achy feet soaking in a hot bath with Epsom salts. When my heartbeat quickens, I imagine her interest turning toward the electrocardiograph machine beside me.

"Tell me—my once dear friend—What were you doing with my fiancé on the day of my accident?"

But she's unable to provide an answer because my question is never spoken.

Tamar's voice is calm, not demanding, as was her usual demeanor. I suppose seeing my mangled body lying in a sterile hospital bed is unnerving. She approaches my bed several times, whispers her request, then walks away. After each round, she pokes or pinches my finger. I know this because each time she does it she says, "did you feel that poke?" or "can you feel this pinch?" I feel nothing past the first pinch to my fingertip.

"Wake up, Emma, don't make me snatch you up out of that bed," she demands, and I almost laugh. This is the Tamar I know. I'm sure she doesn't appreciate being ignored by my unconscious body. If I could answer her, my question would remain the same; *why were you arguing with Orion in the rain?*

"I want to tell you everything, but not like this," says Tamar. The sound of her short, quick breaths signaling her frustration. She takes a seat, then is up again, moving around the room.

"I'm no coward, what I have to say will wait until you're awake," she huffs.

For a moment, she is quiet, and then after some thought moves to the chair beside me and sits. There is nothing but silence upon silence; her calm matching the stillness of my body. When I think she's left the room, she blows a gust of wind from her mouth before speaking.

"The twins are doing well; in case you're wondering. Me and Beaumont are separated, but you would know that if you were more concerned with us than spending all that time with Naomi," she says.

Ah, yes! She has expressed her feelings about my new

friend before.

"I blame her for this confusion, filling your head with all that hocus pocus. Everything was fine before she stuck her self-righteous nose in other people's affairs," Tamar says. Her opinion is now bordering on jealousy and her argument getting old.

"Did you feel that?"

She is back at my side, poking or pinching but only she knows which of the two. When there is still no response from my body, her footsteps leave my hospital room.

"Don't go yet," I imagine myself calling out to stop her. *"What is it you need to tell me?"*

After she has gone, I turn my plea toward the dark contraption masquerading as a hospital bed. *Loose me, let me be!"* I demand.

Beep…beep…Lub-dub, lub-dub, lub-dub

The orchestra begins to soothe, or is it to distract me?

* * * * * *

I have fallen asleep, and when I awake, the Corridor returns like a recurrent dream. I run toward the Garden in search of Suniva, but it is the Gentleman who greets me this time. Gesturing to me with an outstretched hand, He leads me back to the door.

"Why would you make me go back there? It's so unkind," I *protest, following closely at his heels.*

"This is the only way, you must go through the process," He *explains while walking ahead of me. When we approach the door, His*

16

eyes guide me to the worn doorknob.

"No," *I shake my head, backing away.* "It's dark there, and I can't feel anything. My mouth doesn't speak, and my body won't move. It's that bed, it won't let me be," *I complain.*

"The point is to listen; you must hear what needs to be said," *He tells me.*

"At least help me out of that bed, let me see something. Even Ebenezer Scrooge was able to see, to feel…and move." *I debate with the Gentleman to no avail.*

"The Scrooge is a fictional character," *He laughs.*

"Well, I'm not really here, and I'm not really there. I'm not alive, and yet I'm not dead." *I tell Him.*

"Your heart is still beating; have you not been listening?" *He questions me.*

I nod, Yes. How could I not hear the concert of my body and the machines? They are like the slow rising horns and shimmering violins of the Blue Danube Waltz. Only my rendition differs from the classical piece, which was beautiful and lively; the version I'm left with is slightly off-key, never quite reaching its triumphant peak.

The Gentleman raises an arm toward the door. Shaking my head, I continue backing away. Forgetting He's able to hear my thoughts, I consider running away from the corridor. Before I can take another step, He touches the door, and the darkness of the hospital bed returns.

❉   ❉   ❉   ❉   ❉   ❉

"I don't care how long it takes, my niece will remain on every life-sustaining, life-giving machine known to man!" says my Uncle Eli.

He is the one who now controls the bag of money left behind from my grandmother, Rosemary St. Roman. He also stands to inherit what belongs to me from my Father's will. So, I am grateful to hear of his tenacity for my life.

"I want those machines on, if you can't take care of my niece, I'll move her somewhere else, but she will live!" He boldly defies the Surgeon, who pronounces another grim diagnosis over my body.

"Don't worry we will try—"

"TRY? Oh, you'll do more than that!"

"A-a-are, WE ARE providing the best of care. Please, Mr. St. Roman, you must calm down. Look, your niece is stable, it's really the best scenario we can hope for," the physician says and then pauses. "Her body must do the rest," he finishes after a moment of thought.

Listening to the exchange, I'm ashamed of my temper-tantrum in the corridor. Like me, my Uncle Eli has lost too many family members within a short period. Because of this, I know he'll break the entire St. Roman trust fund to keep me alive. I want to tell him that I'll be back shortly; just give me a little more time. If I could somehow tell him that his mother, and his brother, had come to me in the garden, it would bring him peace.

My father was first to greet me in the garden— comforting and stoic—reminding me to forgive; especially my Mother, because he knew the ugly details of my abduction.

18

Afterward, Grandma Rose had come to say goodbye, restating her charge: don't forget to pray. She was the one who challenged me to examine myself, and before leaving gives me 'the look' I know to mean; *I didn't raise you to be this way*. But I'm unable to tell my Uncle Eli any of this, having been betrayed by my defiant body and this menacing bed.

"Well, since you insist on staying in this bed, I guess I'll have to keep you company. I'm sure you won't mind," says Uncle Eli.

The chair squishes beneath his weight, and to everyone's relief, my uncle settles down.

"This gives me the perfect opportunity to fill you in on everything you've missed these last few years," he begins. "I told your parents, many times throughout the years; send Emma to me, I'll keep her during the summer months. But did they listen?" he huffs.

Uncle Eli grumbles on about how not having extended family has left me vulnerable during a time of grief. After he is through complaining, I learn that my cousins, his two children, were both doing well. His oldest, a son named Micah, has graduated from college with a Master's degree in engineering and is following in his father's career path.

The younger, a daughter named Amelia, was more of a challenge for him. It had all been planned out carefully, then discussed the day of her high school graduation. Obtain a similar degree, if not construction than business management or finance. Unbeknownst to her parents, at some point during the first semester, Amelia had switched her major. It was at her college graduation when she was handed her degree in Marine Biology, they realized she wanted no part of the family's land development and construction business.

"How are we doing in here, need anything?" a hospital staff interrupts Uncle Eli's confession.

When he grumbles his response, I hear the door close. To my surprise, he remains at my bedside throughout the night; sharing stories of Micah and Amelia's childhood. Occasionally questioning some of his parenting decisions, pondering the things he'd done well, regretting a few mistakes. But I remember three children.

"What happened to the other child?"

One minute he's talking, the next moment I can hear him snoring. Whenever he awakes, the story picks up where he left off. The third child, he later says, sadly drowned in the ocean near their beachfront home. Late in the night, during what I believe to be sleep-talk, Uncle Eli shares his vision of developing landmarks across the United States, for starters. But this is hard to accomplish, and he needs the entire family on board.

My uncle's internal operating system functions best at far and wide plateaus. As a result, his marriage bears the stretch marks from years of the forced vision. His wife, Miranda, has sacrificed her artistic dreams to oversee the company's bookkeeping. His son abandoned an athletic career to help his father. With Amelia's act of defiance, he fears mutiny is at hand.

"I thought this was what we all wanted as a family. We discussed this years ago; build our empire together—I don't know—somewhere along the way the plans have changed."

He goes on like this until morning, mixing grief with tales of family trips; sighing at times, questioning some decisions, laughing at cherished memories and other times he sobs.

"Good morning, Mr. St. Roman, would you like something to eat?" One of the hospital staff asks. He accepts the tray, but without taking a bite. He moves closer and whispers in my ear.

"I must go now, but I'll be back. Don't worry about a thing, your Uncle Eli will make sure you're well cared for," he assures me. I imagine he kisses my forehead and stares at my face for a response before leaving.

Uncle Eli's conversation has kept me from the garden that night. After he's gone, I realize how focusing on the present inhibits my journey to the corridor. Remaining in my body allows me to hear confessions of those visiting at my bedside. Providing an ear, I become the stranger on the park bench. It means less time with Suniva, but each day that passes, I find myself more present in body.

My aunt Miranda visits on another day, expressing remorse over missed opportunities to bond with me. She doesn't grumble, or complain, as my Uncle Eli had; her conversation is hopeful, but at times indecisive. She believes in my full recovery but is unsure if I'd want her at my bedside. In one sentence, she tells of painting portraits and starting a side business. In the next breath, she stresses the importance of staying focused on the family business. Aunt Miranda discloses that she has disappointed everyone, including Grandma Rose; who adored her other daughter-in-law, my mother, Reba.

"There are many reasons they connected so easily, I won't name the obvious, but Reba has a way of remaining the center of attention," she says.

It's an interesting view-point she presents; I'd always thought attention was the opposite of what my mother desired but considering her antics over the years, I can see how my aunt has drawn this conclusion.

On another day, Tamar visits again. This time, she is offering her home for my recovery.

"The kids will love having their auntie Emma around…" she pauses. "Your Dad wanted us to look out for each other…and it would be nice to have you around again. What do you think?" she says and when I fail to respond her heels echo across the linoleum as she turns and leaves the room.

Naomi sits at my bedside often. When she's not praying, she reads from the Bible. When she's not reading, she encourages me to rest and get well. During one of her visits, Uncle Eli storms the room, interrupting her prayer.

"Sorry—I didn't know, please forgive me," he begs, apologizing as if he'd somehow exposed her nakedness.

When he leaves, Naomi giggles at his obvious embarrassment. Orion often visits, confessing his love, disclosing insecurities about his future. I listen more intently when he speaks, to the point of eavesdropping. When he answers his cell phone, I strain to hear every word. A phone conversation between Orion and his mother reveals doubt over starting a law practice. His mom is supportive, telling him to follow his heart.

At another time, a mysterious visitor enters my room—twice. The first time I assume, it's Tamar; hoping to find me awake and then leaving disappointed. The next time, I think it's Naomi, offering silent prayers. But now I realize the footsteps are different; softer, almost gliding across the floor. This time the visitor doesn't leave after circling the room.

"I have to sneak in to see you." A female voice speaks. Her voice is raspy, and she has noisy breathing. When she coughs, I can hear the phlegm build-up in her chest.

"Mmm, do you mind if I eat this?"

Her voice is muffled as she takes bites from the food tray offered to my visitors.

"Would you believe this is the first decent meal I've had in weeks?" she says and coughs from shoving large amounts of food into her mouth. I imagine her quick bites as she watches the room door.

"I'm sure you wouldn't know anything about starving, or going days without eating, Princess Emma!" She all but snarls.

My enemy, Victoria, has come to gloat over my lifeless body. Anger flows from my ears throughout my limbs; a charge I thought for sure would spring me from this bed. I wait to see if my body responds to her presence; still no movement, the darkness remains.

"NO, you wouldn't know what it feels like to fight off those dreadful rats, or what it's like dodging two-legged creatures hiding in dark alleys." Her voice trembles before falling flat. Victoria and I hated one another, but as she speaks, I feel compassion for her.

"This city is cruel, it's a mystery how you've made a home in a place like this. It's filthy, cold, and run down... just like you are." She is whispering, but her hatred screams at me. "I only came here for revenge," she admits. In the silence, I hear her tears.

"When I leave here, I'll have to walk and hike back to Brooklyn. Do you see my shoes? Oops, silly me, you can't see. Sorry about that, but they're worn through, and my feet are blistered."

She shuffles around the room, wincing in pain. I can hear her murmuring about needing a break, some money, and a safe place to sleep—free of roaches and mice. Victoria has tried to survive in New York for three years, alone, stalking me mostly. Because she was barely eating, her emaciated body earned her a few modeling jobs. After mismanaging the money, and several complaints about her pay, the gigs ceased.

"They don't care that my belly touches my spine because

24

I'm starving," her voice screeches.

When she walks away from my bed, I listen to her movement as she opens and then closes cabinets and drawers. I hope the time is nearing for a vitals check, or someone to chase her misery from this room. A part of me feels responsible for her hardship. I remember the brief time during high school when we were at peace; before I betrayed her friendship, claiming her boyfriend as my own.

After her search, Victoria returns to my bedside. She tells me that when the soup kitchen isn't offering a free meal, she must pilfer through garbage bins behind restaurants for food; which wasn't easy to do considering most of the dumpsters were now locked.

"Ma'am, can I help you?" A man's voice asks.

"I'm fine," says Victoria, and then mumbles her goodbye.

When she leaves, I worry about her walking with worn shoes, and wonder where she's been sleeping? The intruder bumps around my bed, making sounds and clicks I'm unable to decipher. His presence annoys me, but somehow, I fall asleep.

*　*　*　*　*　*

Within the span of three full respirations, I am back in the Corridor. The Gentleman waits for me at the entryway to the garden.

"How do you expect me to get better listening to the woes of humanity?" I say.

Then he steps aside, allowing me entry to the garden. When He doesn't answer, I try a different approach. "At least let me stay here in the garden, with you and Suniva, until I'm well? I doubt the anger in that room is good for my recovery," I debate.

"Is anger the only thing you've heard in the room?" He asks.

No, I shake my head, because there's no use lying to Him. There are other things I've learned from listening. "I've learned that expectations are subjective, and some people express love by making sacrifices," I admit.

"Very good, you are beginning to understand."

"My surgeon doesn't expect a good outcome for me. When I recover..." I pause, afraid to repeat the prognosis.

"Your first question is, do you want to live?" He waits for my answer.

For all my uncertainties about staying in the garden, or returning to my body, I choose to live. "How long do you think it'll take for my body to heal," I ask after taking a moment to think.

"Your healing comes when you accept that what's done can't be changed, and what's to come is already written. Through listening, you'll gain insight; the hearing will bring you peace." He watches me, evaluating my comprehension.

I remember my Grandma Rose saying that no one could take the peace that was inside of me. Even Naomi had spoken of peace during difficult times. Now here was the Gentleman saying I could have peace if I listened.

I try contesting that my hearing wouldn't change the others. When He entertains the discussion, I'm grateful for the delay back to the

26

corridor. Though I detest the door, I know through this process the confusion in my mind is unraveling, like a ball of yarn; the hearings serve as thread, knitting and weaving me back together like a warm blanket.

I will miss Him when the time comes for me to leave this place for good.

"But I'll always be with you," He answers my unspoken words.

ORION SITS AT MY side, huffing and puffing every so often. Then he exhales before declaring, "It's been three weeks!" By now, I'm accustomed to my loved ones, and the hospital staff, announcing the duration of my condition whenever they enter the room.

"I was hoping to find you awake today. Our baby is perfect—sorry to break the news to you—she looks just like me," he teases.

"It's not just my opinion, the nurses think so too. Looks like you'll have to wake up to disagree."

As he speaks, I imagine his familiar scent—fresh soap, and citrus—I can almost see the indentation of his cheeks when he smiles.

"Did I ever tell you about my brother? Probably not, I don't usually talk about him, to anyone. My mom and pops say it's best not to talk about it…"

In his pause, I hear a stifled groan. Then my fiancé

begins telling the story of how he became an only child. His parents gave birth to two sons, Rigel and Orion while living as missionaries in Ghana.

"It's an Arabic word for leg or foot because he was born breech. Rigel is also one of the brightest stars in the constellation which I'm named after," he says proudly. Besides the memory of a field where his brother was laid to rest, Orion admits to having few memories left from his birthplace.

"I loved him... I miss not having a brother," he says. His tongue smacks against his clenched teeth. I listen to every word, as the Gentleman suggests; especially when Orion speaks. After his silence, Orion tells me he doesn't like how his parents never mention his brother's name. It's shameful to him how they've carried on as if he never existed.

I learn that Rigel and Orion were born eleven months apart, and were inseparable, up until his mysterious death. "The last time I saw him was on the morning of his tenth birthday...for some reason, he stayed home from school that day. When I came home, the neighbors were comforting my mom. At first, I thought they had come to celebrate his birthday," he explained. It didn't take him long to realize their wails were not celebratory, but tears from mourners.

"Either I was too young to understand, or no one bothered telling me, but whenever I'd ask, what happened to Rigel? There was an accident, that's all anyone would say." He smacks his lips again and then releases a long breath.

29

When he became overwhelmed with grief, Orion turned his attention to solving his brother's mysterious death. He had gathered all the facts and drawn his own conclusions, even though the adults had dismissed his claim. To this day he suspected foul play, but he couldn't say for sure.

After the funeral, his parents became preoccupied with their return to America, which took time considering proper papers had to be obtained for a child born in another country. When the family arrived in New York four years later, Orion was 13 years old. He was multilingual in the native language, Twi, and was fluent in French and English as well; causing him to speak with a rather unique accent.

The change in his diet from traditional African foods to American cuisine caused him significant weight loss, and by the time he entered the public system he was a scrawny kid, with an uncommon name, who spoke with an accent; making him an easy target for bullying.

His mother considered a legal name change, but not for the same reasons. One night he overheard his parent's discussion of her superstitions. She worried that a shaman from the village of his birthplace could use his name to locate them during a seance. His father reminded her that they were Christians and had no need to fear such an ineffectual practice.

"I'm glad my Father talked her out of the name change," says Orion.

When he stops speaking, I eagerly await sleep, hoping to

awake in the garden. I want to ask the Gentleman about Rigel's death, and what kind of practice could locate an individual across seas? Moments may have lapsed, or maybe hours, but sleep nor the door draws me away from the sounds of Orion resting at my bedside.

At some point, Orion begins to speak again. This time, he shares more of his mother's concern about ancient superstitions. During his adolescent years, her paranoia leads to an unofficial name-change, a byname, "Blessed by God."

"Orion, blessed by God, can you take out the trash?" She would say, or, "Orion, blessed by God, did you finish your homework?" Other times it was, "Orion, blessed by God, where have you been?" And when she was upset with him, "Orion, blessed by God, let me give you wisdom," as she paddled his backside. This continued until his high school graduation.

"Maybe she thought by then whatever curse the shaman tried to put on me was gone. I never questioned her," he says before preceeding to share and then shares that no one, up until this very day, had ever replaced Rigel as his best friend. The closest he'd come to having a connection with another person, outside of his parents, was with me. Maybe he is feeling sentimental because I have given birth to his first child, or it's his exhaustion speaking. I imagine myself reaching over to embrace him, but this forboding bed refuses to loosen its grip.

Beep, beep, beep…

31

In my delirium, I imagine the beeping to sound more like the heart monitor laughing. It's mocking the foolhardy idea that I could raise up at-will, defying my bruised body. "I started talking to Rigel on the plane leaving Ghana. My mom wouldn't like to hear this, she'd blame the village shaman. I don't think Pops would take it well either, but having Rigel to talk to has helped me through the toughest times of my life. He was the one I confided in before enrolling in law school, even before proposing marriage to you," Orion admits.

As I listen, I remember how busy his days had been. He worked full-time during the week, with a crazy commute from Harlem to North Jersey; law school several nights a week, and he volunteered at a community center on the weekend. He feeds the homeless on Sunday mornings before attending Church with his parents, and somehow, we manage to have a relationship.

"Even though it's his ten-year-old voice in my head, talking to Rigel soothes me. We talk man to man…if only face to face. In my dreams, he's still the same skinny kid with an elongated face and round eyes. I tried envisioning him as a man my age, but I can never see past his innocence." Orion's voice chokes, causing him to stop speaking.

I want to tell Orion about the corridor, and the Gentleman; of all the things I've learned during my rest while my body heals. How I was able to meet and speak with family members who have passed on. I didn't wish for him to be lying in this bed, but it would be helpful for Orion to have the same closure.

I have known my fiancé for five years, and this is the first I hear of his brokenness. He heard voices, like I had, except his were kind and comforting; not cruel and angry as mine had been. This was the reason he never complained about being over-worked; he needed to fill in a void—like I had tried—only his method was more productive than mine.

I want Orion to know about our similarities. He should know where the depths of loneliness could lead him. But how can one understand without being told? The same way I couldn't have known until the Gentleman exposed the hidden, dark places within me.

"Anyway, I'm rambling about things that don't make sense," he says.

When he stops speaking, this time, I pray for his peace. I don't like how hard he works. If Orion was tired before, he is about to experience exhaustion on a different level. Left alone to care for a newborn baby, I'm afraid will tip his overloaded scale.

Because he never asked, we never discussed our finances. I didn't see any point in offering needless information, but I realize now how important it is to have such discussions. I'll tell him of my trust fund when I regain consciousness, I make him a silent promise. I'm unsure how much time passes as I listen to Orion's breathing change from pressured, and then softer when he relaxes.

*   *   *   *   *   *

Finally, I'm standing in the corridor, looking down at the golden floor beneath me.

"Everyone is on a journey," the Gentleman says when I approach Him. "You mustn't interfere with their process. If you fix Orion's problems, it actually cripples his growth."

"What's wrong with being informed? If you could somehow tell the others—as you've told me—it would eliminate a lot of pain."

"It doesn't make sense, but then it makes perfect sense," He says. "Your life will impact someone else's; just like Orion, and even Victoria's life will."

I think to tell Him there's no way my story could help anyone, but I'm reminded of the survivors from my Grandmother's nonprofit organization; PAHST (Parents Against Human and Sex-Trafficking). I recall the women who stood before packed crowds to share their stories. It's plausible I've gained the strength to survive because somewhere deep within me, I hold their faces, and their stories, close to my heart.

"You've been here with me for quite some time," I say, rather than questioning His wisdom.

"Twenty-two days to be exact," He answers.

"That would be three weeks, have I been this way for three weeks?" I turn to face Him, my expression indicating profound astonishment. Then I walk to the oversized chair across from the door and take a seat. Inhaling the lavender-scented air centers me. Glancing at the worn doorknob makes me question how many others have passed this way before?

"I'm a little concerned about Orion taking care of our newborn baby alone, but I don't feel like I'm quite ready. Otherwise, there's really no need to rush back. A week in my body there is like one day here," I muse.

"I guess there isn't if you've considered all things. There is the matter of your baby, she'll need—"

"And what about my child here? Doesn't she need me as well?" Before he could correct me, I hold up a hand to stop him. He doesn't say aloud, but I hear His response—I am the one who needs Suniva.

"Your body is healing, as well as your mind. It has taken you this long, and some more days before you'll be well enough." And with His answer, I know at the right time, I will return to my body and leave the garden for good. But what happens to Suniva?

"She is here at your request - until you're able to accept what is, and the things that can't be undone," He says.

But when would I be able to let her go? Suniva will never know what it's like to have parents who love her. There won't be any birthday celebrations or friends to play with. No new memories, just the ones she has up until four years old. I wish for a way to make things right. The only thing I could give her was my time.

"I'll be ready after..." it seems foolish to say the words out loud.

"After you've spent a little more time with her," He finishes my sentence. The Gentleman understands me. I remember our first encounter, His words were, *"I want to help you."*

"I need more time." My eyes plead with Him.

"Time won't change things for her, but it will help with your healing. There's more living for you, a great work to be done," he advises.

35

"When you're ready, that is."

I find the idea that anything good coming from my life absurd. Me, the irresponsible heiress who single-handedly dishonored Rose Mary St. Roman's legacy? I have been mad at the world, and angry at life, for the cruel things that have happened to me. Once I grab hold of the doorknob, trauma awaits my return. For me, love and every good thing I've known is in the garden.

"And still there are people in life who will be greatly influenced by your story, and what you offer. You only need to keep on living."

"Tell me, please, what are these great things I'm going to do?" His compassion makes me want to believe for good in me. In my mind, I calculate the many ways to be of service using my financial inheritance.

"There's no dollar amount, or price tag, you can affix to your works," He says.

"Well, it would be nice to have a hint, I've made quite a mess back there." I nod toward the door and roll my eyes.

"You have an opportunity to impact someone's life every day," the Gentleman chuckles. "Sometimes all it takes is lending an ear."

"I heard Orion talking about his brother who he lost in Africa. I had no idea he was hurting like that. Why didn't he tell me this before? I would have listened," I try to convince myself. But no sooner had the words left my mouth, I knew they weren't the truth. The Gentleman says nothing, but the towering walls glare down at me. I understand the language of the Corridor; a stern reminder to watch my manners and mind my tone. Only truth can dwell behind these walls.

"Imagine how many others, like Orion, who are walking around with deep-rooted pain they can't understand. How do you feel now,

knowing you're not the only one with secrets in your past?" the Gentleman asks

"I feel less alone, more normal actually," I say. But the more I talk, my concern grows; when my understanding is full, I must leave this place.

"More money doesn't equal fewer problems, and less money doesn't equal more suffering. The human experience is a journey to love; in every face, whatever their race, with no regard to status or position," He says, then watches as I nod my head. I know He hears my concern about leaving.

"When you're ready, you will walk over to that door, and turn the doorknob."

When He points to the door, I look away, firs to the majestic walls, no help from it's scolding presence. Then down to the golden floor, it even appears that my reflection peers over to the worn doorknob.

EACH TIME I return to the Corridor, the choice is offered, "Are you
ready to turn the doorknob?" When I refuse, the voices of those at my
bedside pull me back into my body. This time it is the southern woman's
voice calling to me.

*   *   *   *   *   *

"Alright now, Miss San Romun, four weeks done gone
by and you still lying here like this."

I listen to the peculiar drawl of her tongue, and the odd
swishing movements of air as she walks.

"They gonna take you off that ventilator soon, no matter
how much your Uncle pitch a fit."

After her caution, she swishes around the room several
more times, humming as she goes about. When she leaves, a
tribe of physicians enter my room. They discuss concerns

with my ability to withstand additional procedures. Their main worry seems to be "raised intracranial pressure" and "irregular heart palpitations." As I listen, some of Uncle Eli's anxieties become my own; but the thought of having the beeping machine silenced over-rides my fear.

After the procedure is over, Uncle Eli, Orion, and Naomi stand at my bedside. My Uncle is quieter than usual, Orion is breathing heavier than normal, and Naomi whispers words I know to be prayers.

"Well, it's done. The rest is up to you, niece, I know you'll pull through this," says Uncle Eli.

"Me and the baby are still waiting for you, we have a wedding date, remember?" says Orion.

* * * * * *

I'm not exactly sure at what point the shift occurs, or what triggers my voyage, but within a heartbeat, I am back in the corridor. As I stand, staring at the door, the Gentleman's words return, "When you're ready, you'll turn the doorknob." Then, and only then, I will return to my body and end their suffering. I look down the corridor, back to the door, and without hesitation, I turn and walk to the garden.

"What do you think about our prayers?" I ask the Gentleman who appears to be waiting for me.

"I love them!" He answers. "But your question is, why do some prayers go unanswered?"

I nod, yes. "Like Naomi, praying at my bedside, her prayers won't bring me back. I'm not well, and you said so yourself, the choice is mine,"

I say and look back to the entryway, picturing the doorknob that awaits my final decision.

"That doorknob is worn down for a reason." He doesn't shuffle me back to the corridor yet. Instead, makes Himself comfortable by taking a seat on a bench.

"What purpose do her prayers serve?" I ask again.

"What purpose did your prayers serve when your father passed away, is your real question?" He says.

"Yes, and what if I decide to stay here? Naomi's prayers don't get answered."

This time, for the first time, I hear faint murmurs from the hospital room; Uncle Eli, Orion, and Naomi are praying at my bedside.

"One day, when you are mature and much older, you'll find your way back to this garden; but how do you think the people standing around your bedside will feel if you choose to stay now?" He asks.

"Orion will feel guilty, I'm sure. After all, the last time we saw each other was on the day I caught him with Victoria and Tamar. Naomi would be hurt, and my Uncle…"

"Oh Yes, Uncle Eli, he's certainly rattled the entire hospital over your care…but what of your mother?" He searches my face for a reaction.

"What has she to do with me?" I ask. "Reba would be glad to have me gone. With me around, she fears I'll finally speak up and tell everyone what she and her boyfriend did."

"Losing you this way would be devastating. Who knows what will become of her then," He says.

There's no point in saying how I feel because He already knows. I haven't seen my mother in nearly a decade. In fact, another ten years could pass between us, and I'd be okay with that. But knowing how it's hurt me to lose Suniva gives me some empathy for Reba.

"It wouldn't be easy for her," I admit. "She's already had enough bad breaks in life. When I think of it all, I don't know how she copes."

By the time we finish our talk, He extends a hand and walks with me to the corridor. At the door, I shake my head, No. He must be the one to lead me through. This way, I know my visits here can continue. Even though the time is drawing close to when I'll no longer be able to refuse.

* * * * * *

When I return to the dark, stillness of my hospital bed, there is no improvement. The room is silent, and for an extended period, there are no visitors. I sleep a lot, sometimes I remain in body, other times I'm in the garden.

Darkness here; in the garden, there are vivid hues of violet, red and orange—and Suniva's giggles as she plays with me. This whimsical state continues until someone enters my room, pulling me from the garden and back into my body.

With each return, hope grows within me to hear Reba's voice or her tears. She should be the one at my bedside, not as punishment, though it's what I initially think. I know as a young girl, she fled from a lifestyle that made the room in Breaux Bridge acceptable, and less frightful.

The Gentleman said Reba-Lynn had been born and raised in a brothel, but I want to hear the story from her mouth; what had she endured as a child? How had she felt after exposing me to the nightmare that was my birthright? I need her here, in the same way, I always had; desiring her presence, then despising her flaws. It was the game I'd been taught to play. We craved each other but then hated one another for our expectations.

"I feel bad for not being there for you that morning," says Naomi. "I saw your missed call but waited until my break to play your message. You said you needed to tell me about your daughter, the first one?" She pauses, leading me to think she expects that I will answer her now.

"When I heard your voice, I'll admit it scared me some. By the time I got to your apartment, there was no answer…I feel awful, I should've been there for you!" she says.

I'm sure the message caused her some concern, as did my condition now. Of course, she isn't to blame. It was my unhealthy reliance on her that produces this guilt. If I were able, I would tell Naomi that none of this was her fault. I was needy, and she always made herself available, except for the one time. When my Father passed away, she slept at my home—abandoning her own—to nurse me around the clock. Naomi knew I was having a nervous breakdown, and that was the reason she stayed with me.

How could I blame her for going to work and not answering my every phone call? She had done all that was humanly possible considering I hadn't told her the whole truth about my past. She didn't know about my battles with guilt and shame over leaving my first baby. To her knowledge,

I was carrying my first child. I must tell her the whole truth when I'm able. For now, she is left with hopes that I can hear her prayers for my recovery. Soon, Naomi, it shouldn't be much longer, though I still desire more time in the garden.

On another day, Tamar's voice draws my body back into the hospital bed.

"Do you remember the day we met?" She asks. "I didn't like you at first, the way you and your Dad threw money around. Well, I guess it was jealousy. And he…" she swallows hard before continuing.

"He was so attentive to your needs, wanted only the best for his princess," she exhales, and then says, "You don't know how good you've got it."

I know this is Tamar's truth. It has been the driving force behind our friendship throughout the years. Most people assume me to be a trust-fund brat; they only see the material; the fancy apartment, my couture wardrobe, and Mercedes. But I would trade it all to have my Dad back, or Grandma Rose, or even my dog, Biscuit.

"I thought you were a spoiled rich kid, and I was right, You are," she giggles.

Tamar continues, explaining how her jealousy stems from not being raised by her parents, who lost their parental rights when she was a toddler. She has since learned of her mother's whereabouts but is unsure of whether to reach out. Tamar describes her childhood in foster care as traumatic and negative in every way imaginable. There was no sexual assault to report, but she wonders if that kind of abuse would've been more tolerable.

"They whipped me for any reason, and every occasion, for years, in the first home they placed me in—up until the age of twelve. That's when I learned to throw a punch," she says, and the chair squishes when she sits.

When Tamar began fighting back, placement became a challenge. Foster parents complained of her violent nature and said she was combative.

"The day I left the last home, I did something I still don't regret to this very day. What I don't get is how could they not know it was me, I started that fire," she smacks her teeth and lets out a rather wicked chuckle. "I didn't know a house could burn that fast," she says.

Her next placement barely lasts a year. The home after that, even less; the third too short to count. By sixteen, Tamar decides to take off with a friend she'd met at school. While living with her friend's aunt, she is taught work ethics and the importance of saving money; and between them, they save enough for their own apartment and tuition for trade school.

"Compared to your fancy apartment, my place was a shack, but it was mine, and I worked hard to keep it. You don't know how hard I worked on closing that sale with you and your Dad. I drank at night to drown out your bratty whining and to calm my nerves. Then you called to invite me to celebrate with you. I don't know, you turned out to be alright," she admits.

44

"Do you remember when we found out our birthdays were on the same day?" When she laughs at the memory, I try to smile remembering how we partied for a week straight— every roof-top, night club or pub we could find was ours. We were called the Irish-twins.

"Remember when I forced you to cook gourmet meals with me on Friday nights? You didn't like it at first, but you must admit, gossip and drinks mix well with good food. Those were good days Emma, I miss those days," she says, and when she shifts in the chair this time I know it's to cover the sound of her sniffles.

"I couldn't tell you this before, but I'll tell you now; those times when I was on your case for drinking too much, was because I had got a DUI. Yep, wrecked my car one night after leaving a pub. I was embarrassed to say it before, but I've been in treatment ever since," she confesses.

Tamar says her reason for not sharing this with me sooner is because I was always going on about "what's her name? Nancy, or Nina." She couldn't recall the name, but says it was "the one who was making you go to all those church meetings." Tamar believes that I am brainwashed by Naomi.

"Sorry, I know how much you like her; I guess it wasn't such a bad thing, just another thing I'm jealous over. You were doing something without me, and I was having such a hard time. I owe you an apology. I'm waiting for you to wake up, so I can ask for your forgiveness—can you forgive me,

Emma?" she begs.

"When I started drinking again, I wanted you there with me, like old times. Then you were pregnant, and…well, that's something else we need to discuss," she mumbles.

"Please wake up, we can't end things like this, I wouldn't be able to stand myself."

This time, I hear her sobs before she stands.

"I have to go, I'll come again…" and when Tamar asks, "Who are you? Why are you always in the way?" My heart rate quickens, believing my Mother has finally come.

"I know her, we're friends from Colorado," Victoria says.

"Hmmm, why are you always lurking around?" Tamar asks. I pray my hospital bed is bolted to the floor because the last time these two faced off things went flying, and I crashed into a wall. I brace myself for what's to come.

"I can't do this here, I'll come back another time." Victoria's footsteps retreat but then stop abruptly.

"Why were you there? You keep getting in my way, and I don't like that," says Tamar.

"Remove yourself from the door, please, let me leave," Victoria pleads.

I hold my breath—if you can call them breaths—and wait for the sound of their scuffle. When one of them exhales, I relax.

"Okay, Orion was helping me with a lawsuit," says Victoria.

46

"Mm-hmm, so you were having an innocent meeting with your so-called attorney?" Tamar wasn't buying the story, and neither am I.

"That's what happens when you hire legal representation; and why were you there? Wait, are you both dating him, is that why you're so angry?" asks Victoria.

"No, she's my friend; but he and I do have unfinished— like you said before, this isn't the time or place," says Tamar, letting herself off the hook. I assume they've left the room, but there's another voice now.

"Hello ladies, am I interrupting?" says Naomi.

"Nope," Tamar answers.

"Not at all," says Victoria.

"No? Well, it seems like we have a problem here," another says. I know the voice, it sounds like my tough friend, Faith. And for those who don't remember, she makes it known. "Don't let me call my dude from the Bronx, he owes me a favor," she reminds Tamar, then informs Victoria.

"No need for threats," says Naomi. "But there's trouble in this room, and it's not coming from…" When the silence grows, I imagine their eyes falling on me.

"*Save your pity,*" I wish to tell them. I can finally say, *I'm okay.*

"Well, I got a switchblade in my pocket, in case anyone is wondering," says Faith. Tamar knows not to push; I wait to hear Victoria's response to her threat.

"I'm leaving," she says, without any objections from the

others.

"Tamar, let me have a quick word with you," says Faith. "See this lady right here, I'm real cool with her, and she also happens to be a really good friend of Emma's. So, when Naomi's here, you need to leave. Period!"

"Oh, so this is the one. You've got quite a following," says Tamar. There is nothing more said, until her heels smack against the floor at her retreat. The others sigh, but I know this won't be the last word from my friend.

THIS MORNING I dreamed of my twelve-step support group. I wonder if anyone misses me after having only attended three meetings. If circumstances had turned out as planned, today would have been my eighth class. I remember the faces of the others. There were at least twenty, all joined by the same goal; get sober and stay clean.

This group was nothing like the one Tamar urged me to attend a few years back. That first group was comprised of sobriety-bullies, positioning themselves as twelve-step gatekeepers. Of course, their self-appointed authority was fraudulent; people seek to do better when there's nothing left except change. It was a matter of one decision—many times over—until an internal switch signaled to act, get moving, and to evolve.

My new group consisted of younger, supportive members, who understood the need for help. We - yes, I include myself among them - lacked the tools that would bring us closer to our desired outcome. I wonder if any of them knows about my condition?

It's a shame Tamar and I haven't been honest with one another. We could've attended the meetings together and laughed about it afterward. Instead, she pretended I was the one with a problem, and she had the perfect life with her husband and children. After having attended the meeting she scheduled for me, I bolted from the group and ran into the first liquor store in sight; the end of that story leads me here to the hospital bed, fighting for my life.

Someone returns to my bedside; the chair squeaks, and then a cough. After a moment, the unidentified person stands and moves about my room. A toilet flushes and water is left running inside the sink. When the person gargles, I know this is someone who has slept beside me through the night. Their footsteps are light, too delicate to be Orion's; besides, he would whisper good morning before getting up. If this visitor were my uncle Eli he would make a routine phone call, first to check in at home, and then to his office. No, this was a female visitor. I can almost hear the sashay of her hips, the arch of her feet as she tip-toes across the floor.

She leaves the bathroom and then stands on the right side of my bed. Coughing and blowing her nose, she whimpers, maybe from pain or exhaustion. If this were Naomi, she has a terrible cold. My visitor leans in closer, her breathing whistling through mucus plugged nostrils. She is going to speak, but instead, a sudden fit of coughing causes her to back off and leave the room.

I want to believe Reba has finally shown up, but it wasn't my mother, it was Victoria. I could hear the inflection of her voice as she struggles to breathe. When her symptoms improve, I wait to see if she'll return, but she is gone.

Later in the day, I return from a short trip to the garden at the sound of someone entering my room.

"I didn't mean to wake you, Mr. Stone," a woman says in a melodic voice. "Would you like to come down and feed your baby?" she asks. Orion says yes, and then the weight of the cushion fills in as he stands. I wait to hear my baby's name, but no one ever says it; she's just, "our baby," or "your baby girl." I'm ready to see my newborn baby. I picture her small delicate face, like Suniva's, except with Orion's eyes and maybe my smile.

"She's adorable, looks just like you...and hardly cries at all. You couldn't have asked for a sweeter baby," says the nurse. Orion tells her how thankful he is for at least that; and then makes an inquiry to the day of discharge.

"I'm not the one to ask, but considering she was born preemie, could be several more weeks or months even. Best to speak with the Doc about that question."

Orion says he is looking forward to having his parents help, who have offered to convert his second bedroom into a nursery. His mother will be around to care for our newborn until they leave for vacation in Madrid.

"Who knows, maybe Emma will be better by then,"

Orion says.

"We can only hope, Mr. Stone, we can only hope," the woman finishes.

I imagine the day is sunny outside. Cherry blossoms have perfumed the air. People jog through central park, and others are strolling with their small children. The ones who are less active, or those who have heavy hearts and cloudy minds, rest on benches; it's a perfect autumn day.

I feel a warm sensation today, not in my body, more like my soul. If it were up to me, right then and there, I would lean against the bed railing, and plant the sweetest kiss on Orion's lips. I try to wiggle my toes, stretch an arm, or kick a leg; still, nothing within the darkness moves. I need to see him.

Maybe if I try to levitate again? No, that doesn't work; I've tried twice before, but that was a onetime occurrence. The Gentleman could explain how I was able to levitate; where is the corridor? It's at the door, and the door holds the answers. The door with the worn doorknob. I need to find the door; I must get back to the corridor.

Once I return to the garden, I will tell Suniva about her sister, who is a good baby, just like she was. We will come up with a name for the baby together because big sisters should be included. I suppose the Gentleman wouldn't want me thinking this way though.

"Except what is, and what can't be undone," is what He keeps telling me. Whether my body heals, and I recover, or I

get worse; either way, I'm exchanging one child for another. That's the way my mind views it.

"I wish you could see our baby. She looks—sorry—but she looks just like me," says Orion. He uses this tactic often. "She does have your nose though, and maybe your lips, but really she just looks like, well, she looks like a baby," he snickers.

"I must admit, she does have a lot of your features," says my uncle, Eli. "Yep, no denying that one even if you wanted to."

"I've never held a baby before, let alone change a diaper, how am I going to do this on my own?" Orion asks.

"Don't worry about that, we'll hire a nanny, just until Emma's better. You just tell me what you need son, and I'll make sure you have it," says my uncle. "In fact, let's make arrangements to meet at your place in the next day or two?"

I suspect he has no idea how my Uncle Eli is about to shake-up his world. Orion lives a modest lifestyle, never needing more than he has, at least not until he wanted to marry me. I know he wouldn't be impressed with my bank account, it's one of the reasons I never discussed money with him. He will try to resist any offer's for help, at first, but Uncle Eli will insist and probably end up telling him this was the lifestyle his niece deserves.

"No sir, I don't want to burden you. Me and the baby will survive on what I'm able to provide," Orion humbly declines my uncle's offer.

"I'm sure you can. Nevertheless, I'll see you in two days, and we'll get you squared away with the baby. I must get going now, excuse me," says Uncle Eli and then yells to another as he leaves. "Ma'am, I'd like to speak with the surgeon for a moment," and with that my uncle Eli exits the room.

"Something tells me I'm in for a ride with this dude. Emma, why didn't you tell me about your Uncle?" asks Orion. "I'm a humble man. I may not be able to buy you a house on prime property, but I can make sure you never go hungry, and we'll always have a roof over our heads," he says, chuckling nervously.

"One more thing…" Uncle Eli whispers as he reenters my hospital room. "I'll need your address."

"Oh, didn't I give it to you before?"

"No, you haven't, I'll need that. I've just had some things ordered."

And when he hears the address is in Harlem, my Uncle grunts, before asking how the neighborhood was? And, is it a good place to start a family?

"It's ok, there are lots of families in the neighborhood. It's a tight-knit community, and everybody knows one another, we look out for each other," Orion says proudly.

"Oh, well, that won't do. Emma and the baby will need a quiet place to live. Do you have a yard? She loves gardens," says my uncle.

"Really, that's funny because she doesn't have a garden at her—"

54

"Never mind that, we're talking about a family, son, a home. Her father wouldn't want it any other way, and my mother—Emma's Grandmother—she'd jump out of her grave if she knew her princess wasn't properly cared for. There's much work to be done, but luckily for you, I've taken some time off work to dedicate to my niece's care. See you on Thursday," he says, then leaves for the second time.

Orion is probably giving me a look. The one he uses when he's frustrated; eyebrows almost touching, nostrils flaring, but not where you can tell unless you knew him well enough to notice the change in facial expression.

"Now I understand why you haven't introduced me to your uncle before. It's going to be interesting dealing with him, but for you, and our baby's sake, I'll accept a little help. My mom says you're hanging out with God, so if you can hear me, pray for my patience," Orion says.

I love hearing Orion speak the most. Listening to him makes me want to leave the garden. Not only because of my obvious love for him; but he's so forthcoming this way. I still have questions, and conscious or not, I will have answers about that day…it was raining, and I was driving—I am such a terrible driver.

For now, neither Tamar nor Victoria poses any real threat; at least, not with my Uncle Eli on Orion's bumper. Once my uncle learns of his community involvement, I'm sure a lecture on monetizing his endeavors will follow. My uncle has years' experience on how to demolish an old vision and rebuild afresh. As a contractor and land development mogul, his company constructs various shopping malls, apartment complexes, and specializes in custom-built homes. When he sees Orion's living quarters, I'm sure he'll insist on making changes, starting with the address.

Uncle Eli is more aggressive than my Father was, who had been successful by way of diligence and patience. He knew what needed to be done and accomplished his goals quietly, like Grandpa. But Uncle Eli was like a military jet fighter—sharp, precise, and explosive—silent only when preparing for another strike.

I take note of how my uncle's tone softens when speaking to Orion. He's somewhat subdued; maybe this is his way of showing empathy or respect. Once or twice I overhear my uncle's thunderous commands in the hallway, but then when he finds Orion at my bedside, he is calmer.

A baby's cry pierces through the darkness, awakening a yearning in my womb, stimulating the orifices of my being. The baby relaxes after hearing Orion's voice. She suckles, exchanging air for gulps, as she drinks from what I believe to be a bottle in her mouth.

"When she settles, I want to tell you more about my brother," says Orion.

I AM BACK in the Corridor, inhaling the floral-scented air. Turning away from the door, I refrain from running to the garden. I must speak with the Gentleman about what is happening. It began with the sensation in my womb, now my nose tingles, and even though I'm not able to eat, I can smell the food left on the tray for my visitors.

Locating Suniva in the garden, I observe as she quietly stalks a small butterfly. Hopeful hands extend to wings that have landed on a lavender stalk. When she is close enough to touch it, the butterfly flutters out of reach. Turning in the direction of the winged creature, I catch a glimpse of the Gentleman sitting near the pond. His hands are clasped together, and when I approach, they open, revealing a vibrant purple-colored butterfly.

"I thought you would like this," he says. "They're almost extinct."

Extending my hands, the butterfly lands within my cupped

palms. Together, Suniva and I, make careful inspection of the creased, iridescent purple and bluish wings. I shush her when she squeals from excitement.

"It's the Purple Emperor. They have a rather unique way of behaving. Other species feed on flowers, but these prefer honeydew from aphids and tree sap," the Gentleman says.

"His voice is sad, I don't think I can stand it much longer," I interject, turning my head away hoping to shield Him from the sorrow in my eyes. When He asks, "Is it time?" I pinch my lips together, afraid of what they may speak next.

"Well, then if you're not ready, patience is what you need. What you're hearing, and feeling, will all come together after a while. Like this butterfly, I'm sure you know about the butterfly's life cycle?" He asks.

I nod my head, "the butterfly is a caterpillar at first."

"Larvae," He adds.

"Then it turns itself into a cocoon."

"In this case the chrysalis," He corrects me.

"After a while, the larvae grow into a butterfly," I mumble.

"The butterfly emerges, but first," his voice raises when he holds up a finger. "It takes some time to harden its wings."

His eyes are twinkling, as they had when we discussed sleeping, and dream cycles; He seems to adore long talks and discussing the intricacies of life.

"I hear their secrets, their confessions. Is this normal for someone in my condition?" Not waiting for a response, I continue. "I'm causing them all so much pain." When my shoulders hunch, allowing my

head to hang low, the Gentleman reaches for my chin and lifts it toward the sky. Though His lips don't move, I hear Him saying, "trust the process."

First, my tears appear as moisture, like condensation on a coffee mug. My thoughts are jumbled, making it difficult for me to speak. Then as my mind clears, it empties my troubles that spill down my cheeks. Most of my tears fall onto my blouse, absorbed by the fabric. A few roll and splatter onto the butterfly still perched in my interwoven hands. Each time a teardrop lands on the Purple Emperor's wings, it flutters and then expands; unnoticeable at first, but hard to ignore when the wingspan doubles in size. Blinking away my remaining tears, I watch as the Emperor stretches out it's stronger, hardened wings and prepares to take flight.

"How—how did you do that?" I ask the Gentleman.

He retrieves the Purple Emperor from me and sets it in Suniva's waiting hands. And when He proceeds to the entryway, knowing the routine, I follow without complaint. Before stepping inside, I stop to look back at Suniva, who continues admiring the Emperor's beauty.

As the Gentleman and I walk through the corridor, the gleaming golden floor winks with approval, the majestic walls nod their support. At the door, He waits to see if I'll take hold of the doorknob, but when I don't, the Gentleman touches the door, sending me back into my body.

* * * * * * *

"The year we met, my brother's voice had already started fading," says Orion. It seems like hours have passed while I was in the garden, but now I know it's only been seconds. He clears his throat before continuing.

"By that time, he only spoke when something was urgent or life-threatening, like a warning. He rarely speaks these days, that's why I started to seek a higher power."

Orion mutters some words, I believe something about getting baptized and mentions being angry. He needed Rigel, the one person who knew him best, to listen and give him advice. He remarks on the changes in my life, and how his parents always preached about having a relationship with God, so he gave it a shot.

"The morning of your accident, I heard two voices speaking to me."

The first was Rigel's, during his 4 am workout, imploring him to skip work that day. "Naw man, there's too much to do," he remembers saying. It was a Monday, and missing work on a Monday would throw the balance off for the rest of his week. When the other voice spoke, it came with instructions. *"Work from home today, avoid Tamar's phone call."*

"At the time, it made no sense, and it felt like I was on the verge of a mental breakdown. I was hearing voices and talking to my reflection in mirrors." He scoots the chair forward and leans in closer. Maybe it was my imagination, but I felt his lips press against my cheek.

"I wanted to tell you about Tamar long before this… but there's no other way to say it except that I was a coward. You didn't want to hear it, and she was so angry. I should have told you anyway, but I didn't," he says.

I recall his attempt to tell me about an "encounter" with someone I knew. Now I wonder how far that encounter had gone?

"Tamar is incapable of love or loyalty, she's not your friend. Snakes travel alone, live in the dirt, waiting to strike at your heel," he mutters.

"It was my first time in the office, so feeling a little uneasy, I took my clipboard and pen out into the hallway. I waited for Rigel's voice. I asked him, 'what am I doing, is it really coming to this?' But he didn't answer me, so I was left to my own reasoning." Orion breathes long and hard, then takes a few more breaths before continuing.

"It meant father.ng children I'd never meet. I wasn't sure if I could go through with it, but what I did know was every dime I had went into tuition, law books and the travel back and forth from Harlem to New Jersey. Cash was tight, and I refused to ask my parents for help."

This is the story of how Orion became entangled with my best friend. He had completed the application to become a sperm donor, but while standing in the hallway, convinced himself he wouldn't be okay with fathering children he'd never meet. After making the decision, the elevator door opened and out stepped Tamar. She wore round, dark shades, with a brimmed hat, but Orion knew it was her. She had that familiar, confident walk - upright and proud. Tamar hadn't seen him, so he turned his back, and pretended to stare out a window. He almost got away unnoticed, until she glanced over her shoulder, just before entering the clinic. Orion tried to act as if he hadn't recognized her, but Tamar couldn't refuse her curiosity.

"Orion, what are you doing here?" she wanted to know. And when he waved hello and said, "work-related matter." She nodded, then headed in his direction.

He had hoped Tamar would settle for a polite greeting and then continue about her business, but she came closer, asking, "what are you really doing here?" He was shocked at her boldness, but I wasn't. Orion didn't ask her the same question, though he wanted to. Instead, he inquired about her husband, and as he does notices the way she averted eye contact.

Knowing her as I did, I knew neither of them made it out of that hallway until he gave up the information she wanted. Tamar knew she was an attractive woman. When she smiled, her veneers cast a sheen on her smooth, dark skin. If she had cornered him with that smile, it was a miracle I still have my fiancé.

This was when she looked Orion in the eyes while disclosing that her husband was unable to father children. In the silence, he contemplated her dilemma and his own predicament. When he asked, "where is your husband," she rolled her eyes, before telling him that no one, not even me - her best friend - knew about her situation.

"That was my third mistake, my financial problems, the clinic, and then running into Tamar," says Orion.

He agreed to keep silent, binding the two of them with a secret covenant. After their agreement, a nursing assistant stuck her head into the hallway and wanted to know if he had completed his paperwork. Tamar was confused, only for a second, and then he saw something different in her eyes, like a light switch turned on. He told the nurse he changed his mind, and excusing himself from Tamar, left the clinic.

Later in the week, after the encounter was long forgotten, he received a phone call from a private caller; it was Tamar. When asked how she had obtained his phone number, she explained having gone through my cell phone as I meal prepped our dinner—it was probably the penne pasta. She always brought me bad news with a penne pasta recipe, but I can't count back to the exact day. Tamar had free access to my home, so it was nothing for her to answer my phone calls.

"I know what you were doing there," Tamar told him straight out. Orion decided there was no point in lying to her. Besides he was keeping her secret, so she had to keep his. "I thought about becoming a sperm donor but changed my mind," he admitted. To which she said, "I'll pay you double."

Orion claims he told her it wasn't a good idea; the point of sperm donation was to ensure anonymity. But Tamar wanted to discuss her offer further, and when he agreed to hear her out, she insisted on a face-to-face meeting.

"If only Rigel had spoken to me that day, but like I mentioned earlier, he was fading away," Orion admitted.

They met on a Wednesday, across the street from his

office. When Orion arrived, Tamar was already seated, and had ordered their drinks; maybe she knew it would take more than a conversation to persuade him. She spoke while Orion sipped from his glass. Expecting the dark drink to be cola, he took a gulp. When he asked what it was, she told him, Brandy, causing him to spit the bitter substance back into the cup.

Orion never drank alcohol, so it's plausible that he would push the unfinished glass away and ask the waiter to bring a cup of water. When she apologized for assuming, he could no longer conceal his annoyance. That's when he asked, "Why me, why not an anonymous donor?"

Tamar launched into a detailed account of how she discovered her husband's infertility while eavesdropping on a phone call. He had no intention of telling her about his condition, which she viewed as a betrayal. This was why she had to take matters into her own hands; and if he couldn't tell her about his problem, she wouldn't tell him how they got pregnant. What did her problem have to do with Orion? "We can help each other," she said.

Tamar had done the research and figured out the clinic would pay $1,000 for the specimen; she offered him $5,000. Despite her attractiveness, there were no sparks between them. Tamar warned their transaction was business only. She was paying for a service, and then he'd be off the hook.

"I have to be honest; I did the math quickly and thought about her offer...the money. I needed extra cash, but I knew it meant shaking hands with the devil," says Orion.

"Did you think about me at any time during that meeting?"
I want to ask.

Curse this bed that refuses to release its grip on me. Then again, thank God for keeping me from my rage. This was the safest way for me to have heard his confession. Orion, and Tamar, should be grateful for my restraints.

Orion says they discussed his concerns with accepting her proposal. First, it meant betraying the woman he loved, especially since she was swearing him to secrecy. He preferred that I knew about her offer, and maybe I would be okay with him being a donor, but I wasn't buying his story.

Then there was her husband to consider, who he was sure wouldn't want his children fathered by a friend or someone he'd see often. Finally, Orion never turned in his application and wasn't sure he wanted to.

I wish for the garden. Instead, I'm trapped in this dark pit, hearing confessions the Gentleman said would aid in my recovery. And now, if things aren't bad enough, my body begins to play it's 'lub-dub' concerto. Searching in the darkness, I wait for the door, hoping for the Corridor, but it doesn't appear. Orion continues to speak.

"It was a foolish decision, nothing good came out of that meeting. I had so much guilt, by Sunday morning, I went to church and threw myself on the altar. My Pops didn't know what to think, I couldn't tell him what was wrong."

And for all his guilt, he still goes through with a

scheduled appointment at the clinic two weeks later. He would say it was due to Tamar's persistence, but I know that's not entirely the truth. Tamar instructed the staff that Orion's donation was hers, and refused all other protocols; three hours later, she handed him an envelope with $5,000 cash.

I wish Orion would stop talking long enough for me to process this information. My fiancé is the father of my best friends' twins? That would make our children blood relatives, half-siblings. If I had heard this news before, I would have died. This was the reason they argued the morning of my accident; but something is missing, Tamar's side of the story.

I AM IN the corridor, reasoning with myself and hoping to persuade the Gentleman who sits at my side.

"...seven weeks now, and if I'm here another five weeks, it'll count towards my sobriety goal," I say.

"You're doing well, soon you'll be ready to return." He casts a long gaze at me.

"What's the rush," I say, shrugging my shoulders.

By now, it makes no difference to me when I return. In fact, my Uncle could do what he wished with my possessions and the money. As the words leave my lips, I hear the familiar lub-dub cadence and feel the gravitational pull toward my body.

＊　　＊　　＊　　＊　　＊　　＊

With another beep, the familiar *lub-dub, lub-dub* rhythm follows; my eyes go dark, and my limbs stiffen as I reenter my body.

"I just came from seeing your baby, oh how precious she is," says Naomi.

I'm thankful to hear her voice because it means this time I will listen to praying, not another upsetting confession. She offers to help Orion with childcare on weekends, so he can meet his community center obligations. I smile at the idea of the two of them spending time together. Naomi was serious about her Christian belief, and anyone fortunate enough to have a discussion with her knew they had encountered a woman with great faith. Knowing Orion had some curiosity about Naomi's beliefs - as I had when my world spiraled out of control - he could use this as an opportunity to answer his own questions.

I admire her conviction and even tried to emulate her behavior when we first met. What did she have that made the difference between us? Better yet, what had Naomi experienced in life that resulted in this deep-rooted reservoir of faith? I can only hope that my time in the garden, and with the Gentleman, will leave me with a mere portion of what Naomi possessed.

I look forward to the day when I can tell her about the journey I make as she and the other's wait at my bedside.

"I...I've been meaning to speak with you about something," she says, her voice low and hesitant. "Do you know any of Emma's friends, well besides me?" she asks.

"Mm-hmm," says Orion.

"Well, it's just that…I'm the last to judge another person, but I get a bad feeling around one of her friends. I know they like to party, I even went with her once—"

"You, you went with her?"

"It's not what you think, I went as support. It was when she wanted to change, live a more righteous life. She asked for help, so of course, I went. Besides, I've been in worse places than that," she confesses.

He was quiet while she spoke. I sensed who her concerns were about. I'm guessing Orion had a hunch as well.

"My point is, the women I met that night were mostly harmless," she went on. "They seemed to just want to have a good time. It was sort of a rough crowd, but mostly of their own opinion. But there is one friend I'm leery of…"

"That would be Tamar," he says before she finishes, "they're as close as sisters.—the first true friend Emma's ever had in life. They met during her early days here in New York, and I'd have to say, they've been through a lot together."

"Yes, I'm aware of their history, but I get this terrible vibe when she's around. Not because she's deliberately trying to intimidate me, I'm used to that sort of behavior. There's something I see when I look into her eyes like she doesn't have good intentions."

"I will say this, she's self-centered but harmless. Tamar sees something she wants and plays her whole hand to get it," he exhales.

"Do you think she means Emma well? Sorry, I must sound like I'm over-protective—"

"No, don't be sorry. I'm sure Emma appreciates your concern. Tamar is harmless. She just has a high threshold for survival. I was thinking, maybe you can speak to her? You were a big help to Emma. I know she cares a great deal for her," he says. But Orion is misinformed about my desire. Even before their betrayal, my friendship with Tamar was beyond repair.

"From our brief encounters, she doesn't seem to welcome advice or help. If it were left up to me, I'd have nothing to do with that woman," Naomi admits.

"But doesn't the Christian faith encourage us not to give up on people?" he asks.

I'm sure Naomi gave a response. Within the pause, I listen to her concern. Naomi knows my friendship with Tamar has become toxic. I want to tell Orion that her concerns are valid. Naomi changes the subject, saying she's not sure what to do about Tamar, but what she knows for sure is that I will wake up and hold my newborn daughter, any day now.

"What's my baby's name?" I ask as they are saying their goodbyes. Hoping that my question has somehow pierced through the barrier that holds me bound and mute. I listen for an answer from the footsteps that retreat and leave my room. Out of frustration, I scream into the dark abyss

70

surrounding me.

"What's her name? Please, tell me my baby's name?"

No one here can hear my voice. I am crying until the silence within me sounds like a horn, reverberating off walls down a long dark hallway. Then the machines at my bedside begin to beep, after which the pulse from my heartbeat chimes in on key. The noise surrounding me blends into perfect harmony with the sounds within me; brass, percussion, and stringed instruments playing together in concert. I fall asleep to the orchestra.

* * * * * *

I'm awake, standing in the corridor. This time I run without restraint, past the towering walls, and across the golden floor. I don't stop until I find my daughter.

"Suniva! I'm so happy to see you," I say, holding her small frame tight against my breast.

"Have you seen her yet?" she asks, her brilliant hazel eyes smile at me.

Reaching out to her, I lift her small body onto my lap and sit on the same bench as Grandma Rose, and I had on the first day of my visit to the garden. Sometimes we sit for innumerable hours, always until I fall asleep or the Gentleman appears with instructions for my return to the door. These are the moments Suniva chooses to ask questions about my life. Other times, we sit like this, cuddling and holding one another.

"What should we name your sister?" I ask.

"Hmmm, how about butterfly?" she giggles.

"I'm not sure that name will work…something for a little girl, like the beautiful name you have." I laugh at the idea.

"Okay, how about my name? We can share it," she beams as her chubby bare-feet sway back and forth. I want to tell her that there will never be another Suniva, but seeing her this way, carefree in a natural state reminds me of Shelly.

I remember the day Shelly found me alongside the roadway as I made my escape from captivity. Her bare feet galloped on the pavement before she guided me to her car and handed me her water bottle. My heart ached for her now. This wasn't the outcome either of us hoped for. She believed the universe had bought us together; me, her, and our gift from the sun, Suniva.

Like myself, Shelly had endured more pain than good in life. After our meeting, it became her self-proclaimed mission to protect us from "the takers." Usually men, in her opinion, who preyed on the kindness of humanity and used it as a weapon of destruction. For about a month or so, we were happy together in Sebec Lake—before my pregnancy was exposed.

"Do you remember your mommy?" I ask.

"Yes, you play with me and tell me stories," Suniva offers.

"Yes, I do. How about your other mommy, Shelly?" I tilt her head slightly so I can see her eyes.

"Oooh, my funny mommy? She liked to dance at night, outside by the lake. She makes up lots of games for us to play," she grins.

As I wait for her to reveal more of their time together, I hope she isn't able to hear the thumping of my heart, which quickens in my silence. As before when the thought crosses my mind, I'm unable to muster the courage to ask the question. Suniva adjusts in my lap and makes herself comfortable for a nap.

"You can give her my name. That way when you call us, you won't know which one you're talking to, but you'll always be talking to the both of us," says Suniva.

How clever she is, I think. Beautiful and clever. She is my pride and joy.

"I'd like you both to have separate names so that way I'll always be able to tell you apart," I say while stroking her hair.

The sound of my heart beating lulls us both to sleep.

* * * * * *

"I want you to know I'm taking good care of your baby," says my Uncle Eli.

I awake back inside my body in the hospital bed.

"And I was able to persuade your fiancé into making a few changes I'm sure you'll be pleased with," he continues. Keeping good with his promise, Uncle Eli convinces Orion to move into a larger home suitable for the three of us, and to my surprise, a business venture between the two of them.

That week my uncle and fiancé meet with investors eager for community projects aimed at providing resources to at-risk youth. Together they draw up plans to build a new community center on the south side of Harlem. The facility will feature a program to strengthen employable skills and mentorship opportunities. A dance studio for those

73

interested, and a nutritionist. There will be a counselor on staff along with reading, and math tutors, in addition to other academic assistance. The food pantry, basketball court, and weight-training room are Orion's contribution.

Their plan is to build on a full-length city block, a three-level structure that will have metal detectors at each entrance, and security cameras at vulnerable spots throughout the building. The exciting news for my Uncle Eli is the number of interested investors, making it possible to break ground on a second facility in North Jersey, not far from the five-bedroom house that is to be our new home.

It's no surprise to me when Orion mentions the amount of time needed to invest in this project, but his sudden change in business is curious. With a little persuasion, he abandons his dream of a law career for my Uncle Eli's proposition. Orion is a hard-worker, my Uncle is a visionary, so combined the colloboration makes sense.

Sometime later, Orion is back at my side with more details of his encounter with Tamar. The plan was to mail her a check, but she insisted on a meeting. Even after repaying Tamar I can tell he is bogged down with stress and he often sighs when mentioning her name.

"I told her it would have to be at an open place, with lots of witnesses," he continues, "and when I gave her the money, the only thing she wanted to know was, why? Why did I betray her this way?" He sighs, and then says, "so I told her, it's because I love Emma too much. It would kill her."

As I listen to his confession I try my hardest to understand why he would return the money he obviously has earned.

THE DARKNESS GREETS me once again as the bed tightens its firm grip around my stiff body. Although my reception is chilly, a warmth from the room increases, inviting me to rest within the black edges of mortality. Someone is here in the room with me, though they're silent at first, I can hear the bend in the quiet as it wraps itself around my visitor's respirations.

"It's going on eight weeks, and I've been coming in here cleaning and checking to see if you're comfortable. Everybody's worried, don't you think it's about time you wake up now?" the southern woman whispers so no one else can hear.

She comes to my hospital room every week or so, always on a Sunday. I know this because she announces each time how good the morning service was.

"I just can't help it," she exclaims, "that choir sang a heavenly tune this morning," she attempts to imitate their notes.

"But I know what you're doing Miss San Romun, um-hmm, you're going up to that place where peoples go when they leave their body," she says.

She has my full attention after her mention of "that place," as I wonder if she is speculating, or had she really known about the corridor?

"What's that verse...to be absent from the body is to be present with the Lord," she pauses for a moment. "Yes ma'am, I know what you're up to...well, you get right back here 'cause you got a beautiful baby to raise and a mighty fine man waiting on you," she whispers close to my ear.

"Excuse me, am I interrupting something?" says another woman as the hospital room door opens.

"—uh, my Lord, you scared me, ma'am!" exclaims the southern woman before she shuffles away from my bed.

"Not at all, I'm just making sure everything is fresh, you know it'll be any day now, and this one here going to raise straight up."

"Yes, I believe that too," says Naomi.

Her voice is different today, flat and somewhat distant. In fact, hers is the same tone as my other visitors had been just before their confessions. Naomi approaches my bed, and I assume she has leaned over to kiss my cheek or forehead. She is close enough for me to hear her pulse, allowing me to catch the scent of a cherry-flavored candy that tantalizes my taste-buds. My sense of smell is inconsistent, not as precise as my hearing.

"My earliest childhood memory is of six women standing beneath a humungous Ceiba tree," she begins.

"They were facing each other, with the same expressions reflecting their matching outfits and hairstyles. I remember it being a cool afternoon, and I watched as the sunrays stretched through the leaves of the tree above my head. When the wind blew, the leaves moved, so I had to lean in the direction of the sun to catch the warmth against my face and skin. I still love sunbathing to this day," she moves away to sit in the chair beside me.

Her mother and aunties—whom she called her tías— would hide underneath the shade of this big tree as the men performed a dance ritual with arrows and painted deer skulls on their heads.

"This was my home, Guatemala. Sometimes we were in the city, and then other times we retreated into the forest," she explains.

Most of the town's people had been converted to Catholicism, while others stowed away to practice traditional rituals in secret. Her family had adopted a mixture of Christianity, like accepting Jesus was the son of a God, but still holding onto a polytheistic opinion which allowed their practice of ancestral worship and offerings. During their transition from the old way into the new world, a hidden war arose within the culture. The blending of cultures had opened their eyes to a broader world view.

"Mujer clara vs. mujer obscura."

The light-skinned women against darker ones. Darker skin was viewed as ignorant or uneducated, even from those who were raised in the same household and afforded the same socioeconomic lifestyle. So her mother and tías hid them underneath the Ceiba tree, whenever they were forced by the elders to journey into the rainforest for the expected rain and harvest rituals.

Naomi remembers a time when running from underneath the shade, one of the tia's snatched her back with a rubberband grasp, yelling 'No salgas al sol, no salgas al sol! Dios migo, regresa a la sombra,' she laughs.

"My tia was saying, 'Don't go out in the sun, don't go out in the sun, My God, get back in the shade!'" She laughs at the memory.

Her small group of aunts and uncles preferred fair-skinned, darker skin would be rejected; she overheard an auntie whisper on one occasion. Naomi was born dark. She had a small face with round baby-doll eyes and dimples set in smooth, reddish-brown skin. It was a face like an angel, but still, because of the skin-tone, she was reminded that her chances to marry were feared to be narrow and slim-pickings.

"I know this will be a shock to you...but, tengo seis hijos," she says in her native language.

"You'll be the first to know this, even though I'm not

sure you can hear me, but I think you can," she pauses and after taking a somewhat exaggerated breath, continues. "I have six kids!" she blurts out.

"You've been so honest with me, letting me into your home, even allowing me to go with you to Denver to bury your father," she sobs.

I hate to say it, but I am shocked. Not by Naomi's admission, but because here sits another person at my bedside baring their soul, believing that I'm the honest one. I continue listening as her voice trembled from the weight of her secret; a secret not much different from my own.

"You heard me correctly, amiga. I have six children in Guatemala—ages sixteen, fifteen, fourteen, thirteen, eleven, and ten years old. It's been at least eight or nine years since I've seen them though," she says between sobs. Her tears are like hiccups, and then the room is silent.

"I had to leave them. There was nothing I could do…I tried going back for them, remember after Denver? But they wouldn't let me see my children."

I remember the time, it was right after our return from my Father's funeral. That's when my faith had been put to the ultimate test. I couldn't understand why Naomi chose that most painful time to abandon me, but now her actions make sense. I remember her note saying,

Emma, seeing you tie up loose ends at home gave me the strength to face my own family. You're stronger than you know. And Brave. Pray for me, as where I'm going will be a great challenge.

At first, I had been disappointed at the way she left, no warning not even a goodbye. Then after a month, my annoyance turned to frustration because I was forced to drive myself to church on Sundays—let's not forget I was a terrible driver. Although her note said she would be facing a challenge, it never occurred to me that the woman I relied on for my spiritual growth was facing her own trials.

I imagine her children's faces, round and brown, like their mother. Naomi had taken such good care of me during my time of grief and had always been a nurturing and caring friend, she possessed all the characteristics of what a mother should be.

"I was married as a young girl. I know why my parents agreed, but you know, it was just wrong. I was too young, forget about getting an education and what I wanted for my life. One day we were introduced, and then we were married. The babies came one after another," she says while taking a laborious breath. I imagine her face, wet with tears, her eyes swollen, and red.

"Most of the other girls my age wasn't having babies, if they were at least not at the rate I had been giving birth…I couldn't keep count of how many times I was pregnant Emma, and then I started to lose my mind," she continues.

As she speaks, I'm reminded of how my perfect world spun out of control after having to give up one child for adoption. Naomi had to leave six children behind, how had she managed to keep it all together? The day Naomi left their small home in Guatemala, her husband, Mateo, had no idea she was carrying her seventh child. She was twenty-two by then and pleaded with her mother for help. At the rate she was delivering babies, she thought surely to have twenty more by the time she turned thirty. Their one-room home was so tiny it required creativity with bed space.

"The babies were everywhere," she says. "One in a bassinet, two on the pallet beside our bed, one in a dresser drawer and the oldest in the bathtub. There was even one in the bathroom cupboard," she laughs. I couldn't help but to wonder if she were exaggerating the story some, but this was Naomi, she had never lied to me before.

Naomi continued speaking, baring her soul for some time, sharing fond memories of her children. She explained how much she loved them and especially enjoyed playtime with them, reminding herself that a younger adult still had child-like ways— this was the reason she enjoyed their games. All of her children had been born with her darker complexion, except the youngest, who was fair like his father. She loved the newborn but found his screeching cries deplorable, just like his father. Naomi never loved Mateo who, despite her being "mujer obscura," couldn't keep his hands off her narrow waist and surprisingly slim figure.

On a night when the older children ran through the house, unheeding her commands and provoking the younger children to tears, she told him—I want a divorce. Mateo ignored her because he was tired from a hard day at the warehouse. So, he disregarded his wife's plea for help, as he often did. Their religion shunned divorce, her mother reminded. Besides, he was a good provider who never stepped outside of their marriage, her mother cautioned. Her Father's reaction wasn't as kind—he would disown her if she left her husband.

"So, I left," she sighs into the stillness surrounding my bed.

On the day Naomi fled their tiny home, there was no time to consider a carefully thought out plan. The babies were crying, as the older siblings provoked the younger ones to tears. Naomi paused to assess her life within the walls, wiped the sweat from her brow while attempting to scrub a sticky substance from her favorite pink, and red hand-woven skirt.

When the newest baby let out another shrilling wail Naomi covered her ears for fear her eardrums would burst, and ran from the bedroom into the kitchen, then to the bathroom where she barricaded herself away from the chaos. Locked inside the small room Naomi braced herself against the door, as her head continued spinning from the noise.

After her hands stopped trembling, she took several deep breaths and then left the bathroom to resume her regular duties. Another hour passed by and Naomi observed her severe exhaustion. She had spent hours hunting for missing socks, wiped vomit and milk spills from the floor, swept and picked up debris blown in from the front door the children refused to keep closed. One child had been pulling at her hemline, another tuggd to nurse from her breast, and Mateo's poking hands and other parts had just returned home from his day at work.

Naomi stopped a few feet away from the front door to survey her life within the frenzied walls once more. She concluded that running was the answer; running would stop the children from crying, it would recalibrate the spinning in her mind. Running would stop the swell of her belly from yet another babies arrival.

Each time one of the children screamed she told herself, "just leave," and when the next one let out a yelp she thought, "the screaming will stop if you leave."

Then she watched as Mateo sat engrossed in a television show, how easily he tuned it all out, that's when she was able to convince herself she could escape too. When she turned to face the door that was never shut, she ran straight out the front door and kept on running.

"I couldn't stop myself—I'm sure I suffered a nervous breakdown," says Naomi.

She remembers little more of the day she fled from her home, except at some point as she ran, crying and confused, down an unfamiliar roadway, a vehicle approached her, and she entered without hesitation—the same as I had done on the day I escaped the room in Breaux Bridge, running until I was full of delirium but free.

Naomi encountered many people during what she called the "blank-days." Some were helpful, but there were also others with shady dealings and manipulative tactics. Mostly it was an American couple who helped her cross the border. The woman, she remembers, was round-figured and spoke bad Spanish. The man was snarly, short-tempered, and only spoke English. Somehow within days, she was in the United States unable to figure out why, how, and who she was? Still, Naomi vowed to never look back because she lacked the courage to face her family; not until she met me and witnessed my bravery as I returned home for my father's funeral.

"Your bravery inspired me to go back and fight for my children, even if they couldn't forgive me," she says. Then I must strain to hear her mumbled words.

"They must know their mother loved them…I love them, I always will," she mutters.

I now understand why the Gentleman said my healing would come from hearing, listening to the confessions from my friends and loved ones. For years I wasted irredeemable time trying to hide my past from Orion and Naomi. Why had we been so afraid to be vulnerable with each other?

"I've helped so many young women here in America. I can only hope someone is there to watch over my girls, my children. My parents are growing older, maybe Mateo has a new wife. Anyway, when I went back, no one would talk to me. My parents gave me a place to sleep but said nada. I couldn't understand it—but guess what?" Her voice swells with excitement. "I saw their pictures, all six of my children, and I'm not ashamed to say that I took the pictures with me when I left...all six of their pictures," she boasts, then the quiet returns encircling the stillness around me.

After what seems to be an hour, the time lapses between our silence. Finally, she continues her story. When she speaks again, Naomi shares that her mother knew she'd taken off with her children's pictures but said nothing. It was the least she could do knowing that Naomi came to her first for help. Her father was not as understanding, called her every unkind word you could think of. He pointed out that someone like her, a dark woman, had few chances of finding another husband, or even a decent-paying job, besides fieldwork.

After all the tears, the yelling and what she referred to as the "shame-game," her parents remained tight-lipped regarding the whereabouts of her children. She'd left them without giving thought to how they'd manage without her, so it was best to leave them at peace; especially since Naomi made her intention clear; this was just a visit and not a homecoming.

"You think I'll ever see my niños again?" she sniffles, and I hear the gurgle of her throat as she swallows saliva and tears. Poor Naomi. I know she wouldn't want my pity. She'd expect me to pray for her, and I will pray, after the shock of her confession wears off. Of course, I could relate to her initial plight, the desperation of entrapment, and the marriage at fifteen…was it even legal?

I remember the day we were introduced at the advertising agency. Naomi seemed lonely to me. She was different and opposite from me in almost every way, and that's what drew me in closer. I was curious about the attractive young woman who defied scrutiny as she read from the Bible on her lunch breaks.

The other's in the office gave Naomi space, taking care to keep her area drama-free. She had set boundaries with our coworkers, and they respected her for it…until I came along—desperate for relief from the angry voice in my head—searching for answers and for help. How would they react, knowing I had succeeded in coercing the sacred Naomi to accompany me into a night club?

"It had to be the protection of God on my life that brought me here safely," she clears her throat.

"I was exhausted, dehydrated, and bleeding in multiple areas on my body. My mouth ached from unexplainable sores, my nose was bleeding after the American woman smacked me for speaking to her in Spanish, and I was hemorrhaging my last baby from my womb," she says.

A concerned Latino officer found Naomi writhing from pain in an ally where the shady couple had abandoned her. She spent her first week in America hospitalized, hen after being released, Naomi thought to find a mission for food and shelter. Following behind a small – but rowdy - crowd of what she believed to be homeless people, Naomi made her way from the clean brick front of the hospital into the colorful side of town.

Turning down a trash-littered alleyway and tagged buildings beside empty lots, concern for her own safety became apparent. The group in front of her would occasionally glance back to see if the quiet, small-framed woman still trailed behind them. Just when she feared the next step around an approaching ally wasn't the best of ideas, two Spanish-speaking women stepped out from a doorway and intercepted her misstep.

"Amiga, vente aqui," shouted the women.

One grabbed Naomi's bruised arm and gave a sharp pull near the area where the nurse at the hospital tried numerous times to find a vein for an IV, the one Naomi had ripped out during one of her fits. She winced, biting her bottom lip to keep from alerting the crowd she was obviously being saved from.

Then they were standing inside a dimly lit apartment. Each woman's dark, round eye's questioned the others as Naomi scrutinized the scuffed wooden floor and dust lined windowsill. When a cockroach scuttled across the base of the wall Naomi gasped; her mother would have taken a peeled tree-branch to their backsides for such shameful housekeeping.

They wanted to know if Esteban had helped her make the journey from Guatemala to the U.S.? It was their job to care for those Esteban sent. Naomi didn't know how to respond, so she nodded her head, yes! Next, the women instructed that her main focus was to learn English, and her housing was free—so long as she pitched in with housecleaning and the cooking, which pleased Naomi, she yearned for the opportunity to buff the bare wooden floor and air out the dark rooms.

Naomi never met Esteban, but another man came in his place, Octavio, who had been sent to teach her English lessons. He would visit on Wednesday evenings for two hours; the first hour they all ate together, talked about who was caught crossing over, and how many had made the journey safely. Afterward, when Octavio had drunk the one can of beer the women poured into a frozen glass, her lessons could begin.

Naomi was fascinated by Octavio, who looked nothing like an English teacher. He wore combat boots, black jeans, and a leather jacket; and his hair was always damp as if he'd purposely splashed water on top his head. His stare was deep and intense as if he was studying the hidden recesses of her soul. Naomi remarked how his gaze moved from her lips that spoke broken English, to her eyes as they blinked after she fumbled over the foreign words.

Her two housemates complained when Octavio bumped their lessons up from one night to three times a week. "She needed more help," he had argued. They each knew the increase in sessions had little to do with Naomi's supposed struggle over syllables—Octavio wanted more time to stare into Naomi's eyes, compliment her smile, and watch her dimples when she pronounced certain words.

She found herself looking forward to his visits. He was a good listener, one of the characteristics that drew Naomi further into his world. Then one day Octavio asked to give her a tour of the five boroughs, and when she accepted his offer, they began spending time outside of the apartment, away from the protective eyes of the two women.

It was during a ferry-boat ride across the bay on an early spring day when they shared their first kiss; pulling her bottom lip inside his, gently biting, Naomi realized in all the years married to Mateo she had never been kissed that way. Octavio was passion, mixed with a little bit of danger, and she grew curious about the two conflicting sides of his nature.

Naomi continued her story, recounting the romantic times they had shared together. How it was on the city transit and subway rides that she gained the most valuable English lessons; how to pronounce objects, people and places as the city rolled by before her eyes. After about three months or so, Octavio moved her into his home. Not long after that, the lamb shed it's wool, revealing sharp fangs and claws that resembled a wolf.

Octavio had a drug habit, which kept him up at odd hours of the night. So, he'd spend his evenings at local bars or dancehalls, whichever stayed open the longest. Naomi figured the only way she'd get any time with him was to hang around where he hung out—at the bar and nightclubs. On occasion, he would ask Naomi if she wanted a "hit?" She refused each offer, saying drugs weren't her thing. She was with him the night he overdosed.

"I held him in my arms watching as he struggled to breathe, believing each breath would be his last," she says.

A friend of theirs pulled her out from beneath his limp body, saying they had to leave before the police arrived. Naomi recounted of how she cried like someone had ripped the beating heart from out her chest. Afterward, she made her way back to his apartment and waited there for days, and several weeks, without a word from Octavio or his friend. On the day she paid a visit to her old roommates to ask if they'd heard from Octavio, a note was left on his apartment door. He had been in rehab and wouldn't be coming back.

The landlord said she could stay, so long as the rent was paid by the fifth of the month. So, that day, Naomi left the apartment and refused to go back until someone offered her a job. Finally, she had found work at a bar, cleaning floors and restrooms.

Naomi once told me that she had been in worse places than I could imagine; I didn't believe her then, but now I did. It was at the bar where she worked that she met a woman sitting at the counter drinking seltzer water. When Naomi went into the lady's restroom to check the toilet paper supply and soap dispenser, the woman approached her with an offer.

"Come to my church," she said.

Naomi wanted nothing to do with a religion that would allow her to be married at a young age and then brainwashed into staying with a man who used her as his human waste bowl. She thought to tell the woman to keep her church to herself. Instead she politely declined before continuing about her duties. A short time after, Naomi saw a promising position listed in the classified section.

With limited job skills, she decided to apply at the Advertising agency. What could it hurt? There had to be more to life than having babies and cleaning floors. She applied for the position, and miraculously was offered the job, two years before I showed up at the very same agency.

The owner of the bar hated to lose Naomi because she showed up on time, minded her own business and worked her entire shift. He pleaded for Naomi to at least finish out the month so he could find a replacement. It was on her last night working at the bar when she encountered the woman who made the previous offer.

"You should come to my church," she said once more, but Naomi looked the other way and pretended not to hear the request. Relieved that her last shift was over, she left the bar for good. When the night ended, she closed the door behind her, and there was the woman and her friend waiting outside. Their conversation was relatable, as they discussed regrets and ways to be free from shame.

"I was impressed with their words of hope, and when I asked them about their faith, they invited themselves to my apartment so they could tell me more," said Naomi.

On a chilly autumn day, the woman and her friend paid Naomi a visit. She had set out hot tea and a plate of jelly-filled donuts; a treat she often cherished because it was a reminder of the snack Mateo brought their children on his paydays. There they introduced Naomi to a study plan that would help her read through the Bible.

"Would you believe, when I started reading the Bible, the colors around me became brighter, no lie. The sky wasn't just blue; it was periwinkle and turquoise, sometimes sapphire, or painted with melon and apricot hues," Naomi mused.

Her apartment was now more than white walls and dark furniture. She noticed the flecks of red in the rustic brown carpet, cotton white walls, accented by shimmery metals on light and bathroom fixtures. She even took notice of the orange and yellow butterflies in the abandoned flower bed outside her apartment window.

Naomi was feeling better about life the day her old roommates came knock.ng. They had seen Octavio earlier, who had come looking for Naomi. She silently hoped he wouldn't come home, at least not that night. Otherwise, he'd be interrupting their fourth bible study, which she planned to celebrate by preparing a meal; roasted pork shoulder with potatoes, and carrots.

As she feared, Octavio arrived thirty minutes later, right after her friends were seated and their plates sat before them. Naomi noticed how his eyes seemed darker, less passionate, and more dangerous. He pointed one boney finger at the two women and then snapped in the direction of the front door. Without protest the two women packed their belongings and left the apartment. "How dare you let those people in here?" He asked.

Naomi was disappointed and hung her head in shame as her new friends scampered down the sidewalk, leaving her without a goodbye. The last time she saw Octavio had been eight months ago as she held his lifeless body on that cold bathroom floor. She had more pain over the two women's departure then joy from seeing the man she once loved.

In that time, the landlord had canceled his tenancy and drew up a new lease agreement with Naomi. When the women had disappeared out of ear sight Octavio wanted to know why she would repay his kindness—their love this way? What kind of woman would abandon someone she claimed to love while he had been fighting for his life?

The accusation was a tactic he used to wiggle back into her life, but Octavio had no idea how much truth rang out from his argument. Naomi who was already weighed down from guilt after abandoning her family in Guatemala, allowed him to move back into their apartment and into the neat new existence she had begun creating for herself.

"I don't know how I made it through those next two years, but somehow, I did," she says.

Naomi shared that things were good between them

94

for the next three months—only. During the day she worked at the advertising agency and picked up shifts at the bar on weekends to cover other household expenses. Octavio would find work soon he assured her. Then after another month passed with no offers of employment for him, they came up with an idea, though in hindsight Naomi realized it was Octavio who had actually proposed the plan.

"At his persuasion, I asked the owner at the bar if he would hire my guy, he did it as a favor for me," says Naomi.

The first month with them working together was not so bad. Octavio would work his scheduled hours and left promptly at the end of his shift. By the second month he was thirty minutes late getting home, a few weeks later he came home an hour, or two, late after his shift. Then one night he didn't even bother coming back.

"I went to the bar the next day, and that's when the owner told me Octavio never showed for work the previous night."

He proceeded to tell her that her guy had been romping around with a female bartender, who liked to party in more ways than one.

"I never saw him again after that night, and I can't tellyou if he's dead or alive."

The joke was on me for thinking I had been the one who corrupted Naomi. This was why the party she had accompanied me to was a breeze. I had placed my friend into a neat little box without any regard to what her past experiences had been. If Tamar knew this side of Naomi, she would show her some respect.

Naomi was more than a Bible-thumper, she had been tested and came out with a testimony; stronger as a result of her trials, like gold smelted from the fire, she was solid. I hoped to remember her confession once I was conscious. I wanted to let her know that we were not so different, after all.

"I'm not sure if you can hear me - I believe you can - but everything I just shared with you, I'm prepared to repeat when you're awake. You deserve to know the truth," says Naomi.

IF THINGS HAD gone as planned, I'd be three months sober by now. My second child would be approaching full term, and I would be planning a wedding.

"Another week, I hoped to find your eyes open today..." says Orion, and then I hear the familiar breathy tone signaling to me his desire to confess yet another secret.

"...the day Tamar's twins were born I tried to avoid the hospital—do you remember? I had hoped to never see her baby, at least not the day it was born—they were born," he corrects himself.

I remembered the day Tamar's twins were born like it was as recent as his confession. She was angry at me for allowing Orion into her hospital room. At the time I had blamed her vanity for the outburst.

"Emma, she only wanted the baby," he says, predicting my thoughts.

"I was paid for a service, and there was no further need of me… that's why I figured my plan would be easy, but when she changed the rules, I was trapped."

Orion tells the story of how he had received a cryptic phone call two years after the birth of Tamar's twins, she wanted him to know that her marriage was ending. Because he was studying to become a lawyer Orion assumed she sought his legal counsel, but Tamar made her intentions clear; Orion was the biological father, and the children shouldn't suffer for her mistake.

He tried reasoning with Tamar, explaining that other people in their lives could be hurt, but there was nothing he could say to persuade her to leave the situation as it was. Tamar had no regard for her relationship with me, or how having a baby by her best friend's fiancé would impact our friendship. She wanted Orion to be what he was, her children's father.

"I was angry," he says through locked jowls. "Because her marriage was over she wanted to destroy what we had," he points out. So, Orion told her some things she was never supposed to find out.

In my mind, I call him every bad and foul-mouthed word I can think of. They are both to blame! I pray for the ability to remember it all when I pull through this nightmare—all of it—everyone's dark secrets. Each one of them who sit here at my bedside hoping I'm able to somehow hear what they say, but I'm willing to bet a year's worth of trust-fund payments if I awoke today and told them, "I remember what you said," one-by-one they'd fall down from a heart attack.

"I knew things were about to get ugly, and I thought about you most...the hard part was coming clean with you. Remember the day I wanted to tell you about an encounter I had with someone you knew?" says Orion.

As I continue laying here in my bed of restraints—straining to hear every syllable of his confession I begin to recount the time-period of that year. Orion spent most of his time volunteering at the community center, and the other half studying for his upcoming bar exam. He interned at a firm in North Jersey, and probably wasn't bringing home much money, maybe had taken out some financial aid to pay for his classes; that was my guess.

Orion was in love with a woman who lived like she'd never see the bottom of her money bag. He was careful never to discuss his financial burden with me, so I assumed he had it all under control. I can hear him now as I am constrained in this bed, forced to listen. Orion's budget was tight, and I'm sure freeing up his weekends to pick up extra paid work was out of the question. He loved volunteering and helping out with the youth in his community. This is why the consideration to make a donation at the fertility clinic was tempting.

Tamar seized a perfect opportunity, I remind myself, and her mesmerizing smile most certainly baited him in further. Orion wouldn't be able to refuse her even if he'd changed his mind. Tamar had positioned herself as my dearest, best friend, but she is the opposite—she is my enemy. Tamar stood by close enough to strike and then waited for me to fall after her poison had been secretly injected. She encouraged me to drink alcohol while I was pregnant, had even brought some of the bottles. Were they all hoping I'd miscarry my baby—Orion, Tamar, and Victoria?

"She was never supposed to find out that I never gave my donation," Orion admits, silencing my rage.

He says they had arranged to meet at the clinic on a Monday morning. Tamar sat beside him and watched as he completed the required paperwork. Then an appointment was scheduled for him to return on another day. When the nurse slid the appointment card across the counter, Tamar had her head turned to look at her cell phone. That's when he tucked the card into his pocket and never told her about the next appointment.

During his follow up exam, Orion was honest with the physician. He didn't think it was appropriate to go through with providing his specimen because not only was Tamar someone he knew, she was his girlfriend's best friend. With a wink of an eye, the doctor told him not to worry. Scheduling another visit on the same day as Tamar's pre-op, the staff ensured that her injection was supplied by an anonymous donor. On that same day, Orion's appointment was for consultation only, should he ever reconsider his options in the future.

This was the reason for Tamar's rage. The day of my accident when Orion, Tamar, and Victoria argued outside in the rain, Tamar had found out that he was not her children's father. When she went to confront Orion, placing a demand on the money she paid for his donor-sperm, Victoria's presence was a fluke. Neither of them expected for me to drive all the way from Manhattan to New Jersey; I was a terrible driver, and they all knew it.

Can someone in a coma sigh with relief?

Yes, because that is precisely what I did—I'm sure of it—though Orion must've thought the sound came from the hose and machines surrounding my unconscious body. What an awful mess, I wonder if Tamar's husband knew the true paternity of their children?

We are all to blame in some way. Our ignorance, vanity, and selfishness created this civil war amongst friends. And it seemed like the babies were always caught in the cross-fire; mine, Tamar's and Naomi's. Not just our children but even ourselves were profoundly affected. We were the children that had suffered in our youth and somehow survived.

"That's why I had to give Tamar her money back," says Orion interrupting my silent discourse. "But now it's more than that…" he pauses.

I discern his angst while listening to his pressured breathing; Tamar is out for revenge. Orion is worried about my safety as well as our newborn baby. I recall Naomi's earlier concern about the look in Tamar's eyes, now I wish he had confirmed her suspicions.

A nurse enters my room and then informs Orion that his visit must be cut short today due to some tests that the physician has ordered. As his footsteps leave the room, and the door opens, I hear my Uncle's voice as he greets them all. "How do you like the new place?" he asks. "Good, and don't forget about our meeting on Tuesday. The investors are eager to come on board," he reminds Orion, who grunts his approval.

After Orion has gone my uncle charges the room, igniting the hospital staff with his lengthy checklist of concerns. He demands more tests, new procedures, things I don't understand, and the surgeon questions. My uncle tries pronouncing a few medical terms neither of us have ever heard of before, leading me to believe he has recently researched similar cases to mine. He has probably studied the other trials and sought out second and third opinions from specialists near and far.

The condition of my skull was discussed, and the shaving off of my hair—my thick hair that resembled my Grandma Rose's and defied my mother's curls would need to be sacrificed. The surgeon wants my uncle to understand what life for me would be like should I regain consciousness.

"When she regains consciousness," Uncle Eli corrects.

Then he kindly instructs that no one should ever speak negative about my recovery—his niece will make a full recovery, and he expects the support from everyone on my care team.

Because I'm not able to feel, it's easy to forget the damage to my body. The more they talk, the more I understand the severity of my condition. I have suffered such trauma that my soul left my body to avoid the pain. The length of time I remain in a coma will determine the extent of rehabilitation. I will most likely need therapy to relearn how to walk, grip objects, and a host of other skills that most people take for granted, like tying a knot in shoelaces.

Of course, the Gentleman was right, hearing all of this helps me to prepare for what's to come. Listening to my family and friends confessions has given me more in-depth insight, it has become my healing balm, soothing the inflamed areas of my soul, drying up lacerations and oozing wounds from my past.

After my hospital room clears, uncle Eli approaches my bed and whispers to me, "I heard from your mother today," he says, and the chair beside me squishes as he takes his rest.

"Emma, I didn't tell her a thing...I don't trust that woman."

He wants me to know that my mother was an addict and that they've all known for some time now. Because of this, it wasn't a good idea to have her around.

"Forgive me, I'm just doing what I think is best in this situation. What I can do—only for you, is keep in touch with your mom and when you're up again, and only when you're ready, you give her a call," he concludes.

My heart sinks, realizing Uncle Eli's concern for me. He knows the danger that Reba presents. Somehow, he knew, and he is prepared to protect me like one of his own children; knowing this brings me comfort. Although I desire to hear my mother's voice, I understand his decision, my life is fragile as I float between life and death. If Reba were to show up with Ogre who knows what will happen.

My Uncle says that Reba mentioned being in a detox program. Then she hinted around about needing somewhere safe to go after her treatment ended. He wants to know if I have objections to my mother living in my Grandparents' home?

"I'll put her to work, of course, there's a lot that needs to be done around the yard and inside the house since..." when he doesn't finish the sentence I know he means to say *since Grandma Rose passed.*

"She'd be earning her stay, and the groundskeeper and his wife are still renting out the converted barn so they'll keep an eye on her," he says.

I'm not pleased with the idea of Reba and her crew pillaging through my Grandparents' home, and the remote location almost begs for Ogre to continue his chosen profession to exploit innocent young girls. This was my concern, but thugs like Ogre don't stand a chance with my Uncle Eli, who has keen intuition and leaves no corner unchecked. Ogre wouldn't stand a chance against my uncle's eagle eyesight.

I can hardly bear the image—the home of Rosemary St. Roman, founder of the PAHST organization used as a human-trafficking headquarters. My thoughts are running wild, and I almost fail to realize as parts of my spirit began to float, drifting toward the door. I'm not ready to deal with all this, and that's why I keep returning to the garden, at least this is the story I tell myself. The good news is I have enough information to incriminate Reba and Ogre's operation.

Yes, I say silently to my uncle, put them both where I can point them out quickly.

"Let's talk about this fiancé of yours, shall we? He's a rare find, Emma. I sure wish you'd brought him down to meet me before this," he teases. "You might object, but I found a five-bedroom home for you and Orion—you'll need a decent place to live with the baby."

Uncle Eli has never seen the inside of my apartment but says he believes it's just as lovely as Orion's studio. He reminds me that I was now part of a family unit, and decisions had to be made with that in mind.

"Orion doesn't know what to do with me," he laughs. "I like all that community involvement he's got going on. I can use his help in making some big changes down in Harlem."

My uncle likes that Orion had a vision that involves community and he admired his motivation to help others. As I listen to him speak I am delighted by his excitement and pleased that he approves of my fiancé. I hadn't known much about my uncle before, but it is apparent that he was more outgoing than my father had been. I was sure his grand way of thinking clashed at times with his brother's modest goals.

My uncle's dreams were even from high altitudes, far greater than the mile-high city of Denver. For all this ego and loud speech, he was still thoughtful and giving, and although he was tall in stature like his father, uncle Eli had inherited his goal-driven personality from Grandma Rose.

Considering Orion's recent financial struggles, I'm relieved that he's agreeable to working with my uncle. I can only hope their honeymoon-phase will outlast the duration of my recovery. Listening to Uncle Eli's advice leads me to consider my ways. I need to make some changes, with my resources there shouldn't have been any excuses. I could have sought the best therapist in town and hired a blood-thirsty attorney to take Ogre down; he needed to be arrested for the sake of others.

When I'm better, I must do my part and stop acting like a spoiled princess. One thing I'm sure of, I will never take another drink—and I will learn to be a better driver. It was time to bury my self-pity. I had to shed light on human-trafficking and bring justice to the girls lost in trashy, underground rooms. I let this all sink in for a moment, admitting that I am a victim of sex-trafficking. When I awake from my ordeal, I'll call myself a survivor; I suspect my mother had been as well.

My father had done his research at some point, and he knew, the woman at his funeral said it—he knew. I spent wasted years, refusing to go home, shielding my truth from my Father. He had somehow traced me from Louisiana to Maine. He knew about his first grandchild, Suniva. He was sure to have known about Reba's family ties.

I couldn't let the cycle continue or be passed down from me to my daughter. I will honor Suniva's memory by living a life of advocating for the daughters and sons around the world. I want to use my anger to fuel my mission. I may not be physically ready, but my mind was healing.

I am ready, so ready that I can now feel blood as it circulates through my veins and pulsates through my arteries. This was not my imagination, I can feel my other senses as they are stimulated; my body is preparing to awaken.

THE SOUTHERN WOMAN seems excited this morning. She wants me to know the time has come for me to awake.

"Miss San Romun, I know it's 'bout time you wake up because a May beetle crossed my path when I came into work," she says, whispering close to my ear. I frown within, annoyed by her attempt to provoke me to consciousness.

"A May beetle, Miss San Romun, you know what that means right? It's time—June beetle coming soon," she whispers again.

For all her odd speech, I understand what the southern woman has been trying to convey to me. My visits to the garden are less frequent nowadays, and on several occasions, I sat alone in the Corridor admiring the large door, as I contemplated what it will feel like when I muster enough courage to turn the doorknob. I still detest the wobbly knob that disrespects the immaculate hallway. I should ask the Gentleman to replace it before my time comes to turn and open the door. Then maybe the decision would be easier— less offensive.

*　　*　　*　　*　　*　　*

I still need them; the Gentleman and Suniva. If only there were a way to have both my world and this secret place combined together. Coming here to converse with the Gentleman helps me to make sense of my chaotic existence.

"Today is the day," announces the Gentleman.

"The day?" I repeat, unsure of what he means.

I continue my search around the garden peering through hedges, observing blooms that can be used for another flower crown.

"I'm not ready," I tell him.

"Your baby will be released from the hospital today," says the Gentleman. Then I remember overhearing a conversation between Uncle Eli and a nurse that my baby was thriving and could be released any day.

"She's in good hands, Orion and my uncle will make sure she wants for nothing," I assure the Gentleman while trying to convince myself. Although His lips don't move, He looks at me and says something.

Is she okay? The one I entrusted to another the first time? If it wasn't His thoughts, then they're my own.

"It won't be like before," I say facing Him.

* * * * * *

I don't recall the conversation ending, or the shift back into the hospital bed but now I'm listening as my uncle speaks. When he excuses himself to make a phone call Orion tells him to take his time. His breathing is heavier than at other times as he paces the floor.

"Hey Mom, yes I'm here at the hospital now," Orion says, after answering his cell phone. "It's almost noon, I'd been calling here since 5:00 this morning. I thought the message was about Emma waking up, but she's…"

Inwardly I tell Orion to hold on, my recovery will happen at any day now. Even if the Gentleman hadn't warned that my time was drawing nearer, I know my body is growing stronger.

"Every time I called another person said her doctor would get back to me," Orion complains to his mother. Something thumps against the floor, and he stops to pick up the fallen object. He is frustrated and beyond ready for this nightmare to end. I imagine his mother encouraging him to remain calm, that all things will work out for the best.

"Why isn't she waking up? The longer she stays like this, the more I worry," Orion wonders aloud.

I'm not sure what his mother says, but he takes a deep breath and agrees with her several times.

I did move my hand today. Unfortunately, no one is watching so I can't be a hundred percent sure; and there is still minimal sensation in any part of my limbs—but I believe

110

my hand moved. It was almost like I waved at Orion, but he didn't notice. Perhaps he isn't looking in my direction.

"Here's your baby, Mr. Stone," says someone who enters my hospital room, and by the sweet tone of their voice, I know Orion is holding my baby girl.

"What is her name?" I ask, though no one hears me.

I hope Orion has picked a pretty name like Jasmine, or Willow...or Suniva. As I contemplate name choices, their adoring coos begin to fade, one-by-one, until my room is empty.

The next morning, Orion returns to my bedside, saying that he expected to hear that I'd woken up today.

"It's a good day for a miracle, Emma. I'm settling in with our baby, but I could sure use your help." Then Orion explains our daughters features the best way he knows how; chestnut-brown skin, high-forehead like his, her lips furl like mine.

"And she hardly cries!" he exclaims while releasing a long-winded breath.

Suniva had been a good baby too, I remind myself. The next time I'm in the garden, I'll tell her about her sister. Then my hospital room door opens as well-wishers enter to pay condolences and to see the miracle baby born to a comatose woman. Apparently, my story has made headlines: Pregnant woman veers off the road during monsoon rainstorm, is how the news was reported.

News reporters had been encircling the hospital for

days waiting for the first opportunity to update their story. Naomi was the one who read the articles to me, she especially liked reading ones which included prayers and mentioned the vigils that were offered daily for my healing.

My Uncle Eli allows for one interview at my bedside from an ethical, conservative broadcasting channel, which I believe to be at Naomi's persuasion. Unaware that I had been drinking and out of my mind that morning, she wants to spread the message of God's protection. Initially, I didn't think it was right to spin my story this way, but then I thought about the impact the accident has had on my body and must admit, a full recovery could only come as a miracle from God.

Orion gives a brief interview about the conditions on the road that day, and how his pregnant fiancé bravely endured torrential rainfalls, drove through the Lincoln tunnel, and safely to Union City, only to hydroplane and lose control just as she reached his workplace. Even I am impressed with the skillful way he spins the story, and it now feels like a waste of talent for him to give up a law career. Once the interview concludes, uncle Eli recharges, giving commands to the hospital staff as he inquires about new tests and procedures.

"All her vitals are steady," says one nurse, after mentioning some improvements to my condition. When someone enters the conversation, I presume to be a surgeon, he reasons with my uncle the benefits of allowing my body to heal naturally before considering experimental treatment. I am relieved when Uncle Eli agrees to wait.

Then the room settles into a calm as he exits, I believe to bark orders in another direction. When I am ready to relax from all the excitement, my room door opens again.

"How are you holding up?" Naomi inquires.

When he grunts, I realize Orion is still at my bedside. She offers to babysit on the weekends, and two nights during the weekdays. He is grateful for her steadfast support, and then they are gone.

On the next day, I find comfort in having fewer visitors. Hopefully, less activity around my bedside will allow me to journey back to the Corridor. The room has been quiet for hours as I doze on and off to sleep, each time still waking up in the hospital bed. Where is the door, with the majestic walls, and the golden floor? Where had Suniva gone? I hadn't imagined it all.

Then my hospital room door opens, and someone tip-toes around my bed. The movement is different from the hospital staff or of Orion and Naomi. They would all approach me first, making a slight fuss about the posturing of my body or ask if I was ready to wake up now. This was a stealthy person, creeping along the baseboards, melding into the drywall. This person is barely breathing, if at all, squeezing their boneless body in between the cracks of the cabinet doors.

Had I imagined it all?

When my hospital room door opens again, someone gasps.

"It's you, what're you doing here?" Orion asks my phantom guest. There is a pause before the person answers.

"Funny running into you here, I'm looking for a friend," says Victoria.

In his silence, I know Orion to be weighing her response, preparing to challenge her defense. He approaches my bed, and after leaning in close to me—I assume to kiss my lips or cheek—his inquisition continues.

"And who do we have here?" she asks with an attempt to elude his questioning.

"This is our baby girl," Orion answers.

"I never heard back from you after that day, is this her, your fiancé? I saw your interview, I'm sorry about all of this," Victoria pretends to be ignorant. I listen as the sound of her footsteps moves closer to my bed—closer to Orion.

"If there's anything I can do to help until she's better, I'm not working right now so, if you want my help…" Victoria offers.

A great silence falls about the room as we both await his response. I force myself to listen to the adjustments of their bodies, the language of their unspoken words. I wait in the silence for the sound of an embrace or heavy breathing from a passionate kiss. Orion says nothing that I can detect. The only noise comes from stretching vinyl as he sits in the chair beside me. Then Victoria seems to surrender, with a sigh of defeat she creeps back across the floor and leaves my room. When she is gone, Orion inhales deep and exhales long.

"There she is, that's your mommy right there."

I listen to my baby's soft gurgles and grunts, her body squirms to adjust in muscled arms instead of the tenderness of her mother's touch. I'm sure I can smell her breath, sweet with baby formula, and her skin rubbed over with sensitive-care products. The scent of my baby serves to stimulate the olfactory glands of my nostrils, my nose has awakened for good. I can smell other things in the room, like an apple core in a nearby trash bin, cleaning products the southern woman uses in the bathroom, and I can even smell the citrus soap that Orion likes to use.

My finger twitches again, though I'm sure Orion won't notice because he's musing over the cuteness of our baby.

"Say her name," I plead again, I want to hear him say her name. *Is it Suniva?* If it is I can return to the garden and give her older sister the good news.

"Let's give mommy goodbye kisses, for now. We've got a tribe of people waiting on us," says Orion.

At another time I awake from sleep, frustrated because it has been days—possibly weeks since my last visit to the Corridor, Orion is speaking low beside me.

"I'm not sure if I'm doing this right, I worry about dropping her," he complains, and a few moments later she releases the tiniest belch.

"I know, daddy's girl. I'm not doing this right," he says when my baby begins to whimper. When her cries increase, he stands and marches back and forth across the floor, the sound of her grunts falling low then high each time he bounces her in his arms.

"Ssshhh, daddy's got you...look at that, you have eyes like your mommy," he coos, whatever slight adjustment he makes seems to settle her discomfort.

I've come to understand that Orion wants to appear strong for the baby and me. He knows how vital the first moments of a newborn's life are and worries about the bond a mother and her newborn must make. I imagine him, with underlined weary eyes, cuddling our baby like a football he'd won at a championship; our baby objects to his grip with another whimper.

"It's like looking in the mirror..." he says, whispering a name I'm unable to discern. I think he says something like, Sienna, or maybe Lilah—why is he talking so low for heaven's sake? Then he moves closer to me, and I feel the closeness of them. When Sienna - or is it, Lilah - makes more grunting sounds I know he's holding her in another awkward position. Then he kisses my lips and mumbles something I fail to catch because I'm listening carefully to her grunts and gurgles. I enjoy the scent of her that to me smells like fresh cinnamon and night-blooming jasmine in late spring.

When the nurse comes to check in on the three of us, Orion mentions needing to make an urgent phone call, and then hands Sienna, or Lilah, to the nurse. After they have gone, my baby's scent lingers with me until I fall asleep. It is then his words come back to me.

"I don't know how to do this without you. I need help at home," were his words.

I am sure Orion is doing better than he gives himself credit for, and there are many offers from family and friends to help. His parents, my Uncle Eli, and even Naomi have agreed to pitch in. As his words replay in my mind, I realize there is a slight tremble in his voice, Orion was panicking and is about to make another desperate decision—Victoria!

Tell her no, there's nothing she can help us with, and you aren't in any position to help her!

If only Orion had known of our past, how Victoria is now out to destroy me and take everything that I love – she can't be trusted. Then my hospital room door opens again, and I am relieved to hear his voice.

"I know we'll be fine, I've had many offers for help, but I need you, Emma—my heart needs you. I'm not complete without you," he confesses.

At this moment my hand moves again.

"Emma—Emma? I saw, did you...wait," he stutters as he rushes to leave my bedside. "I saw her-her hand moved," he calls out. "She's awake, I know she is," he almost shouts.

"Stand back, sir, please, Emma, can you hear me? Move your hand for me, can you feel this?" asks a hospital staff.

As the commotion surrounding my bedside

117

increases, the commands of the hospital staff becomes overwhelming making it difficult for me to focus on who wants me to do what; Orion is calling me, a nurse is ordering me, the southern woman is encouraging me...someone is calling for me.

Suniva was calling for me.

No, she couldn't have been—a girl was calling for me, I'm sure of it. I had to get back to the garden first and say goodbye one last time. I search for the door, for Suniva in the darkness.

* * * * * *

The glowing light returns, toying with me as I reach out; I am in the garden.

"She hasn't left you, think of it as though she has moved," says the Gentleman.

"I can't go like this, what will she think if I leave her again," I stammer, almost in tears.

"Will it help that you now have another Suniva?" He questions.

"Never, there will never be another Suniva," I shake my head bitterly, then an image near the pond moves.

"It's okay Mommy, the baby needs you now," says Suniva.

"I'm not leaving you, do you hear me?" I run to her, but she doesn't answer me. Suniva is calm—as is the Gentleman, I'm the only one here in a panic. She reaches for me then places the flower crown in my hand.

"Your great-grandma is here somewhere, have you seen her?" I say, kneeling at eye-level with Suniva. She nods her head, yes. "And your

Grandpa, my father—have you seen him too?" Yes, she nods again.

"Good, when the time comes for me to leave, go to them," I say.

"We're all happy here," says Suniva, "I want you to get better, and I want them to be happy," she points in the direction of the Corridor.

"Don't you want me to stay here with you?" I ask, but Suniva doesn't answer me, she reaches for the flower crown lying on the ground and then places it on my head.

"This will help you, the crown will help to keep your head lifted up, so you don't fall down," she says. Then she grabs hold of another flower crown and places it on her head. "Like this," she demonstrates, walking with her chin extended putting one foot in front of the other.

The gentleman appears, standing in the entryway of the garden, but I refuse to look Him in the eye. "Only when you're ready," He says.

Finally, I go over to Him, and we walk together in silence down the Corridor. He stops in front of the door. The worn doorknob stares back at me, begging to be turned. How many others have stood before this door with a choice between heaven and earth?

I can hear the beeps from behind the door and murmurs from hospital personnel as they continue to exam my responsiveness. Someone else has come to the Corridor, I look to the entryway of the garden and see them. Grandma Rose and my Father are smiling; she looks younger with her hair pinned up, his hazel eyes glisten like a young man in his prime. My Father, Emanuel, is the first to speak.

"I'm happy to know he's with you," says my Dad. Then he approaches, pulling me into an embrace. Next, Grandma Rose reaches for me, making sure to stop and straighten my hair. She lifts my chin and holds me there until I agree with them.

119

"The Gentleman and Suniva have been more than helpful, I don't think I'd be sane without them," I say.

My father shakes his head and says, "No, my brother, Eli, he'll look after you the way I would, even more. He's always had a hands-on approach don't push him away the way I had. It would make me very happy if you love him—show him that you love him, for me?"

I understand his plea is a regret my father has been left with, his wishes are many, not only with his brother but with most of the people he loved.

"You were always working too much," I'd said to him before just as my mother used to complain.

"You're ready, princess," says Grandma Rose. "You'll go on to accomplish many things I always knew you would, far greater than my contribution at PAHST," she winks at me. I miss her winks.

"My little girl is here, will you look after her?" I ask them both. I have convinced myself I'll be okay leaving if they promise to look after Suniva.

As we continue holding onto each other, I sniff the air around them, savoring the smell of my Grandma Rose's jasmine-scented perfume and the English lavender on my father's fingertips. I knew he'd be happy tending to the lavender bushes here in the garden, as he'd done at home many years during my youth.

"Go easy on your mother," he says.

"Extend mercy to your mother," says my Grandma Rose. "Continue my work, the two of you together will stretch PAHST far and beyond what I was able to achieve. Your story and Reba's will restore hope in so many others."

120

I had to be imagining this whole scenario—this couldn't be real, I thought. All of this has been part of some drug-induced hallucination the entire time, I am sure now. Reba would never agree to stop a sex-trafficking ring she profited from.

"Reba can't help me, she's to blame for all of this," I say, demanding to be heard. "She locked me in that room, in Breaux Bridge—that's how Suniva was…"

"Reba was in that room long before you got there, even from her childhood," Grandma Rose explains.

"I know you're angry, as I was, but things have changed; your mother is ready, and so are you," says my father.

"Have you seen my little girl, Suniva? She's here somewhere with you." I attempt to change the subject.

"You must go to your new baby now, she needs you," they both agree, and each take turns to embrace me. Then I am back at the door with the Gentleman he says nothing, only waits with me. "What if I'm not ready?"

"You're ready, but there are still several more days left before you turn the doorknob, and I need to prepare you for what you're about to hear," He says, as the expression on his face changes.

"Please tell me she's okay, what has happened to my baby girl?" I ask. When He nods for me to sit, I take a seat in the overstuffed chair across from the door.

"You are about to hear from someone who is suffering from a great deal of confusion, her actions will be life-changing, but I want you to have patience with her. Love her, Emma." He says, grabbing my hands in his.

I want to ask if this person is Reba? Knowing how I feel about my mother would explain the delicate approach. Or was it Tamar who has spiraled out of control? I would need more Jesus in my life to forgive her after she had betrayed our friendship.

"What she has to say will be somewhat of a surprise, but you can handle it, if you weren't ready I wouldn't allow for the timing," He says.

"It's Naomi, she's trying to find her children—can't you help her?" I ask.

WEEK ELEVEN

"THAT LADY COMING back soon, I watch her every time she comes, snooping around, and following behind your boyfriend—" the southern woman whispers.

"Oh, good morning…I'm just about finished in here," she moves away from my bed, as the swish from her broom quickens.

After sweeping around the room, the southern woman leaves me alone with my visitor. Someone sits in the chair beside me, releasing a plume of ammonia and a tinge of soiled clothing causing me to regret the return of my sense of smell.

"Destroying you wasn't supposed to be this hard," she whines. "I came to this awful city to ruin your life, and still you have outsmarted me." Her laugh is slightly manic, and then she stops to inhale the mucus accumulating in her nostrils from crying.

"Uh-uh, where is your suffering? You lie here without a care in the world. If you die like this, you die in peace, I don't want you to die..." she says, but forgets to finish her sentence, which should be, *"I don't want you to die in peace."* I chuckle at what sounds like a plea for my life.

"It was supposed to be easy, but it's not," she admits. "I hated you from the day we met at your Grandparents ranch. Twenty years is a long time to wish for vengeance," her words are soft as she confides in her dying enemy. Afterward she laughs, louder this time, and I wait to hear the door open—hoping for a nurse, or maybe the southern woman, to chase Victoria away.

"I was seven, so you had to be about five years old then," she pauses to double-check her calculation.

It is apparent now that Victoria has no satisfaction from my grave condition, nor does she sound like a person who has come to hurry along my death. She is always around me, here in the hospital room and even before my accident, lingering in the shadows—watching—always watching me.

What will life be like for her if I die? She mentioned how hard living in New York has been. So I wonder, had she been sleeping here at the hospital—somewhere in a secluded, hidden space? She is always there, even during times that most people shouldn't be.

"The first time I came to see you, I leaned over your

barely breathing body and wanted to smother you, I was going to tell you that I won I-finally-beat-you… All those years you've turned up your nose at me. You had it all. You had what was supposed to be mine," she snarls.

"The men that were supposed to love me loved you." Victoria begins hiccupping or gulping for air. As I listen the sounds of her laughter, although quieter this time, fills the room. It shouldn't be long now before she pulls out a knife, or cuts off my air supply. I am at her mercy, praying for the strength to move out of harm's way.

"Wake up, this is not how we fight— do you hear me?" she whispers, the bedrail shakes under her weight as she stands and then leans over my helpless body. "You owe me a fair fight before the dark alleys of this city claim my soul. I hate it here," she says, the ammonia of her urine-stained clothes lingers when she moves away from my bedside.

"I don't want to fight anymore…I surrender, you win!" She declares before flopping down in the chair. "I want you to know I'll take care of them," she says as if fulfilling a dying wish of a dear friend. Then the sound of her hiccups and sobbing reverberate around my hospital room. Some moments lapse before she speaks again.

"By the time we met at the audition I already knew where you lived, who you worked for, and where you hung out. And when I finally saw you with that handsome man— Orion—I came up with a plan to tear him away from you, the same way you did to me back in high school," she admits.

125

Ah-yes, I knew it would come back to this; what was her high school boyfriends name…Tim, or Jeff? No, his name was Seth. It was a long time ago, and we were young. If I could talk to her now, I would call a truce, maybe offer her a place to stay; there was plenty of space at my apartment. It is the least I can do considering her suffering is because of me.

Have I gone mad?

Why not go home, Victoria? You've seen my downfall.

GO HOME, I wish to warn her. Maybe there's another reason she needs to avoid Denver, same as I couldn't go back after my life-changing incident.

"I didn't want you to be happy…but you always were, and you always get what you want—you don't ever suffer like the rest of us, like me," she blubbers through her meltdown.

Victoria's argument is so convincing that I almost forget that Reba ever happened, as if the kidnapping - and Suniva - never occurred. Of course, Victoria doesn't know about any of these things either.

"I followed you on social media, stalking your every move, watching to see what you were doing. When you posted your excitement over the dance audition, I sacrificed everything to be there…I didn't get the part, but it didn't matter because neither did you. I've had enough of your better-than-everyone-else ways," she says, laughing through tears.

Then Victoria goes on to recount how after the audition she turned her attention to my relationship with Orion. It was on a warm night she slept outside my window on a park bench across the street. By then, I hadn't been coming out much, and she soon found out why.

"I couldn't believe you did it, you actually went and got yourself pregnant!" she exclaims. "When did you become so private, Emma?" Wanting to know why I never posted any pregnancy photos on social media? She pauses as if awaiting my response.

"I figured by following Orion I'd learn more about you, but there was even less about him on the web so I ended up trailing behind him as much as I could."

She explains his route from Harlem into New Jersey on certain days of the week. She continued with a meticulous plan, plotting my downfall to steal my boyfriend while I was pregnant.

"I wanted you to regret those words you said to me at the audition, remember what you said, Emma? 'Wow, you sure cleaned up well,'" she says, leaning forward close to my ear. "You remember those words, Princess? Do you know what someone like me had to go through, what I had to go without to be there?" she asks before sitting back into the chair.

When Victoria found out that Orion worked at a law firm she considered approaching him for legal advice, planning to use her poor living conditions as an excuse to seek his legal counsel. After they had met she learned that Orion was not yet a practicing attorney, and she found his personality unbearably patronizing—he asked too many questions, quickly catching and filling in the holes of her story.

Despite the warning signs and his keen intuition, Orion agreed to check into her matter for a possible lawsuit. Victoria used this slight interest to her advantage, believing the way she batted her eyelashes and twirled her curly hair caused him to abandon all suspicions.

"I ruined my hair standing out in the rain with that arrogant fool, then I almost broke my neck when that car came out of nowhere and tried to mow us down—YOUR CAR...the news called you brave!" she said, sucking in her teeth, and blowing out her breath. She is curious about the angry woman who arrived at Orion's job that day?

"I've seen her here in the room too, I don't trust that one. When the car came out of nowhere I assumed it was her, but it was you," she continues. Orion had shoved Victoria from in front of my car. Falling to the ground, she had twisted an ankle, and a stone gashed her knee. Victoria needed medical care, but after calculating the cost of ambulance fees and the hospital bill, she had refused treatment. Orion drove her to the emergency room, insisting she is triaged.

At the hospital, Victoria overheard him ask about the driver—his pregnant fiancé. That's when she realized it wasn't the furious woman behind the wheel, but me. The revelation that her actions had driven me to rage gave her pleasure.

Then Victoria explained her journey from Denver to New York, she wanted me to understand the sacrifice it took for someone like her to make it here in the big city. Back home, Victoria had worked as a salesclerk at an outlet. With one paycheck she purchased a ticket, and another she cashed and then said her goodbyes.

"It was $425.00, hardly enough to survive off, but I was already invested in making the trip," she explains.

Victoria had another plan that included asking her father for money—her real father—the one she'd never met, to do so meant she'd need to make amends with her mother; it had been months since they'd last spoken. After graduating from high school Victoria moved out with a boyfriend who turned out to be a big loser. Her mother had warned her, but Victoria refused to listen. Admitting her mistake, she dropped the "dead-end" guy and returned home. That's when she found out that her mother had become obsessed - again - with my father, Emanuel St. Roman.

I'm sure my nose flares at the mention of my father's name, as does every pulsating vein within my body. My heart taps against my chest like a conductor calling an orchestra to attention; the lub-dub crescendo cues into performance.

I don't like the direction her story is heading.

"Victoria-St.-Roman," she pronounces the name slowly for effect, as I strain to hear past the concert of my heart.

"I like it, makes me sound like someone important."

I need a distraction from the noise, a focal point to keep me from going into convulsions—which I am sure will happen if Victoria keeps antagonizing me. What did the Gentleman say? He tried to warn me about something bad, someone was about to hear something they didn't like. No, his words were, *"What she has to say will be somewhat of a surprise, but you can handle it."* Victoria has something to confess to me, it is the reason she has tracked me down and is always coming for me.

"When I was younger my mother obsessed over him—and her, your mother, Reba."

Then she becomes silent for a moment, as she struggles with time that has come to rob her of the stories she swore to never forget; the memories that justify her revenge.

"I hated your mother," she spats.

Victoria's mother told her the tales of my father, how they met in middle school and became sweethearts in high school. When the time came for him to leave for college he had promised to love her always. His second year away he was home for Christmas break, that was when he'd broken things off with her mother. Not long after he married Reba.

"From what I'm told she pranced around town pretty much the same way you did. She and your Grandmother would stroll into high-end boutiques together, throwing money around as if it fell from heaven like manna each night."

Victoria's mother never got over being replaced, and

she never stopped loving him.

"Did you know they had a thing?" She asks.

Victoria had to know how much I loved my father, this was part of her plan; destroy me by tearing down my father's reputation. If it hadn't been for the Gentleman's words, I wouldn't believe her.

"I found out when I moved back home. My mother was never there, only saying she was reunited with the love of her life. She still loved him after all those years, and they were happy for some time," she continues.

"When?" I want to ask, *"When did they have a thing?"*

Searching my mind for the exact period, I know it had to have been when my mother came for me the night of my high school graduation. During my captivity, and afterward, when I refused to return home. My Dad had been abandoned by his wife, and now his daughter was gone; he sought comfort in the woman who confessed to loving him always.

"Our father was a handsome man, Emma. Those hazel eyes, like mine—or rather mine like his."

She is crying or laughing, or probably both at the same time. I am furious, how dare you sob for my father's eyes, Victoria. I always wanted his eyes, had prayed all during adolescence to wake one morning and by some miracle the brown eyes—that were identical to Reba's—would be gone.

"Mom wasn't ready for me to meet him yet, but I insisted. They wanted me to know you were doing well living

131

in Manhattan..daddy told me where you were, so he's to blame if you want to hate anyone for my being here." When she blows her nose, I hope she's found a tissue and not using her arm sleeve.

Victoria had nightmares afterward, dreaming of the pampered life she assumed I was living in Manhattan. She knew my father wouldn't allow for anything but the best.

"You always had what was supposed to have been mine because your mother stole my mom's sweetheart away. When your parents finally separated, mom was so happy. She had put on her best dress and planned to meet him at his office to confess her feelings. He waited until after you were gone and then he gave in to the reunion she'd always dreamed of."

My father and Victoria's mother had been together.

This is what I didn't want to hear, but the Gentleman said I could handle it. The times I felt guilty for leaving him alone in Denver to pursue my big dreams in New York, he wasn't really lonely. Their romance had picked up right where they had left off.

"I enjoyed seeing them together, my mom wasn't bitter anymore, and she was happy to have been the one with him in the end...after he was gone I got angry, he wasn't supposed to leave that way," says Victoria.

I hate the idea of having to share my father's memories with my enemy. He is mine; there isn't enough space in what's left of him for an imaginary sister. The

132

LAURA GAISIE

Gentleman also said someone had a great deal of confusion, was Victoria confused about my father being hers? I was a lonely child and had dreamed of having a sibling for years if I had one now, I'd feel cheated. She could have slept in my room, played in our yard together with me and Biscuit.

I miss Biscuit.

They took him from me when I ran from the room in Breaux Bridge. Maybe Reba had him all this time; it would alleviate some of my sufferings to have my dog back—my youth and innocence.

I'd wake up in a heartbeat for Biscuit. If you're really my sister, Victoria, you would track down my mother, and find out if she has Biscuit. Then my mind spins with fantasies of a miracle ending. But I know Biscuit was gone, just like I know what Victoria is about to confess.

"Of course, you know we're sisters, I was the parting gift he'd left her with when they broke up. So, I'm ready to face you now. I want to know the sister I never knew I had so you must wake up—wake up!" she demands.

I hear the slap, perhaps across my face or maybe it's just her hands she smacks together; but I feel nothing.

"GET-GET 'WAY FROM HER!" the southern woman shouts.

I hear the shuffle of her feet as Victoria backs away, saying it was a misunderstanding.

"I'm sorry, I-I'm getting something off her, she's my friend from home—Denver," Victoria tries to explain.

133

Then there is another voice.

"You know my Emma?" asks Orion.

He arrives seconds later, missing the assault. Victoria gives no audible response, but I assume nods her head.

"Are you just finding this out, or did you already know?" he questions. "Even then, when you asked for my help with your case?

"I'm sorry, I have to go," says Victoria, excusing herself from my room, and the symphony within me quiets once she has gone. When the room settles, my confusion begins. I want to hear her voice again—sisters, how had I missed so many of the clues? My mind swirls with questions until I fall asleep.

＊　　＊　　＊　　＊　　＊　　＊

When I awake, the immaculate walls greet me in the Corridor.

"Will she come back again?" I ask the Gentleman who waits for me at the door. "Is she really my sister?"

"Yes, Victoria is your sister, and she's unraveling quickly...like you, she has many questions," He says.

"How can I help her? There's no way I can reason with her like this, in my condition, and we've always fought—from day one," I say, and begin telling Him of our first encounter that sent me running from my Grandparents' home.

"That's child's play," He chuckles at the memory and swats a hand in the air. "She's severely malnourished, afraid, and desperate..but she wants to know her sister and I want you to help her."

After being coached on how best to handle Victoria, I am led out to

134

the garden. Suniva has been waiting for me and occupies her time by chasing after the Purple Emperor.

"Remember when you asked me about my family, how important family was?" I ask Suniva.

"Yes, you need your family," Suniva reminds me without taking her eyes off the butterfly; she leaps in the air when it takes flight.

"You asked me to tell you something about me," I say to the back of her head as she continues leaping. "Come sit with me, Suniva." I pat a spot on the bench.

"I have another little girl—a baby, I haven't met her yet because she's waiting for me to get better," I speak softly, needing her to understand that my time here in the garden is coming to an end. "I needed this time with you - to take care of you - because I didn't do that when I should have." It's hard for me to admit this now, but I know there is nothing more I can do for Suniva.

"My father takes care of me," she giggles.

She is a bright child, smarter than I had been at her age. I imagine what fun she and Shelly must've had living off the land in Sebec Lake. Fishing and searching for fresh herbs and nuts, swimming in the lake at dawn, and dancing under the moonlight.

"Yes, I can see that you are well cared for, but I want to be here with you…" I pause, unable to bring myself to say, I would stay if she begs me to. "You're my little girl too, did you know that?" She bobs her head up and down.

Touching my eyes, she trails the length of my nose, across my lips, and then around the circumference of my face, as she had done on the first day. Then she snuggles into my arms, as I hold her close to me, needing

135

to ask her the question.

"Are you okay if I leave?"

Suniva nods her agreement. "You're just visiting so you can feel better...Do you feel better yet?" she quizzes.

Something is different this time in the garden; I feel the heaviness from the weight of my legs, and the mass of my body. In times before my body was airy, void of gravitational pull. The scent from the lavender and orange blossoms are less pungent. When I enter the Corridor, I can hear the visitors from my hospital room; even while in the garden, I could hear them talking—their voices like the gentle breeze along a deserted beach.

*   *   *   *   *   *

Then I am back in my body. Orion sits beside me, pleading that I answer him. He wants to know if it's okay to hire Victoria as our baby's nanny?

"Yes." I murmur to myself, please take her in, I can't bare the thought of her taking off before we have the chance to speak face-to-face. I know there is some concern with the two of them living together, but I refuse to think of the dangers it may pose.

"I just don't want to give her the wrong impression. She seems fragile and hungry—I've caught her stealing food off the hospital tray twice, she wanted to sue the property management for a rat infestation, but I suspect she's no longer living there."

Orion begs for me to wake up, to help him make this

decision. He wants this madness to end so things can go back to the way they were; but things will never be that way again. For me, everything has changed, some of it for the better.

For starters, there will be no more alcohol. I am done with binge drinking and stashing bottles around my apartment. Also, there will be no more pity-parties and no more entertaining guilt and shame. Hope and faith will be my new best friends. The dark voice that once taunted me will remain in this bed and die, but I will live.

When the door to my hospital room swishes open, Orion greets the visitor and then asks about Victoria.

"The skinny girl with the long legs? She was here before, said she was a friend of Emma's from back home, but I didn't meet her when we traveled for her father's funeral," says Naomi.

"That's what I thought, she knows Emma well though...her parents, grandparents, where she lived, even where they went to school. She described the horse ranch and birthday party's there for Emma. I was thinking of hiring her as a nanny," says Orion.

Then Naomi offers her services again, saying she can help on weekends, but she isn't sure about weeknights. Orion is grateful for whatever time she can spare but says he will hire my friend, Victoria. He doesn't think I would mind; besides she needs the work, and he needs live-in help.

"Let me speak to her first, please. Once I look her in the eyes then I'll know what her motives are...if only Emma would wake up," says Naomi.

"Even if she woke up today we'd still need the help, she'll need rehab and therapy after all this. I'll schedule a meeting between the three of us, it'll be like a second interview," says Orion.

As they leave my hospital room, not only does my arm flinch, but my left leg jerks.

"MISS SAN ROMUN, you wake now?" The southern woman leans over to my face, poking my arm and touching my eyelids. She smells brassy—or like an iron supplement; and another scent, citrusy bergamot lingers from around her face. The cold, stiff grasp of the hospital bed reminds me of my lingering condition.

Her touch feels more like when the dentist numbs your gums during a root-canal; you aren't supposed to feel anything, and yet the pressure is real because you know something has happened. Afterward, the rubbery sensation on your lips is fun and confusing; this is what everyone's touch feels like to me.

One of the physicians said it was normal to see my body twitch, or jerk at different times. He was the one who liked to talk honest and direct about my condition to whoever was in the room. Once after he delivered another grim report, Naomi interrupted, telling of how she knew a great physician who could heal all sickness and disease. Needless to say, the physician takes caution not to speak when Naomi is around.

When this death-trap that masquerades as a hospital bed releases its grip, I'll tell them it wasn't nice hearing the way they spoke of me. I hope to remember hearing Orion's confession—Naomi's, Tamar's, and Victoria's secrets; they deserve to know. I feel obligated to make things better, at least not have them worry about me anymore. I have been selfish, this is what I wish them to know.

The door to my hospital room opens. As footsteps hasten across the linoleum and march up to my bedside I notice her effort to bathe although a slight ammonia smell still lingers. After checking around my bed, and then nibbling on the food left on the tray, Victoria speaks. Her mother phoned this morning, asking if she was ready to come home.

"My mom ran into Reba too, she's asking for you, but I couldn't tell her, Emma, I had to lie...I had to tell her I was back in Colorado already, she would be upset if I was here because she knew how much I—"

She stops herself, stepping away briefly, and then returns to the chair beside me.

"She would think I did something to you, because of what I said before I left," Victoria admits, then proceeds to say that our mothers discussed my father's funeral. Hearing the news for the first time, my mother fell to the ground crying inconsolably on the sidewalk. No one had told her anything, why would they? Everyone knew what she was.

"I've met your baby girl—she's beautiful. I hope you don't mind, but I'm going to be staying with them, as her live-in caregiver...I love her already. I could sit and hold her for hours, I don't want her to cry, she shouldn't have to cry," says Victoria.

For the first time since our meeting over twenty-five years ago Victoria seems genuinely happy, although I worry slightly about the spoiled baby she is creating for me to deal with later.

"Thank you, Victoria!" I say in my stillness, for loving my baby despite your feelings toward me.

"And I see why you love him, he's handsome and intelligent," she says, and when she pauses I wonder if she is falling for my fiancé? What would I do if they fell for each other?

"Don't worry, he's not my type—too straight for me, I'd get bored with that kind of man," and when she laughs, so do I, it's a relief that she promises to leave him alone, and our truce could continue. If only Victoria could hear my response because she will never know what this moment means to me. It is like we are sharing our first moment's bonding as sisters.

Then I fall asleep, but I don't return to the garden this time. When I awake, I hear Orion's confusion about moving on with his life.

"What should I do if you never wake up? Wouldn't it be

best to have someone there to help raise the baby?" He asks.

My heart is still for a second or two; I can feel my blood pooling in my arteries as I await the news that Orion has fallen in love with Victoria; knowing it'll feel like I've hit the wall all over again, I refuse to listen to him.

* * * * * *

Somehow, I'm not there anymore. I sit in the corridor and wait. The Gentleman doesn't show, and neither does Suniva; I want to talk to them, not Orion, I won't be there when he makes this confession.

* * * * * *

Against my will, I return to my body, locked into this bed. Victoria is telling me that Orion seems unhappy. He was nice at first, but lately, he refuses to speak to her.

"And he avoids me," she complains. Coming home after she's gone to bed and slipping out early in the morning before she's up...he is like a ghost in the home, she catches shadows of him passing but never his face, only the back of his head as he leaves out the door.

"I don't think he's fit to raise a child; I won't let him hurt her—I'll make sure our baby is safe," says Victoria.

Her statement makes no sense to me. Why would she think Orion would hurt his child—our child?

"He works too much! We both know what that's like...they're never around when you need them, and the children suffer," she continues, admitting her anger. "I hate
142

him—the arrogant fool...that look in his eyes. I will take her away if he keeps this up. You have my word—I won't let him hurt her!"

This is when the hearing becomes disturbing, and my body begins to convulse. Victoria's scream rings in my ears, bouncing off the walls until my soul travels back to the corridor.

*   *   *   *   *   *

The gentleman stands at the entryway of the garden, waving for me to follow him to the bench.

"I can't do this anymore, I don't like hearing them. Why are they all spiraling out of control?" I want to know.

"You already knew your time was coming," He says. "Some things you will remember - not at first - but as your body recovers so will your memory. You will go somewhere for intensive rehabilitation, take the time and get stronger. Don't worry about Victoria, she'll take care of your baby as if it were her own—but it's best that she leaves now."

"I won't let her take my baby...you can't, don't let her take my baby!" I plead with the Gentleman.

He doesn't answer, but simply stands and leads me back to the entryway of the garden. We walk down the corridor in silence, my head down staring at my reflection in the golden floor; the image of the majestic walls shimmering behind me as if they are waving goodbye. When we pass by the over-stuffed chair, the Gentleman leaves me standing before the door. I glare at the worn doorknob, refusing to extend my hand. I can hear Orion's voice on the other side, pleading for me to wake up.

Then I hear my baby's whimper. Victoria gently shushes her, whispering how much she loves "our baby." She wants me to know that it is time for her to take my baby away from here and that I shouldn't worry—she will only take care of my baby until I'm feeling better—then I'll know where to find her.

My baby begins making short agitated grunts, but Victoria's words are soft and warm, calming her cries; there is love in her voice. When she says her goodbye, my frustration causes both of my hands to clench into a fist and remain that way long after she is gone, up until Orion arrives— but he doesn't notice.

"My father tells me you'll be sad today," says Suniva, she is sitting in the over-stuffed chair behind me.

"I know now that my time has come," I say, approaching her for the last time. Then I lift my first-born onto my lap. "I could stay if you want me to," I speak carefully. The Gentleman watches as I sit, brushing her ebony curls.

"No, you can't stay, you're only visiting while your body heals," Suniva reminds me.

After spending a few more moments holding her, the Gentleman walks over and extends his hand to me. Anticipating what it will feel like to finally touch the worn metal in my hand, I steady my breathing.

"Listen," I say to Him as I strain to hear Orion speaking on the other side of the door. He is saying that Victoria is missing with our baby, and God help her once he tracks her down. His footsteps echo as he leaves the room.

"Are you ready?" the Gentleman asks, seconds before I raise my hand toward the door. I nod my head, as He instructs me to "Take a deep breath."

I hear his silent words, whispering to me, "you're not giving up Suniva, she has fulfilled her purpose." Closing my eyes, I lay hold of the worn knob, and give it one full turn. Suniva's laughter is like a gust of wind that encircles me, and then lifts my soul up, carrying me through the door.

* * * * * *

It is the sound of joy that pushes me forward and then gently places my soul back into my body, lying in the hospital bed. Suniva continues laughing, she is happy for me.

If Orion turns around now—a quick glimpse back at me, he will witness the opening of my eyes. The metal tentacles uncoil, releasing me from my prison of darkness. I gasp for air as my eyelids blink open and shut, making sure this is real. The light is blinding, so I close my eyes and peak. The Gentleman is leaning over me.

"Welcome back," He says.

I blink several times, my surprise at seeing him outside of the Corridor is apparent.

"Is Suniva here too?" my weak voice questions.

"You really awake?" asks the Gentleman. But His voice is different here. He speaks with a twang now, and he smells like bergamot. I blink again until my eyes lose focus of the Gentleman's kind eye's and fix on the Purple Emperor hovering above my head, three times its size from in the garden. I want to catch the emperor for Suniva—she wouldn't believe how big it has grown.

145

"Why are you talking like that?" I ask.

"Who's Suniva, Miss San Romun?" says the southern woman. "Stay calm, you alright now," she says as she presses the call button for assistance.

With one act of obedience, I am awake, responsive, and alert. At some point, Suniva's laughter begins to fade, confirming that the portal to Heaven that was opened to lift me up and away from pain has shut, and with the closure my mortality returns. A surge of pain shoots through my limbs, stirring my stomach and moving my bowels. My head is throbbing, and my chest aches. I feel every forgotten sensation from head to toe; this was the reason the Gentleman came for me before my Mercedes hit the wall.

The physician is asking if I can lift an arm or leg, but my limbs are stiff, barely able to move past a flinch.

"Too hard," I say. Even my speech betrays me.

With the little strength I possess, I'm able to flex one finger, then two…and I remember the Gentleman saying, *"Take a deep breath."* So, mustering my limited energy, I fill my lungs, and then my fingers loosen, my toes wiggle, and my neck twists from left to right.

Behind the physician and two nurses, I catch sight of a silver-haired woman wearing a shirt the same shade as the Purple Emperor. Uncle Eli holds the door open for her, and she smiles at me before leaving the room.

"I'll come back later," she mouths the words.

Then my uncle and his wife, Miranda, approach my bed.

146

"It's true, you are awake," says my Uncle. In my confusion, I mistake him for my father.

"Daddy?" I whisper to him. No, he shakes his head, "It's your Uncle Eli—nurse," he yells for assistance.

A fair-skinned woman with rimmed glasses approaches. Then another woman arrives, smiling as she probes my body and checks the monitors surrounding the bed. My Uncle Eli and his wife are asked to step aside, as a battery of questions is thrown at me.

"Who's the president of the United States?" one asks.

"How old are you...do you know your name?" Someone wants to know. I tell them, "I don't know," because it's confusing and I'm not sure how much time has passed.

"Wait—my name's Emma, that's my uncle, and his wife," is all my disordered mind knows for sure.

Then there are more tests ordered, and another round of questions. There isn't anyone I want to see, or wish were here, that I can remember.

"Do you remember being pregnant?" the physician asks. "We delivered your baby while you were in a coma...she's doing well and was released just last week to the father, Orion."

"Suniva," I say.

"Oh, is that the name you chose for her? Beautiful name, let's see about the birth certificate." He instructs for a nurse to retrieve paperwork.

"Where is she?" I ask, looking from the doctor to the

147

nurse, then back to my uncle. Uncle Eli approaches me first, calm with gentle shushing.

"No need to worry, princess," he whispers in my ear. "Orion has the baby; I'll call him now," He assures me.

"You can handle this," I hear the Gentleman's words.

Then I remember what has happened and I know Orion won't return today; not unless he finds Victoria first. I am worried about her—my sister. What will happen once Orion finds her? How will my uncle respond to the news that she's taken off with my baby?

When the room clears, I try reaching for the phone, but I find my hands are unsteady, refusing to cooperate with my desire. A nurse reenters and when she sees my feeble attempt, advises that I should relax for now. It will take some time, and the help of therapy to strengthen muscle before full mobility is restored.

"I need to make a call," I hear my raspy voice saying.

The kind nurse tells me not to worry and proposes she should dial the number for me. I sigh when she offers, grateful for the help. Then she waits for me to give her the phone number, but I can't recall a name, or why the urgency for the call.

"Don't worry, it's going to take some time for everything to start clicking," she pats my shoulder.

As she leaves the room, I see my father standing in the hallway with a cellphone to his ear. His shoulders slump slightly after he ends the phone call. I smile when he approaches, it's been so long, I think to say. But seeing his brown eyes reminds me again, this is his brother, my Uncle Eli. I try to shield my disappointment, but it's too late the expression on my face gives me away.

"It's just me, I know we look a lot alike," says Uncle Eli.

"Sorry, I'm just so confused, everything seems different," I offer a weak excuse. He changes the subject to the weather; it's the first week of October, and rare early snow is falling outside. I'll need warm clothes for when the hospital discharges me.

"Do you mind coming with me to Florida? It's warmer there this time of year, better for your recovery," he says.

I don't mind, how could I refuse? At the time, I can't even remember my address.

"My dad said to tell you hello, so did Grandma Rose, they want you to take care of me," I smile, happy to have remembered the message.

He nods, adjusting the pillow behind my head and smooths the sheet beneath me. When he turns away to pick up an empty milk carton, I catch a glimpse of the sadness he wishes to conceal. He leaves my side and marches into the adjoining bathroom to discard a handful of trash, and with each step I'm reminded of the creeping person who searched the cabinets and stole bites of food left out on the tray; she had been here earlier today, with my baby.

"Your cousins are preparing a room for you, and we're all looking forward to having you stay with us," says Uncle Eli from in the bathroom.

He remains there, cleaning and picking up small debris from the floor, and then wiping down the sink. An opened newspaper lays near the windowsill, and two disposable coffee cups nearby. There are wilting flowers pushed behind freshly budding yellow roses and white daisies. An exotic looking orchard with a jawed lip was placed at the foot of my bed, among many cards and several balloons.

"Who are all the flowers and balloons from?" I ask.

"There from all of your friends, some from me—well, not me, but your aunt bought the roses. She sends a fresh bundle up every Monday," he replies.

"I'd like to read the cards."

He is quick to gather the cards from around the room, placing about two-dozen on the bed. I try to open one, but my hand's fumble.

"Let me," says my uncle, pulling up a chair. "This one's from someone named Faith," he says and reads the card silently at first, but then raises an eyebrow.

"Emma, I hope you get well soon. I miss seeing you down at the spot, all of us do. I don't know how this happened, but I'm telling you if you need me to let my dude from the Bronx know, I'll make sure he takes care of the rat that did this to you. Interesting friend," is my uncle's reaction.

"Where's Suniva, did you see her leave?"

"Orion has the baby, he'll come soon," he assures me.

"Not her—my first baby, her name's Suniva. She was in

150

the garden with Grandma Rose and my Dad, I think she came here by mistake because I heard her laughing." I look around the room for hints where Suniva may have hidden.

"Don't upset yourself, maybe she'll be back soon. I'll go get the doctor," Uncle Eli promises.

IN A DREAM, the Gentleman wags a finger at me. "Let her rest now!" He scolds. Behind Him, Suniva sleeps on a bed made up of tiny white doves that form into cumulus clouds. The cloud rises and then floats, as she continues to sleep—undisturbed—with her hands folded beneath her cheeks. I feel ashamed for wanting to disrupt her rest.

When I awake, the southern woman is wiping down surface space and emptying the trash pails.

"Well, it's sure nice to see those beautiful eyes open, Miss San Romun," she beams. "I was worried you were gonna decide and stay there—it sure is a beautiful place, ain't it?"

"You've been to the Corridor, the room with the golden floors and towering walls that scold you?" I try to prop myself up in the bed.

"Sit still—yes, I been there child," she says, and then places her dust rag down and comes near my bed. "It sure is a hard place to leave," she sighs.

"Tell me about the time you were there, Ms…"

"Violet, but folks that know me real good call me empress—Empress Violet, on account that my hair turned gray when I was in my twenties. I knew it was gonna happen, the same thing happened to my Ma about the same age. So, instead of covering it up, I stick my head up high, and walk like I'm wearing a crown," she exclaims.

"Violet," I repeat her name to myself, "have you seen the Purple Emperor?"

"No, I can't say I've seen that one. I don't get to watch the television much," she says.

I watch her closely as she picks up her dust rag and goes around the corners of the room. I wonder if there's something about her time in the garden she's unable to say.

"When were you there, Ms. Violet?"

I believe she would have answered had not the hospital room door swung open. Naomi peeps her head in and then turns to leave as someone in the hallway calls to her. I can hear the murmuring exchange between them but am not able to make out what's said. Then when Naomi returns, Ms. Violet scuttles her mop and utility cart through the door, but not before stopping to wink in my direction.

They all speak outside of my room now that I'm awake, assuming I don't understand the reason Orion still hasn't shown three days later. They often whisper out of my hearing; Uncle Eli, Naomi, the physicians, and the nurse. Afterward, they'll approach me as if trying to console a two-year-old.

"Emma-It's-going-to-be-okay!"

"Emma-do-you-know-what-this-is? Right, you hold the spoon like this…"

It is my limbs that won't cooperate, not my mind. But I play along with their treatment because it helps me—and them—as we wait. They hope I don't learn that my baby is missing, but I am the first to know. It was Victoria's delusional confession that freed me from my dark dungeon.

They keep watch over me; Uncle Eli taking day shifts and Naomi covers the evening. When my uncle fills me in on my mother's whereabouts, I am grateful for the chatty distraction.

"I'm allowing her to stay at the ranch for now. There are only two horses left there, so not a whole lot for her to do really," he says, and then goes on to tell me of how my mother had surfaced a month after my accident, wanting to know where her daughter was? Knowing of her past troubles with addiction, he decided it'd be best not to tell her what happened to me, for now.

"I'm sorry, but she can be a handful and trouble does seem to follow her," he says.

"I understand," is my response.

Uncle Eli explains that my mother is now volunteering at my Grandmother's organization, and when he pauses I assume he knows what I am thinking.

"It's been going on three months now, and she seems to be staying out of trouble, but don't worry, time will be her judge. If there's any shady business, she's out of there. I have her monitored around the clock," he assures me.

"She won't ever do to anyone else what she's done to me—I won't let her," are the only words I utter. When Uncle Eli nods his head, I wonder how much of my story he knows.

Naomi enters the room, and then my treatment team follows behind her. As they fill the space, my recovery is discussed. First, I will require several weeks' care from a rehab facility. This is a relief to hear being as though my legs and other limbs are not doing what they should. I make a conscious decision not to think of anything, or anyone else until my full strength is restored. My recovery should take months, but who's to say for sure.

On the next day, Naomi and I are practicing a hand-strengthening exercise when Tamar pays a visit.

"I didn't know you were awake," she says.

Naomi looks to me, searching for my approval. When I nod, she refuses to budge, denying Tamar the coveted position closest to me.

"How are you feeling?" She stands far off at the foot of my bed.

"Like I drove into a brick wall, but I'm getting better," I quip. Though I remember we are close friends, there isn't much else about her that I recall. We were close, but I don't feel she is someone to be trusted. Maybe it is because of the look Naomi gave me when Tamar entered the room, and even now.

"Great, we'll have to go dancing when you're on your feet, I know how much you love to dance," she snaps her fingers and does a wiggle with her hips. Naomi gives her an expression of scorn, and Tamar returns the glare.

"Yes, that's what we'll do, I'll plan a party. Maybe we could have it at your place?" she asks.

"My place? Is my place big enough for a party?" I ask because I still don't remember where I live, or if it's true that I love to dance.

"Of course, silly! Don't you re—"

"Emma-grab-hold-of-my-finger..." Naomi interrupts. "Squeeze, that's good!" she exclaims, congratulating me for the small victory.

"I'd say 2,100 square feet is plenty of space—I ought to know, it was me that sold you and your daddy the apartment," says Tamar, watching me close for signs of awareness. "You don't remember your fabulous apartment?"

"Now-give-me-your-other-hand," Naomi instructs.

Small droplets of sweat form around my face, dampening my hairline. Slowly I lower one hand and then lift the other to meet hers.

"I'm surprised you're not praying, or something," Tamar says, turning her attention on Naomi who continues as if Tamar hasn't said a word.

"Why wasn't I the first to know that she was awake?" Tamar fusses. "Her Father asked me to look after her before he—we're like sisters, aren't we Emma?"

"I'm in no condition for dancing," I grimace, frustrated with my hands. "Besides, I'm leaving for Florida soon."

"Florida—why Florida?"

"Because that's where her uncle lives," says Naomi.

I can tell by the smirk on her lips that she finds humor in Tamar's dumb-founding expression.

"I never knew you had an uncle—in Florida. Why am I just hearing about this? You, or your Dad, never mentioned an uncle or any other relatives before. You made me feel like you were all alone in the world with this huge inheritance and no one to look after you."

The more Tamar speaks about the memories of our times together, color begins to spill into tiny pockets of dark blotches in my mind. Visions of the two of us owning the night and partying until daybreak flash in my memory. She had been my first real friend in life, not Victoria, nor Shelly, and long before Naomi. Still, there were many things Tamar hadn't know about me; far more secrets than just an uncle and cousins in Florida or a mother I never spoke of.

"There's a lot about me that you don't know," I say, looking at Tamar first, then to Naomi. "I was pregnant before coming to New York."

The words roll off my tongue more comfortable than I ever imagined. "I gave the baby up for adoption." I pause for a moment to gaze at the clouds forming outside of my window. "I gave her to…a friend," I finally say.

It was the first time I had considered Shelly more than

anything besides 'a kind woman who helped me when I was in need.'

Tamar's eyes are bulging, and when she smacks her lips and marches over to the window I know she is upset.

"I see it took you no time at all to brain-wash my friend all over again," Tamar says, she leaves the window and moves closer to confront Naomi, who keeps her composure.

"She likes to come around acting all nicety, praying all over the place like she's the saint Mary or Mother Theresa!" Tamar's hands are flailing in the air. "Well, say your prayers and get on. I'm here now, and Emma's fine without you," she points at the exit. Just when I fear Naomi will leave, I notice how she stands her ground, still silent, refusing to react.

The more Tamar rages, darker pockets of my memory continue to fill; the last nine years spill into my mind like paint on a canvas. I recall our last encounterTamar had been angry about Naomi being around. She was jealous of Naomi then, and even now. She had been upset that it was Naomi's friendship that helped me to quit drinking, and not the twelve steps meeting she demanded I attend. I remembered standing at the door to my apartment, telling Tamar to leave.

"Come closer, please?" I ask, but she doesn't hear me above her yelling. "Please, come here," I ask once more, but she continues yelling at Naomi, who is now suggesting it is time for Tamar to leave.

"Just leave," Naomi says.

"Emma, do you want me to leave, or her?" asks Tamar,

turning her back on Naomi, who is now headed in the direction of the door. I didn't want her to go, but I don't know what else to say. So, I scream out...

"WHERE IS SUNIVA!" My cry is loud enough for the nurse and a security guard to come running.

"We're going to have to ask that everyone leave now," the guard says.

"I'll come back later." Naomi is compliant, but first comes over and kisses my forehead.

I mope after her goodbye. Tamar stands at the foot of my bed, staring as Naomi makes her exit. When she finally makes eye contact with me, I motion for her to come near.

"When I'm better, I'll explain everything. Please, give me time?" I beg. When she says, "sure," I have a sliver of hope for our friendship.

"Call me as soon as you can. We'll cook a gourmet meal together—like old times," she says.

When I agree, there's a look of remorse on her face. Her happiness depends on us, the way things were before husbands, fiancé's, and babies. Tamar wants nothing to do with my talk of God, and a Jesus that saves. She wants the young howling version - carefree, and immature - all the things we will never be again.

"I'll go now," she tells the hospital staff, her nose high in the air. Then Tamar turns and leaves with her heels slapping against the floor as she marches away; this is the Tamar trot, confidence oozing from every step she takes.

When my guests are gone the hospital staff voice their concerns with having visitors so soon, my recovery could be compromised, and resting is crucial. I'd argue that three months has been enough time to rest, but it's better to conceal my protest because my body agrees with their defense.

The interaction between Naomi and Tamar assists in restoring my memory. Also, after belting out one good scream, my voice does crackle a bit but is no longer raspy and weak as before. For this reason, I prefer to have more visits; I hope Orion will come soon.

It is decided that one guest will be allowed at a time; except for Uncle Eli, who is granted open access. The security guard who sits at my door is responsible for maintaining order; which almost guarantees I won't see Victoria again, at least not here. When the telephone at my side rings, the nurse watches to see if I'll answer it. When I refuse, she offers, "Let me get that for you."

"Emma, is that you—is it true?" asks Orion.

"Yes," I say. "It's me," and we both try our best to speak without crying.

"Why aren't you here?" I question.

"I can't believe you're awake, this is a miracle. I had to leave to take care of something important, but I'll be there soon. How are you feeling?" Orion asks.

"My hands don't seem to cooperate. In fact, there's a very kind nurse standing here holding the phone at my ear. I'm told this is normal for now," I say.

"I can't wait to hold you in my arms...I must tell you about Victoria, your friend..." when he pauses, I remember she has been in my room often. First, it was about how she was hungry—very hungry—and was having a hard time living in New York.

"I hired her as a live-in nanny. She did a great job at first, but it's not working out anymore," he says, but I hear the hesitation again, the thing he's unable to say.

"Do you love her?" I ask, because I need to know the truth.

"Absolutely not, we hardly see one another. In fact, I'm looking for her now, I can't seem to find her today, maybe she has an appointment or something," he says.

"When you do, tell her thank you for me, I'd like to see her soon," I say.

"So-would-I," he adds, then after repeating how much he loves me; he ends the phone call.

At the time, I remember Victoria as my enemy, but there is something else. She has visited often, confiding in me. I don't recall feeling threatened, only concern. It was an old war we fought over a decade ago, and there is no reason we couldn't be friends today.

I remember her visits far more than all the others. What was it she said, "we're sisters," or "we're like sisters?" It was something like that, or had Tamar been the one to say it? She mentioned that she would take care of "our baby." What an odd thing to say, even to someone laying in a coma.

161

Where are you, Victoria? Take care of my baby – *"our baby?"*

The phone rings again, and there is no one around to answer it but me. With the little strength I saved after Naomi and Tamar's visit, I manage to reach for the phone by the tenth ring.

"Hello," I breathe into the receiver.

"Tell her we're fine..."

I can barely hear for the background noise; children squealing, people shouting.

"When she wakes up, she'll know where to find me, I'm at home," says Victoria.

"I'm awake now," I say, but maybe not audibly.

The call goes silent or disconnects. There is a way to trace the call or ring her back, *Think Emma, you know this.* Before I can figure out the code my hospital room door swings open with my surgeon, and a team of nurses; they ask me more questions, and want to run more tests.

"Please, tell them I'm alright now!" I say once I spot my Uncle Eli. When he shushes me, I realize the swarm has gathered at his command. "Do you hear me? I really am fine," I say.

"Yes, you are princess, but we need to get you cleared for the transfer. Your therapy will take place in Florida—don't worry or stress yourself," he says, and then I nod my surrender.

"Have you seen Orion today? I'm waiting for him, he

called earlier." I peer from around the nurse who is poking my arms to inject a needle.

"Yes, he'll be here shortly," says Uncle Eli. Turning away from me he grabs hold of a young man and pulls him into a corner.

I watch as they whisper to one another. When my uncle sees me, he turns his back, so I'm unable to read his lips. Then I am wheeled out of the hospital room for x-rays and CT scan. Finally, I'm out of that room.

Inhaling my lungs expand with air from the hallway, I take deep breaths, allowing my nostrils to fill with the smell of cleaning products, food trays—grilled cheese maybe, and chicken noodle soup. Someone exits a restroom, the scent of their waste-matter trailing as they pass by.

The exam lasts about 30 to 40 minutes, and after the final scan is complete, I am wheeled back into my room. Exhaustion from the activity causes me to roll onto my side for the first time, and fall asleep.

WHEN I AWAKE, the first person I see is Orion. He stares at me for a long time without saying a word. "What time is it?" I ask, noticing the shades on the window still closed. "It's barely 5:30 in the morning, you know I like to rise with the sun," he answers.

I watch him, his smooth hazelnut skin disrupted by the lines around his eyes, and his lips. Despite the trace of worry, he is still a handsome man. We hold our stare for a moment until his unspoken words cause me to blush.

"I need a mirror," I groan, what I must look like to him.

But he moves nearer, holding his gaze. Leaning in closer, he places his lips near mine, almost touching, and then inhales. When he closes his eyes, I copy him. We stay like this for a while, catching each other's breath. When my eyes open, his are watching me again. When he kisses my mouth, I can taste the creamer from his morning coffee on his lips.

"Seeing your eyes open makes it all worthwhile."

When he moves away, I reach for him to stay close.

"Why were you standing in the rain with her? Is that why Tamar was mad at you?" I ask, needing to hear the story from his mouth—those lips that have just kissed me and said, "I love you."

Orion inhales before moving in close again, kissing my lips and forehead.

"You have every right to know what happened that day— it was a huge misunderstanding...well partly," he says.

I hold my breath waiting for his confession. *Tell me everything Orion, please leave nothing out.*

When he reclines into the chair, I observe the routine he's developed over the past three months. He slides off his shoes, sets the food tray, and a glass of water nearby. The newspaper is within reach to the right side of him. He doesn't bother with the remote, he prefers to sit in silence.

I picture the many days he's done this exact practice, waiting dutifully for his sleeping beauty to awaken. I wonder if he feels remorse or responsibility for what has happened to me. He says that Tamar was angry at him, and in his opinion, she had every right to be. He made her believe he would do a huge favor for her; in return, she'd pay him a large sum of money. When he couldn't go through with the deal, he kept the money. He fails to mention or maybe has forgotten to say what the favor was.

When I ask, "what favor," a lump gets caught in his throat, choking the lie he's trying hard to create.

"She asked if I could be her s-sperm donor because she and Beaumont had trouble conceiving," he says, taking a deep breath. I watch as the knot passes from his throat, freeing his speech. "I lied to her, made her think I'd go through with the sperm donation. The clinic told me she'd never find out, but she did." Then he says that on the day Tamar confronted him he had just met with a new client, Victoria, to discuss a civil suit against her landlord."

I want to forget that dreadful day, but instead, I tell him what I saw: Tamar arguing with my fiancé who's standing with my enemy. When the women turn on each other, he separates them and then afterward, he embraces Victoria.

"She thanked me for taking her case, there was nothing between us," he defends himself with eyes pleading for mercy.

I believe him.

Orion doesn't know about my past experiences with Victoria. So, I tell him we have known each other since childhood, five-years-old to be exact. Then I begin the story of the day she antagonized me to the point of tears at my grandparents' home. I go on about how we later became friends but quickly returned to enemies because of my betrayal. Our physical fights increased in violence, until the point that school policy had to be updated to include strict rules against assault and battery.

"We fought like two cats in a back alley—it's true," I say when his face goes blank.

"Emma, she has our baby!" He says wiping the sweat-

166

beads from his face. "It's time to involve the police."

"I don't think she'll harm our baby," I say as I stop him from reaching for his phone.

"After all you've told me, how can you even think that," he searches in his pocket, I assume for his cell phone he's left sitting on the table. "I must report this—I don't know what this lady is capable of."

"Because she's my sister," I whisper, not sure if he hears my words. When he freezes in motion, I watch as his face contorts. "Victoria-is-my-sister... neither of us knew growing up," I admit, still trying to believe it myself. "And she called me already, she and our baby are fine."

"Are you telling the truth? I mean, are you sure of this? Your uncle never mentioned having another niece," Orion says.

"He doesn't know yet, so please don't mention it, I'd like to tell him in person," I say.

I want to tell Orion that Victoria's decision is partly based on his behavior; working many hours, never available—like my dad had done, but I decide to leave that conversation for another day.

"She didn't want to be in your way. She thought she was helping by taking the baby until I was better," I continue.

"But I never made her feel uncomfortable, I practically gave her my home." He's shaking his head.

I think about telling him that Victoria went back to Denver because she was depressed living in New York, but I can't risk his reaction.

"We'll go together after my treatment when I'm able to walk and hold my baby at least."

"I'll go get our baby and meet you in Florida."

"No! She said I will know where to find her," I protest, almost in tears. He must understand why it must be me—not him, to get our baby from Victoria. But he's worried, I can tell by his questioning eyes. "Look at me, I'm of no use to either of you like this—we still need her help." I plead with him until he stands and faces the window.

"When she calls again I'll tell her to give you our baby," I say, giving in. "Then you both can meet me in Florida."

This solution seems to please him as Orion returns to me, kissing my lips and holding my hands to his face.

"There's more, your uncle is involved," he says.

I worry with my Uncle Eli leading the search he'll use aggressive tactics to track Victoria. I must tell him that Victoria is his niece too.

"Orion, what's our baby's name?" I say, tapping him gently on the shoulder. When he slowly raises his head I can see the frown lines on his forehead.

"Well, I wanted her to have your name. I call her Lynn for now until you decide—"

"No, not Lynn. Her name should be Suniva after my first child." I look him in the eyes, making sure not to blink. I nod my head when his eyes ask, "What are you saying?"

168

Then I proceed to tell him about the evening of my high school graduation; finding my mother in the backyard fooling around with my yellow Labrador, Biscuit. My anger at her for leaving drove me out into the yard to confront her—slap her if need be. I explained how her boyfriend, Ogre, came up from behind and knocked me out with something strong. Orion shook his head, considering the possibility that I might still be delusional from my head injury.

"Yes, this really happened," I say.

When I see that Orion is listening, I take my time and finish the story. I tell him how I awoke in a filthy dark room with trampy-clad women on posters along the wall, boarded up windows and a locked door holding me captive.

"The men that came for me were like monsters walking through walls. I couldn't figure out how they were getting in, when I couldn't find a way out," I tell him. "But I was drugged—some days I took the pills willingly, for the pain."

Feeling a prick in the tenderness of my palms, I look to see both my hands are pulled tight into fists, my fingernails digging into the fleshy center. Orion's eyes begin to swell with tears. He is listening, seeing the woman he professes to love with brand new eyes.

"But there's more," I continue, telling of how one of the men, kinder than the rest, fell for me. Using his interests to my advantage, I coerced his cooperation to help with my escape—and a scheme to give my mother an overdose with her next fix. When the day arrived with our pre-planned signal, I was surprised to see it was my mother who'd come to facilitate my getaway. She had finally realized no drug was worth selling her daughter. No one was hurt, except for Biscuit.

Then I was running, fleeing from the room, my mother, and my past. It was nightfall by then, which made my hiding behind buildings and trees easy. I ran until daybreak and became delirious. By the time the old yellow Volkswagen squealed to a halt beside me, I couldn't remember who I was, or where I was headed.

"So, I went with her, because she said the Northern Lights, along with Venus, paired with the crescent moon in the twilight sky would cleanse my soul," I say, chuckling at the memory, and my ignorance.

I had been fascinated by Shelly—the vegan, aromachologist, new-age spiritualist, and doula. She was the exact opposite of everything my Grandma Rose had brought me up to be, unlike anyone I'd ever met before. I considered her to be a friend I'd never had.

Once we were settled into the cabin at Sebec Lake, I became like a student, absorbing her teachings on organic and vegan lifestyles; up until the day we learned I was with child. That's when the idea of dancing under moonlight and howling under the aurora borealis was no longer fun.

I became consumed with ways to terminate my pregnancy. Shelly fixated on our growing family, tried to convince me this was the universe's design—giving back what "the takers" stole from us. I knew the best outcome was to stay with Shelly, have the baby, and leave what I viewed as a spawn of evil with her. If I went home, there was a considerable risk of my mother catching up to me, and of Ogre laying claim to me or my child, as he'd done before. I was also worried for my Dad and what he'd threatened if Ogre showed his face again. I couldn't go back home now, but I didn't want to stay with Shelly or the baby. Seeing that my mind was set, she agreed to the adoption.

Shelly had a friend that practiced law here in Manhattan. It was after a drive into town to finalize the adoption that I fled like a fox who'd just gnawed off a limb from a steel-clamped trap. I hobbled away in tears first and then found myself sprinting as adrenaline propelled me farther away. I refused to look back.

"No matter what I did, I couldn't stop thinking about the baby. Then there was this evil voice that taunted me day and night—that's why I drank," I continue.

By the time I finish speaking, Orion's mouth is hanging open, and so is my Uncle Eli's, who says, "I'm so sorry."

I'm not sure at what point during my confession he enters the room, so I'm unsure what part he is sorry about. It doesn't matter to me if he has heard it all, or just a portion. I am finally talking about what happened to me, and like so many other survivors at PAHST, this will be the first of many times, I will repeat my story.

"Thank you," Orion says, "thank you for sharing this

171

with me." He loosens my clenched fist and kisses the center of each palm, right where my fingernails left their imprint.

Uncle Eli clears his throat before turning to give us a moment of privacy. As he remains with his back to us. I can see his shoulders square as he tries to anchor the emotions that threaten to capsize his stern, steady ship.

"If I had my way, we'd build one of our new community centers in each borough of this city," he says, walking up behind Orion and patting him on the back. "If you weren't already aware, your fiancé here is the visionary behind my newest development in Harlem," says my uncle.

When Orion grins at me, I see his chest poke out a bit. Orion outlines his vision for the opening of the center; approximately how many square feet were needed to run the facility and the type of doors that would invite teens, but deter criminals. His voice rises when he begins explaining the preventative and early intervention programs.

"You're happiest when working with young people," I remark. I want to ask how his internship at the law firm was going but couldn't for fear of bringing up what had happened to me there.

If the first launch in Harlem is a success, there'll be another center in Brooklyn in two years. My Uncle Eli chimes in with specifics of his building and development expertise; what similarities each structure should have, or slight variances accommodating unique needs of the perspective environment. He just so happens to have a sketch of recent

172

changes with him, and for a moment their backs turn while peering over the notepad in my uncle's hand.

The security guard peeks his head through a crack in the door, announcing that Naomi has been waiting fifteen minutes to visit with me. Uncle Eli and Orion are quick to say their goodbyes, promising to return in the evening; I take no offense in their leaving. The corners of my mouth curl upward as I watch them exit my room, heads still bowed as they scrutinize the plans.

"It's so good to see you smiling, I have a few things for you," says Naomi, matching the grin on my face. She places her tote on the table and unloads a bag of kennel popcorn, sparkling water, and some beauty products.

"I'm not sure if I can have those," I say, pointing to the snacks.

"Those are mine—these are for you," she holds up a hairbrush and nail-care kit. "First, I want to tell you about the scar, I'd like to show it to you when you're ready," she says.

"What scar?" I want to see it," I gasp, my hands tremble as I envision the worst. No one has mentioned a scar; not my surgeon nor any of the nurses. I am sure Uncle Eli is the reason for their sealed lips.

"And there's something else, a section of your hair had to be shaved off," she says and pokes her lips into a pout.

I like that she's the one to break the bad news to me; it's hard to have a meltdown when your messenger is so optimistic about life. After retrieving a pocket mirror from her handbag, Naomi holds the oval mirror up to my face. The scar is at my hairline, my hair shaved about 3 to 4 inches back. What was I to do with a quarter section of a shaved head?

She probably assumes it is the scar that brings me to tears, but she's wrong. I'm crying because I don't recognize the woman who stares back at me; those sad, yellowed eyes, the swollen face and cracked, ashy skin looks nothing like me.

"I'm sorry, "I didn't mean to upset you." She takes the mirror and shoves it down to the bottom of her tote.

"No, thank you for being honest, no one else has bothered to tell me, not even Orion." I shake my head, remembering the way he stared into my eyes. He had kissed me like I was that same girl with the long, thick hair and smooth cinnamon-colored skin.

Naomi goes into the bathroom and then returns with a warm, wet towel and lays it on my face. I sigh with relief when my pores expand from the moisture. After about a minute when the cloth cools, she pulls out a jar of sweet-smelling face cream and begins massaging it into my skin.

"This is made with truffles from France…I know how much you like exquisite products," she teases. Yes, I nod my head, then I close my eyes to enjoy the fragrance.

"Could you tell me more of the things everyone else is too afraid to say?" I ask, and then promise that it will be just between the two of us if she worries about my uncle.

Naomi pulls up her chair, reaches for my hand, and begins filing down my fingernails. She is the one to tell me

174

that Orion had submitted a police report about our missing baby and nanny but then retracted the statement stating he may have overreacted. They had started withholding information from me because of my newfound concern for the sister I never knew existed.

"But she called me, she will only hand my baby over to me, and I'll know where to find her," I say.

"Where would that be?" Naomi holds still making sure not to miss any of the details.

"Home—in Denver, I'll deal with her. I just wish Orion hadn't made that call."

"Well, if there's anyone to blame, you'll have to include your uncle, he insisted on filing the report. Also, I encouraged him thinking it was the right thing to do, it really is, Emma. The more help we have out there to bring her in safe, the better. We're all worried sick," she admits.

I hold my peace knowing my opinion won't make a difference at this point. If only Victoria would call again. I believe she'll come back after speaking with me.

"She'll call again, wait and see," I say.

"Speaking of Denver, I should tell you about your mom as well," says Naomi.

I wait for the news, assuming the worse where Reba is concerned.

"You'll be happy to know that your mother is doing very well," she says.

"I've heard, but has anyone actually seen her—does she

know I'm here?"

"No, and no," she replies. "I must admit it was hard to do, but I promised your uncle not to say anything. I've spoken to her on the phone. She wants you to know that she's clean now. You're going to be so proud of her, she's been helping out at your Grandmother's organization caring for clients."

"It's called PAHST," I say. "Parents Against Human and Sex Trafficking and she has no right there!" I almost yell but quickly remind myself the last time this happened there was a threat of removing visitors altogether.

"She mentioned you would probably have a fit. Your mom admitted some things to me, she's hoping to make amends with you...I've upset you; I've said too much." Naomi stands and places a hand on my arm

I shake my head, "No if we had this same conversation a year from now I'd still have a hard time with it."

"That's the reason I came here and told you my story," she says, "but I'm not sure if you heard me. I want you to know about the children I left in my country, Guatemala." Then Naomi recants her confession, all of it.

"I remember hearing you tell me this—not everything, but some of it," I say.

"Forgive me?" she asks. "I never meant to be dishonest, I just didn't know how to handle the situation. Now everything's a mess with this new president, I don't know if I'll ever see my children again. I barely finalized my own documents without the threat of being deported."

176

"We'll find a way for you to reconnect with your children," I promise her, placing my freshly manicured hands over hers. This was the woman who slept on my floor the night when the ugly voice told me I was going to die; she had gone with me to Denver and attended my father's funeral.

Naomi deserved my help.

A TEAM OF three physicians enters my room this morning. They say they've made these rounds every day since I was admitted. This time, along with my routine check-in, they give me news of my discharge from the trauma center. I am ready, more than ready to escape this bed after its tentacles have recoiled; releasing its hold from around my neck, spine, and legs.

Yesterday a snippy nurse helped me stand on my feet for the first time. This morning the three physicians watch as I take my first clumsy step.

"Not so graceful now," I murmur, and then laugh to keep from crying. The time and money spent on my formal dance lessons are now lost to these wobbly knees. The medical team's recommendation is a direct transfer to Cape Canaveral Hospital, the closest treatment center to Uncle Eli's home in

Cocoa Beach. Then they retreat, leaving me to digest the news and to continue resting before my release.

"You leave today, Miss San Romun?" Violet, the Empress, says when she enters my room. She approaches my bed and runs a finger alongside my face. I'm daydreaming about what a place named Cocoa Beach has to offer a cripple woman like myself.

"I'm awake," I say, opening my eyes.

Her bluish-gray hair shimmers from the sunlit window. "Empress Violet," I repeat her name, reaching out for her hand. "You never told me about your time in the Corridor."

She walks away from my bed and begins dusting in a corner, then another.

"Your folks on the way in, they out there at the nurses' desk working on discharge papers." When she shifts her position, I can see the grin she's trying to suppress. "I'll tell you next time we meet," she says, winking before my room door opens.

Orion and Uncle Eli enter, both waving papers with instructions for home care. Most of what they're saying I cannot understand, but what I know is my Uncle Eli prefers that my treatment be administered in his home and not at a facility. My only request is, get me out of this hospital bed before its jaws of death return.

Orion approaches me, and slipping an arm around my waist lifts me onto my feet. With him holding me this way, I feel confident enough to walk. He releases me sooner than I

179

wish, and the snippy nurse stands before us, ordering for me to sit down in the wheelchair.

"I can walk," I protest when Orion helps me into the chair. I reach for my head, making sure the head-wrap Naomi helped me with yesterday evening is still intact.

"Not without therapy first," says the nurse, "and not on my watch—you have your discharge instructions, along with hospital policy." She smiles, but I think it's for Uncle Eli's sake who has been watching us. This is a small matter, I tell myself; don't make a fuss. Besides, I am now looking back at the machines that have stopped humming, the empty bed, and the room door as it closes behind us.

"Why are we going this way?" I question, noticing as we're led to the utility elevator on the backside of the hospital. Orion looks to Uncle Eli, who clears his throat.

"Well, there are some news reporters out front, they wanted an update—"

"But you didn't want them to see me like this, because of the way I look?" I finger the head-wrap again.

"No, they're expecting to see you with…" Orion begins, his chest heaving as he bites his bottom lip.

I understand his frustration; this was supposed to be a happier picture as he wheeled his fiancé out of the hospital, me holding our baby—the miracle baby—born to the comatose woman. Uncle Eli and Orion aren't pleased with my wish to be lenient with Victoria, but I know she'll bring my baby Lynn to me.

After we load into the non-emergency, patient vehicle, my uncle mentions that we should stop by my apartment first. I know it should be me to pack my belongings for the trip, but I refuse to leave the van.

"Whatever you think I should have, grab it," I tell my Aunt Miranda who rides with us.

When they have gone, Orion holds me as if he'll never let me go. "I'm sorry I gave our baby to that —"

"Sshhh," I say. "You did what you thought was right," I try consoling him. He resists my gesture to cuddle but then reconsiders. After all, we have each other and this moment, which is a lot more than either of us expected a week ago.

"Did you see her?" he asks, pulling away from our embrace.

"No," I shake my head. "She came to my room while I was in a coma—I heard her and all of you talking to me," I say.

"I thought it was her walking by," Orion says.

We both look out the window, scanning through the crowd of people marching along the pavement, and as they cross the intersection over to the other side.

"Are you sure it was Victoria—was our baby with her?" I'm frantic as I continue watching the wave of people flowing past our vehicle.

"I'm sorry, it couldn't have been her the woman was alone, she wasn't carrying a baby," he says. Then he tells me that when Victoria left she took off with most of our baby's

181

items; carrier, stroller, even the bedding.

"How was she able to move it all?" I wonder aloud.

When Uncle Eli and his wife return to the van, we change the topic. The four of us, plus the driver, make our way to JFK Airport in silence. As we're approaching the passenger drop-off lane, Uncle Eli announces he's chartered a personal jet for our flight. It seems a great effort has gone into my transfer, and I can't help feeling that I'm a burden to them all over again.

"Just two weeks, right?" Orion reminds me of our promise to reunite in Cocoa Beach. I nod my response, afraid to speak for fear my emotions will choke my words. I want to say, "Come with me now!" But knowing he'll refuse without trying one last time to find our baby, I keep my mouth shut.

"I'll be there on Friday, that's just five short days," he says, holding me tighter.

My delight causes me to blush, and for a moment, I forget about the scar, my swollen face, and quarter-shaved head. I feel like a desired woman.

"I can't believe I'm alive," I whisper to Orion as we stand holding onto one another, feeling the rise and fall of our chests.

"It almost feels like a dream," he says.

I frown when the smell of the bay enters my nose. This is no dream, and all my senses are now fully functioning.

"FRIDAY," we yell to one another while waving our goodbyes. Then Uncle Eli insists it's time to board the aircraft. On the plane, Uncle Eli sits close to me. When his wife appears to be napping, he checks to make sure I'm comfortable before asking the question. "Did your mother know about your first baby?"

"She put me in that room, and I haven't seen or heard from her since I ran off," I say. Uncle Eli nods his head.

"I knew she was trouble," he says, gritting his teeth. "I'll have her put out at once!" He reaches for his cell phone.

"No," I say, placing my hand on top of his. "Please don't. Naomi tells me she's looking to make amends," I plead.

"She is, but I'm not sure I can forgive her," he says. "I have someone keeping an eye on her—for now she's clean, I'll know if that changes." He places the phone back in his pocket. "She must pay...for all of it!" And I know he's referring to the times I wasn't allowed to visit them for summers as a child, and for abandoning my Dad and me to live as a single, free woman.

"I believe she already has," I say.

From what Naomi told me, she was guilt-ridden and had no peace. It took Naomi's weekly check-ins to keep her from being suicidal. I knew exactly what my mother was experiencing. I hope she'd find freedom without having to crash into a brick wall.

"You do know you'll have to spend some time in a rehab facility, just for two weeks, or less," says Uncle Eli.

I nod my head, knowing that without intense treatment, my chances of regaining strength, or even walking again, are slim. I imagine what it would be like recovering in Denver with my Mom, and Victoria, in a fantasy world. We would all forget the past, and they'd nurse me back to health, but I know my condition places me at a vulnerable disadvantage. My treatment must take priority over family reunions.

Once we land in Florida, I'll have one day to settle into my new lodgings before starting intense physical therapy on Thursday. It worries me that I'm not able to walk, and even talking is a struggle at times. My thoughts are jumbled, so I speak much slower than necessary.

"I'm ready to call my Mother," I say as the wheels of the aircraft touch ground. Uncle Eli looks me in the eye, trying to discern which emotion is responsible for the outburst. My lips bend into a half-smile. I'm not sure of anything really—not even of my decision of flying to Florida.

When we exit the plane, it's dark out. Two young people greet my Aunt Miranda and then kiss my Uncle Eli. Afterward, they reach for me and introduce themselves.

"We are your cousins, Micah and Amelia," they each point themselves out. With a quick embrace, and two smiling faces, my anxieties about coming to Cocoa Beach dissipate.

It is near midnight by the time we reach their home. After Aunt Miranda and Amelia wheel me into the room they've prepared for me, I am helped into the bed. When the lights turn off as they leave, I roll over and weep into the pillow. They are more than generous, loving people, but my heart is aching. I'm weeping because the journey has taken a

LAURA GAISIE

toll on my body, which is now throbbing in new areas. I long to hold my baby, and that Orion was here with me. If only I could speak with Naomi. She would give me sound wisdom, along with one of her spirit-filled prayers.

As my thoughts turn to Victoria, I wonder if there's any truth to her confession. Most of all, I worry that Victoria's actions are part of a bigger game. I try to convince myself she's not sitting somewhere laughing as she declares the winning move...

"Checkmate!"

185

MY COUSIN AMELIA greets me early this morning with a tray of hot breakfast and coffee. Now that it's daylight, I can see that she has wavy, waist-length hair like her mother's, and more Caucasian features, like her mother. Her skin is permanently bronzed partly due to genetics, and from spending many days at sea for work.

"You leave tomorrow to start treatment, so I wanted to take advantage of the time we have together," she says.

After placing the tray on a foldable table, she helps me to a sitting position and holds the first bite to my lips. I should tell her it's not necessary to feed me, but I can't bear the image of such a radiant smile disappearing from her face. Amelia says her bedroom is large enough for the two of us, and when she learned I would be staying alone in the guest room, she worried.

"I think it's better to have someone with you at all times," she insists.

I tell her that the accommodations are wonderful, and I had actually slept like a baby.

In speaking with Amelia, I learn that my Uncle and his wife met during his time of military service. Miranda was living in Austria then and had been visiting family in Germany, where he was stationed at the time. Amelia eludes to the idea our Grandmother never cared for my Aunt, and when I ask why? She shrugs her shoulders and mumbles something like, "some people have a hard time with it."

When I realize she's implying that Grandma Rose had an issue with my uncle's wife because of her race, I am offended. My Grandma was no racist, I think to tell her, Amelia would know this had she spent as much time with our Grandmother as I had—but I say nothing.

From what I've observed, my aunt Miranda is a gorgeous woman with a head full of thick wavy hair and dark features. She is loyal to her husband and plays a significant role in their family business…she was everything Grandma Rose had hoped for my own mother to become.

"I hear your mom's an artist," I say to Amelia, hoping to change the direction of our conversation.

"Yes, she paints portraits for tourists on the pier, she loves the pier, ever since we lost Elijah," says Amelia.

"Elijah, your older brother?" I ask.

"Yes, we don't mention him though… it helps her to think he's missing, but he drowned—it's been over 20 years," she says matter factly before turning to face the window.

187

Amelia stares at the waves for sometime before returning to me on the bed.

A knock on the door interrupts our conversation, and without waiting for an invitation, Micah enters. He is two shades darker than Amelia but about the same build. I recall Uncle Eli saying that Micah recently turned thirty-one years old; which makes him six years older than me. The cell phone in his hand is buzzing, he runs a hand over his curly fro and then declines a call.

"I wanted to see you before I left for work, I'm glad you're here," says Micah, then flashes a smile before leaning over to kiss the side of my face. He pulls away, and the faint smell of marine and mandarin notes linger from his cologne. When the phone in his pocket continues buzzing, he grunts before declining the phone call, but I notice as his attention shifts.

"Let's chat when I get back this evening," he yells from the bedroom door as he exits.

It's not much longer until my Aunt Miranda enters, informing me that my uncle Eli would like everyone to eat breakfast together, like a family. She helps me to bathe and dress, and I use the time to probe her for information.

"How was your relationship with Grandma Rose?" I ask.

"Good, she was an amazing woman," she answers.

"What about my mom, did you two get along?"

"We were close in the beginning, but through the years Reba kept her distance," she says.

"I hear you're an artist, will you paint me someday?" Is my final question.

"I would love to," she beams, but I can tell she's happy to pull the shirt over my head which shuts my mouth for the moment.

Afterward, uncle Eli enters the room. His face brightens after seeing that my aunt and Amelia have successfully helped me to dress. Then he lifts me into his sturdy arms and carries my uncooperative body into the family room. When he sits me in the wheelchair I frown at first, but not for long because he places me directly before a large bay window with a panoramic view of blue skies and white-capped waves.

Their home is what I refer to as casual elegance. The exterior has been painted in a soft seafoam color, with a paved driveway, and manicured lawns. Inside, the walls appear freshly painted, as if they've never been touched by a toddler or raging adolescent. White upholstered furniture absorbs blue and green accents. There are three guest rooms downstairs and three bedrooms on the upper level.

The feature that makes me fall in love with their home is the over-abundance of window and glass doors. From where I sit it looks as though the entire Atlantic Ocean has swallowed their backyard. I can smell the morning sea air, and I listen as the roar from racing waves smacks against the rocks, then recedes; this is a sound heard from every point of the home.

When I'm moved to the dining table, I'm pleased to find

the view of the ocean follows me. Amelia sits close by insisting she should help me with the eating utensils, watching as I stare at the waves. The other's try to include me in their conversation—something about my aunt's paintings and complaints about Micah working too hard. When the garage door opens indicating Micah's departure, my uncle looks to his wife, who twists her lips to show her frustration.

After breakfast I ask them to leave me seated before the window, lost in a vision of the day when I'm able to walk along the edge of the coast with seafoam bubbling in the sand around my toes.

"If you'd like, I can have my dad help move you closer to the beach?" says Amelia, who remains at my side.

It's hard to answer her because my smile stretches beyond words. I nod with excitement, and when my giddiness wanes I answer, "Yes, please." Without hesitation, the three of them; Uncle Eli, Aunt Miranda, and Amelia lift me and my wheelchair from the kitchen, onto the deck and down through the backyard. They are silent as I'm carried along the sandy path that leads to a secluded grassy dune. Aunt Miranda's hands slip a few times, and she uses the opportunity to wipe the perspiration from her temple. Amelia and my Uncle have set their eyes on a marked place in the sand and have determined to get me as close to the shore as possible. When we arrive, my uncle sits me down and declares the spot, "Emma's special place."

For a moment, I am the girl who has just met her first

friend, a puppy named Biscuit. I am running on the lawn of my childhood home, swaying oak trees waving from high above my head. I am the girl doing cartwheels for my Grandpa and his horse, Misty, after spending the morning with Grandma Rose—free at heart and innocent again.

"Will you shave the rest of my hair off?" I ask Amelia after my uncle and aunt have gone, but she doesn't answer right away; I suppose it is a rather odd request.

"That patch is starting to grow back, might as well leave it," she says.

"I don't need it anymore, for so long I adored my hair because it was the one thing that reminded me of Grandma Rose, but it also reminds me of what I became in New York. I want a fresh look to go along with the new me," I tell her.

"Do you think you'll ever go back?" she asks, failing to answer my question.

I hesitate to answer thinking of the many ways to respond. Would I ever go back to Denver, and face Reba? Or back to New York running from nightmares and the ugly voice in my head? Back to excessive drinking and late-night parties?

"I'll go back for my daughter and Orion, besides that there's nothing else," I tell her.

We sit in the morning sun talking for a while, confiding in each other about things we each wished we'd done differently. In between our discussion, we nibble on snacks from a picnic basket my aunt sets between us. I express my desire to be stronger, less ashamed of my past. Amelia too has regrets; letting her longtime partner go after being pressured to meet each other's family. I want to pry and ask for more details about her mystery lover, but she is blushing terribly, and I don't want to embarrass her further. Her heart longs for the one she believes is her soul mate, this is the issue; lost love is a familiar story.

Amelia's eyes remind me of Shelly's when she talks of finding her husband with a new family. Her voice is like the sound of Naomi's as she talks about her children...she will wait for her mystery lover for as long as it takes, the same way Victoria's mother awaited a second chance with my father.

"Hey, have you ever heard anything about my dad having another child?" I ask.

"Maybe you should save that question for my dad," she hesitates to say. I suppose my pleading eyes get to her because then she adds, "There was a baby born the year he met your mom, I think her name's—"

"Victoria," I say, and then proceed to tell her the story of how this other daughter tracked me down in Manhattan and is now watching, or either holding my baby hostage; and how her dad and Orion believe Victoria ran off with our baby, but it was all a misunderstanding because she asked my permission first.

"When did she ask?" Amelia wants to know. I will sound foolish if I say she asked while I was unresponsive, but I am braver now, so I want to tell her the truth.

"She talked to me a lot while I was in a coma…I know where she went, I'll go to them when I leave here," I assure my cousin. "Will you shave my hair first?" I ask again after spotting my uncle approaching in the distance. Amelia follows the trail of my eyes, she waves to her father then goes about picking up our blanket and picnic basket—she never gives me an answer.

By the time we return to the house, it's almost three o'clock in the afternoon. Then I am wheeled into the family room where I'm told a special guest would like to see me. My Grandfather sits in a recliner, hunched back and hard of hearing. His face brightens when he notices me.

"Hi, Emma! How's your father?" he asks in an airy voice, less intimidating than what I recall. I try to picture him as the heavy-handed man who was always gentle with his horse but tough on his workers.

"Pop, you know he's gone, we talked about this on several occasions," says Uncle Eli.

"Did my Rosemary send a message for me?" he asks, and when he looks me square in the eyes I can see a glimpse of the stubborn man he once was.

"Okay, dad you're getting tired, let's eat so we can get you ready for—"

"She said to tell you that she loves you and that we should take care of each other," I blurt out before anyone can stop me. I shiver when a surge of wind blows through an open window that makes me wish I could fetch myself a sweater.

"I saw my dad too; they were both talking to me." I try to convince my uncle, his wife, and Amelia.

"I believe you," says Aunt Miranda finally. "My little boy spoke to me after—I've read about others going to Heaven when…" she pauses, I know she is looking for a better way to say, "when they are near death, or when they are about to die."

The chime from the garage door opening causes each of us to flinch. Soon Micah enters the room, and Uncle Eli uses the opportunity to excuse himself, asking to speak with his son privately. When he is gone, my Grandfather waits for me to turn my attention on him, and when I meet his gaze he winks at me, the same way Grandma Rose used to.

The next day and for the rest of the week, I spend my time at the intensive treatment facility in Cape Canaveral. To my delight, the treatment team suggests that my care is switched to outpatient; I am doing better with my hands and arms, although still wobbly on my feet.

Orion arrives this morning as promised, with a surprise guest—Naomi. Though it's a disappointment he still hasn't located our baby I am happy to have my friend's company. Because we're not married, Aunt Miranda reminds us that it's not appropriate for Orion and me to stay in the same room, though it's obvious we've already known each other in that way—her house, her rules, so I don't take offense to the sleeping arrangements. Besides, I know with Naomi I'll receive around-the-clock care.

I insist that Naomi share the guest bedroom with me, forgetting Amelia's earlier wish to bunk together. It's when everyone gathers in the dining room to watch as I demonstrate my progress in standing and holding objects that I see traces of rejection in Amelia's smile. When I look in her direction, she goes another way. When I ask if she'd like to go down to our spot, she tells me she has work to do. I can't bear the thought of hurting her, so I make a note to apologize the next time she and I are alone.

Later, Amelia comes to my side, saying she forgives the oversight, and that everything turned out as it should because she often works long shifts away from home. Then she smiles and hugs me before leaving for work, and I know we are still at peace.

"I want to show you my special place on the beach," I tell Orion after everyone's excitement begins to fade. So, with help from my uncle and Micah, my wheelchair and I are hoisted down the sandy path again. When the others have left us alone, Orion gives me the update.

"Victoria has been in touch with me, she knows you're awake now," he says.

"Then why does she still have our baby?" I ask.

"Because she thinks you wanted it this way, to keep our baby until you come to get her yourself—is that true?" he wears a confused expression, no doubt wondering when I would tell Victoria such a thing, and why she should withhold our baby from him?

195

"She promised to do everything in her power to keep my baby safe until I'm better... she said you worked too much, that it was best if she was out of your way," I tell him.

"Well, she has your cell phone number now, I know she's doing this because of the way I treated her. I didn't want to send the wrong message," he says, wrapping his hands around his bent knees and hiding his face. I know he regrets his decision, feeling as though he's let me down once more. I refuse to ease his guilt just yet—I haven't forgotten about his arrangement with Tamar.

"I'll get our baby," I say.

For now, I find comfort in sharing more with him about my firstborn. I tell him about her beautiful eyes, hazel like my fathers had been. How she died because the woman who adopted her didn't believe in traditional medicine.

When I begin telling him how I was given a chance in Heaven to say goodbye to Suniva, he blinks his eyes several times. After witnessing the shocking expressions from my uncle and the others, Orion's reaction doesn't bother me as much.

"Let me help you with this, we can locate Shelly together and hear what she has to say, maybe even look into getting her counsel for an appeal. Although I've decided to give up law, I still have some connections," he says.

His decision to change careers doesn't surprise me, so I don't bother questioning the choice; I saw the spark in his eyes when he and my uncle spoke of their plans.

"She took such good care of me when I really needed a friend," I say.

Shelly was odd, but this was the same woman who refused to catch a fish to keep me from starving. "She's a vegan—vegan's don't kill anything!" I'm serious when I say this, but for some reason my statement causes us to laugh.

The sun is beginning to set, and when Orion sees me shiver he suggests that we should probably be getting back inside.

"How will you manage," I ask, then realize he is preparing to carry me. When I wrap my arms around his neck and lay my head against his chest, my eyes are closed, and I almost don't hear him speaking over the roar of the waves.

"Forgive me," he huffs from trying to wade through the sand with me in his arms, "for Tamar…and for all the other stupid decisions I've made?"

How could I not forgive a man who'll carry me over a thousand feet through the dunes? The question is, do I make him sweat a little longer before telling him—yes! I forgive you, a thousand times one thousand.

● ● ●

We have developed a routine, Uncle Eli gets me into the minivan, and then my Aunt Miranda drives me to therapy appointments. Now that Naomi is in town she accompanies us to my rehab sessions. Amelia is gone for the week after being called to observe an aggregation of manatees north of

Sarasota. Uncle Eli, Orion, and Micah spend most of the working week at the construction company.

On one of those days, Orion and I spend time alone outside of the house. We leave early, hoping to catch the sunrise on our drive. Stopping for coffee at a local café first, we then pull over near the pier to watch as the muted blue sky washes away from the yellow and orange bubble that rises from beyond the horizon. This is where Orion reminds me of his promise to marry me before our child was born. He turns to me, looking over the woman that has survived the unthinkable, and declares his love.

"We should get married now," he says, before pulling out his tablet to search for local requirements of how to obtain a marriage license.

"Like this?" my voice pleads, "I hardly look the part of a blushing bride," I dismiss his proposal.

Sometime after 9 o'clock we arrive in front of the courthouse. That's when I begin to romanticize the idea of our eloping, and when I tell him, "yes, let's do this!" Orion wastes no time in getting me out of the car and into the building. We're both giggling like high school sweethearts as we enter the line and ask for the application. After paying for our marriage license, the love-spell seems to weaken, and it's time to reason like sane adults.

"If you think your uncle won't kill me, then we can go through with this now," he warns.

"Please, let's get out of here before we do something

crazy," I beg, and we leave the courthouse in tears from our laughter. Some people watch us with curiosity, but the staff smile after us – I'm sure they've witnessed countless others who've struggled between symptoms of love and sanity.

When Amelia returns at the end of the week, I remind her of my earlier request. "Shave my hair off, please?"

"What do you mean?" Naomi asks.

"This is hideous, my hair's uneven. Besides, it no longer suits me." I poke out my lips.

When Amelia tells Naomi how I've asked her to shave my head repeatedly, I expect Naomi to be upset. I know she wants to remind me of how 'the Woman's hair is given to her as a covering,' but she withholds her objection. Neither of them has answered me, and when my cousin leaves the room, I sulk on the bed, refusing to look up. Before long, Amelia returns holding a pair of clippers, and seeing my face light up, Naomi smiles with me. When Amelia flicks the power switch on, I shut my eyes tight as the buzzing touches my scalp. After several minutes, the room goes silent.

When I open my eyes, Naomi and Amelia remain quiet, waiting for my response. There are clumps of hair around my feet, I imagine them to be the last strands from the cord that held me bound to my past—I am free. Looking at my coconut shaped head in the mirror, makes me almost wish someone else's argument had convinced me this was a bad idea, but this is the real me I tell myself.

Later in the evening after the men have returned, none

of them seem surprised by my shorn head.

"You look beautiful," says Orion, with a kiss on my lips. Then he kisses near my scar.

"Bold and sassy," says Micah, with a thumbs up, that makes me grin.

"Change is good," Uncle Eli announces.

● ● ●

When the morning comes for Orion and Naomi to leave, we each express desires for them to stay. Even Grandpa enjoyed having the house full of family bursting from fun and laughter.

"Don't you worry about anything," says Orion, as I watch him pack. "Soon, we will have Lynn, and then we move forward with our plans," he tries to reassure me.

I hate watching him prepare to leave, but I refuse to let anyone wheel me from the room. It is when I see his laptop that I remember Uncle Eli had grabbed mine from my apartment. On my laptop was the contact information for the mystery woman who introduced herself to me at my father's funeral.

"I believe I know how to get in touch with her," I say, and proceed to tell him about the woman, Victoria's mom.

"Wish you would've remembered this sooner—I can change my flight?" He asks.

I tell Orion to go because he should be in New York in case Victoria decides to bring our baby back. When we have said our final goodbye, Naomi stands beside me instead of getting in the car.

"I'm staying another week," she says.

When I look at Orion, he nods. "Yes, she's staying, and your Uncle is heading back with me. We're close to finalizing details on the first community center."

"I don't deserve either of you," I say, but they each tell me I'm silly. For a girl who has struggled with relationships and friendships her whole life, their love for me is almost unbelievable.

That evening when Naomi and I sit on the deck, the sunset of coral with streams of lilac distracts me from her solemn mood. When I notice her subdued response to my excitement, I turn my focus to my friend.

"It seems as though the ocean air has been good for you," she says, trying to conceal her inner conflict.

"I can't believe my parents kept me from this place." I marvel.

"Maybe because they knew you'd fall in love and never want to come back home," she laughs. Then her face goes somber again before saying, "I want you to know your mom has been calling me." Naomi retells the story of how Reba had managed to track me down – well, not me but my apartment in Manhattan. After weeks of stalking my door, a neighbor told her she hadn't seen me for some time but knew where I worked—even where I attended church.

I know the neighbor in question. I was so excited after

getting baptized I talked her ears numb one day while checking my mailbox. This same person sends my mother to the advertising agency where I used to work, and this is where she and Naomi met.

"I lied—God help me—about knowing how to find you, but I did invite her to church. I told her she might find you there," says Naomi.

I would've woken up from my coma sooner just to see my mother step foot inside a church...Reba, in a tongue-talking, aisle running, Pentecostal Church?

"She didn't think you'd ever speak to her again, but wanted you to know she was four months clean," says Naomi.

"That's not long enough, I gave my first baby away because of what happened. I thought she was a monster, but Suniva was my angel," I say, and then pause before saying, "I'm grateful to have said goodbye to her...when I went to Heaven," I say slowly, wondering if Naomi will believe me.

"What was it like?" she asks.

"You do believe me? I've tried to tell the other's, but I'm not sure they really believe me," I search her eyes for pity or concern.

"Absolutely, I believe you," she nods.

Then I tell Naomi about the Gentleman and his wisdom, how he held me like a father holds a beloved child. How I spoke with my Grandma Rose and my Dad.

"Amazing!" is what she says to me when I tell the whole encounter. "What a blessing to be given that closure, maybe someday when we all get to Heaven I'll get to meet my children again." She looks away, watching the darkening sky as it swallows the remaining sunlight.

"I'm hoping you'll get to see them sooner than that," I say.

The patio door opens, and Micah appears asking if I'm ready to go inside? I can't help but notice the way his eyes linger on Naomi. When I look over at her, she tries to pretend not to see him. He approaches her first, extends an arm to help her stand, then tells her if she needs anything, "anything at all," she should not hesitate to call on him.

At the dinner table Micah seats himself beside Naomi, making sure she has enough to eat, does she need anything to drink—anything at all? Then he offers to drive her to the store and buy some items for the extended stay.

"Yes," she says, agreeing to take the drive with him. When the two of them help me to bed before leaving, I watch their interaction; Naomi's dimples are showing, which means she's smiling more. Micah isn't running off as quickly as he had the previous week. Then I wonder what it would be like if they fell for each other?

Don't be silly, Emma…they have already fallen.

LYING WITH MY eyes closed, I can hear the sound of small birds chirping in a nearby bush, and seagulls screeching over the swell of ocean waves that rise then crash onto the bank. When a lawnmower interrupts the vibration of nature with its own whirling and buzzing rhythm I still hear what I believe the ocean beckoning to me; *Come, let us meet at our private place.* "Emma's spot," Uncle Eli reminded everyone before leaving for his trip three days ago.

In anticipation of the new day stirring beyond my window, I drag my disobedient limbs out of bed and struggle to my feet. I manage to hobble across the floor and into the bathroom by supporting myself against the solid-wood dresser and sturdy wall. Reaching the toilet seat, I am grateful for the daily and repetitive leg stretches that helps to strengthen my gait. Maybe this will be the day I walk from the yard to the beach by myself.

I return to my room without taking thought of my inability. I'm thinking of something warm to wear in the foggy morning air as I make my way for the dresser. Just as I'm about to look inside the drawer, my foot turns in a direction it shouldn't, which causes me to lurch forward. The nightstand catches my fall as my hand jerks and knocks a cup to the floor. Amelia is first to appear. She knocks twice, asking if it's okay to enter.

"Come in," I say without moving because I don't trust myself not to stumble.

Amelia knows something has happened but won't come right out and ask, she watches my reflection from the mirror on the wall, wondering if it was a bad idea to leave me sleeping alone. Naomi moved to her own guest room the week after Orion's departure. Now I am looking in the mirror too, at the horseshoe-shaped scar at my hairline. Without hair, this scar is my one accessory.

"Only a girl with eyes as beautiful as yours could pull this look off." She smiles, misreading my expression; but it's not my shaved head that worries me.

"My hair will grow back quicker than my legs will strengthen," I grunt, turning to face the window.

There is a plate of food on the bedside, I believe Amelia must've placed it there when I left for the bathroom. She waits for me to eat, but now the screeching birds are calling out, and the swishing wind whispers my name, *"Emma, let's meet at our special place."*

"I brought you breakfast earlier," she says then places the foldable table closer to me.

"Thank you, but I was hoping to walk on my own this morning and have breakfast at the kitchen table." I try to appear jovial by showing a few front teeth, but my smile is weak and unconvincing.

"That sounds like a wonderful idea, I can walk with you if you like?" She approaches the window and stares at nothing specific, but her attention is somewhere else, far beyond the issues of this room.

"Would you like to go shopping with me? How about a wig, just to have options."

I'm not sure if her next move is intentional, but she reaches for the string and lowers the blinds. Next, she twists the wand in her fingers, shutting off my view to "Emma's spot," on the beach.

"There's a storm coming," she says upon hearing my exaggerated gasp. "I didn't want the swell from the waves to frighten you, It's a sight to see if you've never been this close to the ocean before."

"Oh, the waves do sound louder this morning." I'm finally able to say. When she turns her back, I laugh at myself; how silly I'd been thinking the wind had been calling for me.

"Sure, I'd like to try on wigs."

"We should also pick up some clothes for you," she continues.

"There you are," says Naomi, appearing in the doorway, "are you ready for—"

"Yes, she's ready for a boring day out with her cousin. I hope you don't mind?" Amelia interrupts Naomi and grins sheepishly in my direction. A secret look is exchanged between them, giving me a reason to question their motives. Amelia shrugs her shoulders, and Naomi stares wide-eyed like the kid caught holding a red crayon beside marked up walls.

"It's nothing really, I just didn't want Naomi to spoil my surprise. I'm taking you to my special place today," says Amelia. I believe them because of Naomi's animated expression; or is this the face of a woman with a love hangover?

"Maybe she'll tell us how her date went," I tease, but she is quick to correct me.

"It wasn't a date, just two people taking a ride," she says. Her face darkens from the flood of embarrassment.

It is only when Amelia tells me to, "pay attention, please," that I quit prying for details and listen to the pre-planned day. First, my scheduled physical therapy—neither of them would agree to skip out on the session. Afterward, we could go shopping.

"When does the special place come in?" I ask Amelia as she helps me to the shower.

"Later in the day."

Naomi remains in my room, picking out an outfit for me to wear. Before the door closes, I see she is still blushing.

"Alright, we may have had dinner too," she says as Amelia shuts the bathroom door.

My mouth gapes open, "they were on a date?"

I have forgiven the morning mishaps by the time we reach the clinic. In the excitement, I forget to have Amelia and Naomi watch as I walk, but my physical therapist is eager to see my progress.

"You're glowing," she remarks, observing the twinkle in my eyes and my giggles when I stumble and catch my balance. I attribute my improvements to the exercises Naomi and Amelia have helped me with daily, and also from having the extra support of my family.

"Emma's spot is where most of my home treatment takes place, and the time flies when we're out there."

I am purposeful in excluding updates about baby Lynn, for fear my mood will dampen. When I finish babbling about how fantastic my life is going, the session is over. I surprise myself by telling no one thus far about my conversation with Victoria last night.

Fed up with Uncle Eli and Orion's handling of the situation I searched through deleted documents to locate Sadie's contact information—the mysterious woman, Victoria's mom. It was a brief phone call.

"I am fine," I told her when she asked how things were going for me since my father's passing. "I've misplaced Victoria's phone number, is it possible to get that from you?" I asked.

"Of course," she said, expressing relief that we have reconnected and are getting along well. I try to find ways to end the phone call because much of the conversation is lost to me. What I do overhear is that Sadie wants me to know she has been hoping for Victoria and me to become closer. After what feels more like thirty minutes than the actual ten, she ends the call.

I'm not sure if it was my nerves or sensory impairment from the accident, but I misdialed the number three times. Finally, the phone rang, and it was Victoria's voice I heard on the recorded message.

"It's me, Emma…your sister," I said after swallowing the knot in my throat. "We need to make arrangements so I can get my baby. Please, call me back."

Then this morning there was a text message on my cell phone.

Victoria: I will gladly place your baby in your hands only.

After the strength training regime, I'm instructed to continue using the wheelchair, for safety purposes, and then my session is over. When we are close enough to the van, I ask Naomi to stop pushing. Bending over to lock the wheels in place, I stand to my feet and then walk the rest of the way. When I make it to the driver-side without fail, the three of us revel in the celebratory moment. I almost don't hear my cell phone ringing.

"I'm so glad you're better!" says Victoria, and the lump in my throat returns.

"Where are you?" I ask, calm but desperate. "Why haven't you given my baby to Orion?"

Naomi and Amelia are quiet now.

"I'll bring her to you, but he's not fit to have a baby," she complains. My eyes begin to water, and as I try to stave off tears, Amelia motions for me to hand her the phone.

"I'm in Florida with my Uncle Eli for rehab," I tell her.

"That's wonderful, but I can't travel with the baby right now," she says.

"You don't have to travel—" I begin to explain, but Naomi interjects.

"What about someone else, will she hand your baby over to me?" she asks.

Victoria wants to know who else is around, and Naomi identifies herself, saying they had met before at the hospital. When there's no reply I fear we have lost the call, but I can still hear her breathing, and then a small whimper in the background.

"Shhh, it's okay baby," she says, and then hums a lullaby. "I will release our baby to you only," she repeats her demand.

I want to scream and threaten Victoria's life. Instead, I say, "thank you for taking such good care of my baby. I'll come—where are you?" If she takes the bait, I plan to send Orion and the whole calvary her way.

"Where else would I be? I'm at home," she says.

Amelia and Naomi exchange questioning looks. They want to say, send someone to her house; but Victoria is homeless, home for her could be in a box, a shelter, or even an abandoned warehouse.

"You're in Denver?" I ask.

The air is sticky inside the van, and each of us begins to perspire from the sealed windows we fail to open. Before she confirms her location, my baby starts to fuss. Victoria's words are muffled while she shifts and moves to comfort baby Lynn.

"It's okay, my angel—I have to go now, she needs to be fed and bathed. How long will you be there—oops! She just made a little messy, I'll call you back," says Victoria. Then the call ends. Because of the love in Victoria's voice, I hold back tears that sting my eyes. My cousin is crying in the driver's seat, and Naomi has her head down, whispering something to herself.

"I'm going to Denver tonight!" I tell them.

Amelia shakes her head, No.

Naomi is still mumbling to herself, and I wish she would speak up; scream, yell, cry at least…because I can't, for fear of a relapse.

Amelia starts the engine, saying we should carry on with our plans for the day after our emotions subside. When Naomi agrees, I decide to continue with them because I'm not sure how else to handle the situation. Then I am taken to a salon that specializes in custom-made wigs. Within two hours, a full cap is placed on my head. I force a smile, although I have no need for the beautiful piece. Naomi and Amelia try on hair-pieces for themselves, which causes us to double-over with laughter from their flamboyant choices. After our purchase, we each don sunglasses along with our new hairdo.

I find comfort in their efforts to enjoy our outing though we continue on, suffering in silence. When we enter a fashion boutique to buy a sun-dress, I try hard to stay in the moment, denying my inner thoughts. By the end of our shopping spree, I can remember purchasing the wigs, but everything else is a blur. Stopping for lunch, I notice another text on my phone; a picture from Victoria as she holds my baby, with a message saying, "She's ready to meet her mommy."

"I want you to borrow this, just for tonight," Naomi hands me her praying hands pendant, "because I want you to remember this as the day your prayers are answered."

When we return to the house, there are several cars in the driveway. "I forgot my mom was having guests tonight, we'll get changed in your room so we can leave quickly," says Amelia then rolls her eyes. There was still the special place she wanted me and Naomi to see.

Once we are inside, I notice the extra lights trickling in from the back yard. There is catered food in the kitchen, and laughter coming from the patio. Because I have insisted on walking from the garage to my room Amelia has difficulty rushing me along. I catch a glimpse of hydrangea flowers trailing through the yard as I hobble by.

"I hope your surprise is as good as your mom's party," I say.

"Trust me, they'll wish to be where we're going," she remarks, and my steps quicken at the thought of the impending activity.

Once we've made it to my room, I'm disappointed to see the blinds still drawn from the morning threat of stormy weather. Naomi distracts me by insisting that I hurry along to shower and dress. I am wearing a white maxi-dress, with blue sandals. Naomi and Amelia are wearing lilac sundresses.

"I don't think this is necessary," I say when Amelia places the wig back on my head. Then she spins me to face the mirror, and the image brings a smile to my face.

"Maybe we should say hi to your mom and her guests before we leave." I pull my shoulders back and flip the hair from my face. Naomi is chanting about "something," when we leave my room.

"Something…something…blue," she is saying.

When we reach the living room, she speaks clearer.

"Something old, something new…something borrowed something blue, that's it!"

"What are you saying?" I frown at her.

When I step through the glass door, I understand why my blinds were drawn this morning. The backyard has been strung with lights, and there are four decorated tables with chairs covered over in ocean-blue fabric. A wooden floor has been placed on the ground, from the deck leading to the narrow path toward the beach. In the distance, I see where a canopy has been erected close by "Emma's spot." A gust of wind billows the white and blue linen draped over the top of the structure.

Something old, something new, something borrowed, something blue: a wedding!

Uncle Eli appears from down the sandy path. He waves for Amelia and Naomi to proceed ahead. Then when we approach, he reaches for my hand and helps me down onto the wooden floor. We walk together, through the yard, down the trail and out before the canopy.

Orion is standing underneath the gazebo, wearing a handsome blue linen blazer and pants, with a wheat-colored shirt. When he sees me approaching with Uncle Eli, his smile is brighter than all the stringed lights combined. I want to run to him, but sensing my eagerness my uncle squeezes my hand.

"I hope you don't mind me being the one to give you away?" he asks.

I give my answer with a hug because there are no words to equal what I'm feeling inside; I am alive, walking on my own, surrounded by people who love me, about to marry my true love. When we finally reach the canopied structure, I notice one of the guests is my physical therapist. She is all teeth from excitement, and I wonder how she was able to keep the secret during our earlier appointment. There are a

214

total of twelve people at my wedding, including the minister, Orion and me.

When the question is asked, "Will you take this man to have and to hold...from this day..." another gust of wind blows the fabric on the canopy top. In the wind, I hear a child's laughter; sounds of Suniva chasing butterflies in the garden. A purple butterfly lands on a wooden post propped in the sand nearby, leading me to believe she has sent the purple emperor to congratulate me on my wedding day.

After the minister says, "I now pronounce you husband and wife, you may kiss the bride." I whisper in Orion's ear, "Victoria called me today, she's ready for us to come get baby Lynn."

"Things can only get better from here," he grins.

Then we turn to greet our guests: Mr. & Mrs. Stone.

I AM NOW, "Mrs. Emma Stone!" I say aloud every morning, the change of name still foreign to my ears. We are staying at a resort in Palm Beach for our honeymoon, and spend our days snuggled together in our room. In the evening we sit on the beach underneath the stars.

"Is it time to go get our baby now?" Orion asks on the third day.

We have managed to keep our anxiety at a controllable level after speaking with Victoria the morning after our wedding. Orion and I had her on speakerphone, so Uncle Eli, his wife, Naomi, and my cousins are a witness at our attempt to reason with her.

"Hope you know you're in deep trouble young lady!" Uncle Eli fired at her before anyone could stop him.

"Why? What have I done wrong?" She played innocent. "I was asked to take care of the baby, and I've done that. Orion's the one who pawned his baby off on me while his fiancé was clinging to life in a hospital bed!" she said, her venom trailed from the speaker and poisoning the air we breathed.

When everyone looked to Orion for answers he shrugged his shoulders and prepared to defend himself. "You were paid to be a live-in caregiver—in my home, nowhere else...you're not even getting paid anymore!" he reasoned.

"That home wasn't healthy for me, it was cold. You already knew what I went through at my last residence," she raised her voice,

"Yes, the rats, what's that have to do with you taking care of my baby?" he demanded to know.

It is a good question.

"Emma, the rats from that hole-in-a-wall apartment would bite me at night. In the morning they hung out in the alley watching me, I still have scars from their teeth!" Victoria exclaimed.

"I'm sorry," I said and told her that I wanted to help.

"I'm safe now, and the baby is happy here." She stopped talking, and we listened as she muttered a few cutesy things to baby Lynn. Victoria doesn't know about Suniva or that this would be my second child to lose if things don't turn out well.

"How are we to know that's even a real baby?" Uncle Eli barked at the phone. "Or your baby for that matter?" he questioned Orion. Then Aunt Miranda calmed him with a look, followed by a shoulder rub. He took a seat and rocked back and forth.

"In case you didn't get the memo, Emma-and-I-are-sisters...I wouldn't hurt our baby, I'll place her in Emma's hands only."

She has made this statement enough that I start to believe her.

"Well, Emma and I are both coming to you, and you will hand over OUR baby!" said Orion.

"I wouldn't have it any other way," she said before ending the call.

Uncle Eli was out of his seat again, a giant mass of angry energy headed straight for my husband. "You tell me right now—did something happen between you and that sick woman!" he fumed.

"On my life, nothing happened between us. That's the problem, I never spoke to her only left notes. If she came into a room, I left quickly," he explained. "I was afraid of sending her the wrong message." He stands against the wall, trying to avoid my uncle's reach. They don't know our story, but I understand why he had reason to fear leading Victoria on.

"We were enemies first," I confessed to my family. "All those years in Denver, she hated me, and I couldn't stand her. She followed me to New York out of spite."

"Now you tell us this!" said Uncle Eli, he was beyond reasoning with. My aunt Miranda was able to calm him again by saying she forgot to give us her wedding present. When she motioned for her husband to follow, Orion steadied his breaths as he took a seat. I notice how Naomi's head is bowed until Micah approached and she cheered up. When my aunt and uncle returned, they were lugging a heavy, wrapped canvas.

"I hope you like it!" she grinned.

My uncle Eli helped her to remove the cover, exposing a floor-length portrait of me and Orion. In the painting, our backs are turned to the artist, and there is a side profile of my face, as I stare at Orion; I imagine this to be the very moment he had asked that I forgive him and I tell him, yes.

"It's perfect," I said, admiring her beautiful work-of-art.

"Yep, she's the best artist in town…and the only thing missing from this picture is your baby," said Uncle Eli.

The room is silent, no one bothering to argue with my uncle's assessment. Then he walked over to my husband and offered an olive branch. "If you say nothing happened, then I believe you," he said.

"Looks like the second leg of our honeymoon will be in Denver," said Orion.

"Let's get packed," Uncle Eli said to his wife.

"Do they look like they need our help?" she asked, stopping him at the door.

It was hard to convince him, but we were finally able to get Uncle Eli to understand that this was something the two of us had to handle—alone. Later, as I packed in my room for our trip to the resort, Naomi knocked on my door.

"If you need me to go with you to Denver I can."

I shook my head and thanked her for the offer.

"You know, it's like she's frightened, not being spiteful. She's holding on to my baby like a lifeline—something worse than a rat bite happened to her," I said.

I know I'm right because my own experience has taught me that victims of sexual abuse don't always respond in rational ways; we need to cling onto something, but we also have a desire to hide.

"What do you think it is?" Naomi asked.

When I don't answer, I believe she reads my mind.

"If it's true it'll be almost impossible to pry your baby from her hands, you'll need reinforcement," she said.

When I tell Naomi that I understand the importance of allowing the authorities to do their job, I remind her that Victoria is my blood-sister, and she needed help.

"And they'll get her the help she needs," Naomi wanted me to understand.

I hoped so because Victoria's crisis was standing in the way of my happily ever after. My baby would be turning five months old soon; Baby Lynn, I still wasn't sure if that name fits. I always hated my middle name, but I would need to look her in the eyes before making a final decision.

"What do you think about the name Suniva," I asked.

"Isn't that the name of your first child?"

"Yes, I'd like to change baby Lynn's name to Suniva—

not to replace her but to honor her memory," I said.

Naomi was quiet, her head down as she squeezed a pair of my shoes into the travel bag. I was doing it again, making everything about me. I reach over and put a hand on top of hers. Naomi's eyes were glossy, but she was smiling. I can't imagine the magnitude of her loss - seis niños - four more than the two I had now lost.

"Helping you locate your children is just as important to me as all of this," I said when she looked at me.

She nodded, not knowing how much I'm prepared to help. I want to relieve some of Naomi and Victoria's pain. The others would disagree, but my sister deserved her share of my inheritance; even though I fear she struggles with a mental disorder.

The evening after my surprise wedding, Orion and I were invited to another dinner in the backyard. When I saw the strung lights still draped across the deck, I put a hand over my face to cover my embarrassment. I thought of objecting to another celebration, but Micah stood and cleared his throat.

"If I can have everyone's attention, please," he said.

Amelia and I looked at one another, and then to Naomi, who is lost in Micah's eyes. They were staring at each other as if there was no one else besides them at the table. Grandpa was also present and occupied himself with the folded napkins and dinnerware.

"This is different and unexpected for me, but I have big news, and I'd like to share it with the people I love the most in this world…" he began. I noticed how he refused to take his gaze off Naomi. I pinch her underneath the table, but she swats my hand away as she blushed.

"I hope you don't think I'm too fast, but you would make me the happiest man alive…" he was saying when I noticed the others now looking in Naomi's direction. They were all smiling —even Grandpa—but I was not.

"Will you marry me?" He asked, bending down beside her, but I was more surprised at how quickly she said, "YES!"

How could it work? She lived in New York and him here in Florida. Then I realized that I could be losing my best friend.

"Why aren't you smiling?" Orion whispered in my ears.

I force a smile when Naomi looks for me, allowing myself to see the gain in their union; this wasn't about losing, but an expansion of my family. I went to her, and after asking for my cousin to step aside, I held Naomi tight.

"I'm so happy for you," I said.

"Now you'll never get rid of me!" she said, holding onto me just as tight. I had so many questions that I refused to ask then.

Where will you live? When will we get to see each other? Are you sure about this?

It was Orion who pried us apart.

"Don't worry, they'll be closer than you expect," he said as if reading my thoughts and feeling my anxiety. Then as if on cue, Naomi finally asked the question that needed answering.

"But you're here, and I'm there—what will we do?"

"Whatever is best for you, we'll make it work," he said.

My uncle chimed in about how they'd better make it work after all his efforts to get them together. It turns out from the moment he met Naomi in New York he had marked her for his daughter-in-law. He was quite the matchmaker, ensuring Naomi would end up here, positioning her in Micah's path, and vice versa. Naomi and Micah were strategically delegated to oversee the details of my surprise wedding; color scheme, flower arrangements, what flavor the cake should be.

My question was, "when did you find the time?"

It was mostly during my physical therapy, and then in the evening after I was asleep that their courtship blossomed. They kept finding themselves in situations together, and in that time learned how much they had in common, and other things not so similar.

Naomi's faith and church community were paramount. His faith dictated his life as well; however, not marked by church attendance. She had been married before at an early age. At this stage in life, Naomi was unsure of her ability to conceive again. Micah had been married young also, at the age of 18, he had eloped with a girlfriend—by the time they returned home to face their parents, they were ready to call it quits. The marriage was annulled three months later, he learned that he had a son a year after the marriage ended.

223

"Are you sure about this?" I asked my friend.

"Isn't it exciting? I've been alone for a long time now."

"Do you love him?" I asked, not wanting a repeat of a failed marriage for either of them.

When she said, "Yes, I love him," I believed her. After saying our goodbyes, Orion and I loaded into the car and drove to a resort. Then Micah and Naomi left for the airport, so she could catch her flight back to New York.

ORION AND I have finally boarded our flight to Denver International. Outside my window, the noonday heat evaporates a thin layer of haze. *Farewell sunshine state*, I say to myself, your shores were to me like the great healing baths of Diocletian; transforming my sweat into healing salts, undressing my wounds, then caressing my weakened bones.

If not for our pressing issue I would protest leaving so soon. But alas, my desire to visit any of the famous themed parks must be delayed. There is no time for Disney World, Universal Studios or Sea World; not even a quick tour of the Space Center in Cocoa Beach. Granted, some of the blame must fall on my physical condition, but I am walking now, albeit with a slight limp.

A large portion of my young adult years was spent running away from family, so it was nice to have them around now; even my Grandpa who on most days didn't remember anyone except my uncle, Eli. There was still the decision of when to reach out to my mother.

"Oh, I will eventually," I told Uncle Eli when he had asked me this morning. I did plan to call her at some point once I arrive in Denver—eventually.

There is an image that replays in my mind of me walking up behind Reba undetected. She is bent over a desk while working, maybe she's writing on a note pad. Her curly hair is thin from age and worry, but she is still a beautiful woman with honey-colored skin and a petite frame.

In my vision, after a quick scan to assess one another's temperament, we embrace; her tears are from remorse, mine are the result of my surrender. I can no longer despise my mother for who she is or what she couldn't be for me. To hate her is to hate myself—for who I was, and what I couldn't be for Suniva, and my baby Lynn.

Once we are in the air I feel safe enough to take my eyes off the tarmac - and then the sky - to focus on journaling. Orion wants to know the story behind the thick book I insisted he help cram into my carry-on bag. Thankfully he was able to find a gift shop in the airport that sold totes, big enough to fit my monstrous journal and purse.

He pretends to nap beside me, but I can feel his eyes bulging from the strain as he attempts reading at a distorted angle. After I have written, *Twelve Mondays*, at the top of my page, Orion's curiosity is evident.

"I need to write about the events leading up to my

accident," I say.

His eyes narrow as he leans in closer. Orion and I have never discussed my alcoholism, nor the twelve-steps group. He doesn't know about the goal I set for sobriety, which turned out to be an epic fail.

"When I found out we were expecting Lynn, I had a terrible drinking problem," I say, pausing to make sure he is listening—really hearing—the message hidden within my confession. I've discovered that most people take words for granted. But how can I fault anyone, it was only after lying in a hospital bed for nearly three months, with nothing but my hearing, that I understand the importance of listening. When he nods, I can continue.

"I kept the bottles hidden in four different rooms in my apartment. When you poured the one from the pantry down the drain, I hid the others as a back-up. My only chance to get sober before having our baby was to try a twelve-step support group," I explain.

I tell him of how the three-month-long group seemed to be a perfect solution as they met on Monday evenings, and I was always alone on those nights. My skin is prickly, and I now feel uncomfortably warm in my sundress. I run my hands over the grooves under the window seal, and above me making sure the air-conditioner still blows cold through the vents.

"I'm proud of you, and I'm sorry for being a little judgmental back then—God knows I've had my own demons to battle," says Orion. He is looking at me at first, and then away at the mention of demons and battling. Which makes me wonder if Rigel has resurfaced. As I study the side-profile of his face, I can almost see the imaginary line where the mask and his true self meet. If I am honest about everything now, maybe it will help Orion to do the same moving forward.

"You do know I only attended three groups? I never completed the twelve," I say.

"No? Well, I'd say three months in the hospital surpasses your goal at some point," he says.

I tell him the morning of the accident I drank one of the hidden bottles before leaving my apartment. It was the grace of God that turned a DUI charge into a miracle birth. But he is right, in the end the goal had been accomplished.

"And I noticed how you refused the champagne after our wedding," he adds.

"Yes, I'm done with drinking, my new goal is to get our baby back, and be better; a better listener, a better friend, a better mom," I assure him.

"And now a wife," he says, as we both smile, hoping to encourage one another.

If our trip to Denver ends with baby Lynn in my arms then my joy will be complete. For now, I can think of nothing else. I don't like the name, Lynn. It is my middle name, my mother's middle name, her mother's middle name; we were all named after my great-great-grandmother Lynn. I hear she was a difficult, proud woman, someone I was sure I wouldn't

228

have liked.

Orion nudges me when the plane touches the ground. At some point during my reflection, I dozed off, missing the best part of the flight—the landing. I like to feel the flutter at the bottom of my stomach as the plane descends from the higher altitudes.

"Are you ready?" he asks. "Let's go get our baby."

The pictorial clouds above our heads are for show only, there is no wind, and it's a hot day in Denver. This place to me has become ancient ruins. Yes, there are new buildings where fields had been, shopping centers have replaced abandoned homes, but the land to me has become ruinous, and my emotional attachment decaying as the year's pass.

"Please tell me we're not staying at the ranch?" I ask once we load our belongings into the rental car.

"No, we will be staying in a room midway between the airport and town."

The plan is to check into our hotel and then phone Victoria for the meeting. As Orion drives the car out of the airport parking lot, my mind considers the few and many places Victoria could be staying. She eluded to "home," on each of our phone calls. Still, her mother has sworn to not have seen her daughter in over a year. She could be anywhere, and the thought of this being a game continues to looms over my head.

I share my suspicions with Orion after we have checked into our room. He tries to show hope in his smiling eyes, not knowing his new bride is skilled in the art of two-faces. Orion has a way of giving me his back to avoid showing emotion, he busies himself with unpacking and talks of the center in New York.

"I want to see my Grandparents' property, but I don't want to see my mother," I say when his full attention returns to me.

"And how are we supposed to do that, become like ninjas and spy from the rooftop?" he asks, then makes a hand and leg movement mimicking some form of Japanese combat.

"There must be a way we could go without having to see her," I say. It is the one place left connecting me to home, and I hoped Reba hadn't been sleeping in my Grandmother's bed—she or anyone else. There were plenty of other rooms she could live in comfortably, including the old horse stalls.

"Do you think she's still…" he pauses to see if I'm following, "…with that guy?"

"I don't think so, but anything's possible with my Mother," I say, not believing she was foolish enough to be with Ogre. Uncle Eli mentioned that she was alone, and so had Naomi. "If he's there it won't end well for either of them, I'll make sure of that," I say before going to change.

While we are having lunch, Orion gives me the go-ahead to call Victoria. The first attempt goes straight to voice mail.

"Don't worry, maybe she couldn't get to the phone," he says and kisses my forehead. "She'll call back."

Three minutes later, I receive a text message.

Victoria: I will call you back in ten minutes, washing baby.

"This is what she said," I say while showing him the message.

"Well, at least she's responsive." His hope keeps my anxiety at bay, whether he believes it or not.

After we have finished our meal, Orion and I hurry back to the room, hoping to ensure privacy for the phone call with Victoria; but an hour passes without a ring, buzz or vibration from a missed call. When I tell Orion I can no longer wait, he encourages me to redial her phone number. This time there is an answer.

"I'm so sorry, I was getting us both washed and dressed. We took a long stroll outside, and we're both pooped and ready for a nap," she says.

"I'm here, Victoria," I interrupt her explanation.

"You are—where? I don't see you," she says.

"Where are you?"

"I told you before, I'm home," she reiterates as she's done on all our communications.

She is home. I want to tell her that home could be anywhere for someone homeless, or had she forgotten? But I don't want to provoke her, so I choose my words carefully.

"I'm in Denver, are you at your mother's house? Or do you have your own place now?"

"DENVER! Nooo, Emma, I'm not in Denver—why

would you go there? I'm in New York, that's where we live," her voice nasal and high-pitched.

Overhearing the conversation Orion shakes his head before taking the phone from my hands, he places the call on speaker so we can talk together.

"Victoria, this is Orion—so, you are back at home, at my place?" he says, in a strident voice.

"I told Emma I would only hand our baby over to her," she whines. I don't like the sound of her voice, and the way she says, "our baby," sends chills down my back.

"Lynn is our baby, me and Emma's, so now me and my wife would like our—"

"You married that man? Why would you do that?" she demands an answer which surprises Orion and me.

"I don't understand, why wouldn't I marry him?" I ask, with a growing suspicion of their living arrangement. I stare at Orion, searching for any clues.

"How could you run off and get married knowing you didn't come back for your baby? You went on like nothing, forgetting all about us—your family!" she says, sounding like a child who's upset that her parents are divorcing.

Now I understand Victoria and her repeated reference to 'our baby.' She came to my hospital bed more times than I'll probably ever know, and at some point, instead of wishing me dead, she saw me as the sister she never knew—and wanted her sister to live.

"Victoria, I am your sister, but Orion is my husband,

and that is MY baby you're withholding from me," I say, cautious but direct. Her silence leads me to believe that she is listening and contemplating the severity of her actions.

"I just don't know why you would do this to us? This was our time to be a family and get to know each other like sisters," she says, reminding me of how I behaved when my friend, Tamar, got married and then had children. Even how I secretly felt when Naomi was recently engaged.

I was desperate to convince her that we will have time to bond as sisters later. I hoped to have her over for family get-togethers and special occasions, but the way she is behaving makes it difficult for us to get to that place. I tell her that she will always be a part of my family, which rubs her the wrong way and makes her defensive.

"Did you or your father have time for me before?" She wants to know.

"You do realize you have abducted our baby? Kidnapping is a federal offense," Orion tries to reason.

"Don't be ridiculous! I'm home—I told Emma when she comes home, I'll place the baby in her hands," she repeats.

My hands are trembling, and my stomach is turning and churning like it wants to spew out my meal. I want to ask Victoria if my baby is alive, but my tears almost choke me when I try to speak.

"Did you hear me?" she says in a calming voice I don't expect. "You do remember me saying I'd give the baby to you, Emma?"

I nod my head when Orion whispers that I should keep speaking with her. "Yes, I-remember…is my baby alive?" I can hardly say the choppy words, all I can think of right now is Suniva greeting baby Lynn in the garden. I don't think there's any strength left in me, standing now becomes a challenge. Orion reaches then sits me in the armchair.

"Oh, Emma, I would never hurt our baby—I could never," she says. I imagine Victoria holding my baby to her breast, staring into her eyes—the ones I desperately need to see. Orion is pacing the floor while mashing buttons on his cell phone.

"I didn't mean to scare you, I will give her to you when you come home…I'm in New York."

I could almost hear the word "silly" added to the end of her sentence. Orion was going to speak but holds his peace seeing my upheld hand.

"Thank you for taking such good care of my baby," I tell her. "Your niece…our baby," I mumble, believing this is what she wants to hear from me.

"You're welcome, and I can't wait for you to see how beautiful she is, and she's a good baby," she adds, pleased with the acknowledgment.

The Gentleman warned that I should take care of her. Victoria was standing on cracked glass, each step she took could send her plummeting deeper into a dark abyss. When the call ended, my body heaved, expelling the pent up tension. Orion holds me until a shivering chill passes. We are both helpless, at the mercy of a woman who claims to be my sister. I envision Victoria's haughty smile, the same way she teased me throughout our youth; now that wicked face has my father's hazel eyes, my thick eyebrows, and the same flat nose.

"I can send a squad car to our house," says Orion, though I believe he has already put the call through and seeks my approval as an afterthought. My concern is that Victoria will get spooked, shut down communication with us, which would make the situation worse.

"Please trust me," I plead with him. "Let's get to her first, I believe she'll hand the baby over to me, as she's said."

Orion has a wild, distant look in his eyes. I have this obscene notion of asking if Rigel has spoken to him recently. A mental break at this point is almost expected; watching me smash into a brick wall, Tamar's wrath, now this. I'm sure he feels guilty for inviting Victoria into our life—an unstable enemy turned sister. Even I must admit this was a hostage situation, with the ransom set at an astounding price of recognition and inclusion.

Victoria assumes I was going on with life without considering my baby. She doesn't understand moving forward helps me to remain sane. My sister believes I've had a perfect life, well, just wait until she hears my side of the story.

"I want you to know that I don't blame you," I tell him when he lies across the sofa and closes his eyes. It takes me longer to reach him from my seat in the chair, but when I do, he uses an arm to cover his face, unable to turn away before I catch a glimpse of his tears.

"We might as well act like newlyweds since we're here," I try making him smile, but this act is more to cheer myself up. When I coax Orion from the sofa, we move to the bedroom. My idea of "acting like newlyweds" is spending the day outdoors, holding hands while shopping. Orion wants those things too, but only after our time alone.

Later in the evening when he asks if we should stay in or dine out for dinner, I tell him about my idea to drive out to Castle Rock. With the setting sun, there will be less chance of being seen by anyone. After deliberating over the plan, we leave our hotel room.

During the drive, I realize the difference in the landscape along the highway. The ride seems shorter then it had in my youth. Outside my window, shopping centers and new housing tracts stand where towering pine and spruce trees once had. When we approach the gate at my grandparent's property, I'm relieved to see the original fence is still intact.

The two-story house is the same, but something is different. The horses are gone, and so are the stalls. In their place are about two dozen tiny homes to the left and right of the property; tiny little homes arranged like a small community, governed by the big house. I'm not sure what to make of the change.

"I don't understand," I say to Orion after my
236

disappointment passes. After boasting about Misty and the red horse, Elektra, I am feeling a little embarrassed.

"Should we get out," he asks, seeing my confusion. I tell him to drive around the block so I can double-check the address and surrounding neighborhood. After driving around several streets, we pull up to the same spot as before.

"Let's come back in the morning, maybe I can speak with someone then," I say.

As we drive, I withhold my thoughts from Orion. It doesn't take me long to calculate who was behind the tiny home community, my uncle Eli was a land developer and has a construction company. He never cared for the "wasted property" needed to shelter the horses.

"Did you know anything about this," I ask Orion when we return to the hotel room.

"No," he isn't aware of any dealings in Denver.

I intend to call my uncle straightaway. When I dial his phone number the voice recording answers. Remembering the time difference, I remind myself it would be past midnight in Florida.

"We'll go back first thing tomorrow," says Orion, when he climbs into bed. Before long, I hear his breathing change as he falls asleep—but I am awake. The day replays in my mind; on one side of my pillow is Victoria's laughter, and on the other side is visions of Reba's face, still bent over the writing desk.

I was falling into a deep sleep when Orion nudges me

saying that my uncle was on the phone. When I inquire of the time, he tells me it's 5:30 a.m., and I groan from exhaustion. "Yes," he is aware of the changes to the property, it was no longer cost-effective to keep the horses or maintain the stalls. Each horse had been sold way before Reba arrived, but there were two red horses left. I hoped one would be Elektra. If there's anyone to be mad at, it is me. The last time I left Colorado, it was me who told my Uncle to do what he pleased—walking away from it all.

After breakfast, we decide it's time to meet with Victoria's mom and let her know all that has occurred. Then we planned to drive back to Castle Rock and maybe speak with my mother. On the day of my father's memorial service, Sadie mentioned that her home was just around the corner if I should need anything. It takes some searching, but I'm finally able to locate the address; a cozy double-wide mobile home. The plan was to enlist Sadie's help to reason with Victoria.

As I stand on her front porch, I wonder if she harbors the same resentment as her daughter had toward me. Orion locks his fingers in mine, and I knock on the front door.

"Emma, so good to see you," she says in a believable pleasant voice.

Sadie is slightly heavier than what I recall, and the lines in her face magnify her concern. When she opens the front door, a white Labrador runs to me. Apologizing, she grabs the dog's collar and then motions for us to follow her inside.

In the poorly lit room, I mistake her dog for Biscuit. It couldn't be him; how could she have ended up with...

"I'm sorry—Rocko, sit!" she says, but I'm not able to make out her first few sentences. My mind has traveled back to days with Biscuit sitting at my side. Rocko sniffs Orion's leg before moving to check me out. The softness of his fur has me in a trance, as I lean forward allowing him to lick my face.

"Did you hear, she asked if you'd like something to drink?" says Orion.

"Your dog reminds me of the one I used to have...I'm here to talk to you about Victoria," I say after she swats Rocko from the room. When she returns to her seat, Sadie apologizes for the troubles she has caused Victoria and me. After taking a sip from the glass of water she brings for us, I notice the way she tries not to stare at my shaved head.

"I was in a bad car accident, it's the reason why Victoria was watching my baby," I say.

Sadie says she is to blame for filling her daughter's head with her jealousy and animosity through the years. She was in a happier place now after having the time to reconnect with my dad, and she hoped Victoria and I could see past our differences and begin to work on a relationship.

"She checks in once a week, I try to keep track of her," says Sadie. Then she tells us Victoria mentioned how my work schedule kept me away from home on some nights. When Orion gives her an account of the correct story, she shows concern for Victoria and my baby.

"If there's anything you can do—please, we wouldn't want to have the authorities involved, but as you can see the situation is getting out of control," says Orion.

Sadie nods her agreement, she will do everything in her power to get her daughter to do the right thing.

"How is Reba," asks Sadie as we prepare to leave. When I tell her that we're headed to Castle Rock where my mother is staying, her request to join us is a surprise.

"I wasn't planning on actually speaking with her," I admit, shyly, but she insists on going with us still.

"I'll go in and speak with Reba while she's distracted you can scope the grounds," she says.

Sadie had always been kind to me, and to my dad. I thank her for being there with him during his last days, for calling me when he became ill; and also for keeping the secret about my first child.

OUR PLANE LANDS at LaGuardia Airport sometime at four o'clock in the morning. I have serious jetlag from jumping time zones twice in less than a month, and that's not to mention my legs still don't cooperate as they should—at least not yet.

I'm hopeful with another round of physical therapy scheduled to start next week my walking will improve, however, the greater challenge for my recovery will be treating and managing long term affects from traumatic brain injury.

During the drive from the airport, Orion tries his best to describe our new home; 2,550 square feet, four-bedroom, two baths; two-rooms upstairs, and two downstairs. There is also a two-car garage and a full basement.

"We're home," he announces, pulling up to a curb outside a quaint two-story brick house. I notice there is a terrace on the second floor which he failed to mention in his description.

After parking the car inside the garage, he opens my door and lets me out. Inside, the kitchen space is clean; black granite countertops and glass-front cabinets complement the drawers and pantry. The sink basin is unmarked and smells of new packaging; same for the floors—spotless, there's no dust or crumbs to be found here.

When I step into the living room, I hope to see proof of life, but there are no signs of Victoria, or that a baby has been nursed here recently. The seat cushions on the u-shaped sectional are taut, accent pillows neatly arranged.

"Doesn't look like she's been here at all," I sigh.

Orion tells me to follow him and starts down a hallway leading to a bedroom on the first floor. "This was her room," he says, before opening the closed door without knocking.

Noticing I've suppressed my breathing since entering the house, I place a hand on the wall to steady my balance. When the room door opens, I try to conceal my gasp, not for Orion's sake, but so I don't collapse. The bedroom has been cleared, save for a stripped bed, and an empty crib. There aren't any clothes hanging in the closet, nothing in the drawers, not even dust on the floor.

Orion has his back to me, but I see his hands draw into a tight fist. He rushes past me without a word, and I hear him running up the stairs then searching in the rooms above. It's not that I can't follow; I'm sure my legs are stable enough to walk a dog on a leash, but Orion has had enough with my so-called sister's antics, and I decide it's best to give him space to seethe.

"Stay calm," I tell myself.

I sit on the bed and close my eyes while focusing on my breaths. Inhale…exhale…inhale… "That's it, Emma, you'll get through this," I say, as the sound of Orion's footsteps echoes above my head.

"There's no time to throw a temper tantrum, you know what needs to be done. Make—"

"We'll have to make the call," Orion snaps. He is standing at the room door, heaving from his sprint.

"Yes," I nod. "Let's do it," I say because if not, I fear what his actions will be once we've located Victoria—or what I was capable of doing myself.

After we have made the call to the Sheriff's department, an officer dispatches and arrives within fifteen minutes. Orion and I take turns giving our version of events leading up to this day—who Victoria is, how long she's been missing, when was she hired, our history together, the misleading phone calls. Then the officer informs us that an Amber Alert will be issued immediately.

I remember the Gentleman's words, "…a great deal of confusion…have patience, love her…"

I have tried in every way to honor the promise I gave him, but after Victoria's story has changed with each phone call I worry this is part of her bigger scheme to destroy me.

The officer leaves after giving us his name and phone

number, and instructions should we hear anything else or happen to contact Victoria first. Orion walks him out, and I watch from the window as they engage in a second conversation outside of my hearing.

"What else did you tell him?" I ask when he brings our luggage from the car.

"I gave him the name of the private investigator who's been trailing our baby's abductor," he says.

In our bedroom, there is a king-size platform-bed large enough to fit us both, a child or two, and even a dog if we choose. I sit on the corner of the bed with intentions to remove my shoes before unpacking. Instead, I lay back onto a pillow and my heavy eyes shut, refusing to open. Exhaustion from travel and disappointment draws Orion into the bed beside me.

When I awake, the bed is empty, and the room has darkened. Reaching for my phone, I check the time: 8:34 pm, it was sometime after 4 o'clock when I laid down. After a search through the house, I find a note on the bedside when I return to our bedroom:

> *Emma, I've gone to speak with a woman from the hospital who has information. You were sleeping so peacefully I didn't want to disturb you.*

It was a good call to leave me out of the chase. I want to explore my new home and envision the three of us happy within these walls. The master bedroom is the only room which seems to have received careful thought. The leather headboard has decorative leaf carvings in the wood, and the dresser has a marble top. A decorative rug on the floor, heavy drapery on the window, and pictures of the two of us on the nightstands. The room down the hallway from our bedroom has a double-size bed, but nothing more; same for the two bedrooms downstairs.

In the living room, along with the gray fabric sectional, there's an oversized ottoman, track lighting in the ceiling, a console table against one wall and a baroque mirror hanging overhead. Down the hallway, there is a laundry room across from the garage door, and to the right is the kitchen.

Once I have surveyed the entire house, including the basement, I retreat back to our bedroom. A writing desk faces a window, and there is a bare cherry-blossom tree that gives me hope for spring. It is now December, and we are fortunate to have made it home before the winter snowstorms begin.

I pull out the desk chair and sit to center my thoughts before writing in my journal. What I learned during my visit to Colorado is my Grandparents' horse ranch had been converted into a housing program for human and sex-trafficked survivors. Some clients from PASHT would live in a tiny home and work around the grounds as pay for their stay, until a set period.

Two horses remained for use as equine-therapy; one of them a red horse, the other was brown. They each nuzzled my face when I approached, leading me to believe the red mare was Elektra—although there was no way for me to know for sure.

There were purple fields beyond the tiny-home community; rows and rows of thriving, vibrant lavender plants. Like myself, my mother had no choice but to learn all about the care of my father's favorite plant, the Lavandula Angustifolia. The mostly women occupants cultivated and harvested the fragrant buds for profit, which were sold to the local farmers market.

When Sadie was inside the house, Orion walked around the homes; twenty in total, arranged in two sets on the west and east side of my Grandparents' home. It was while I was making the acquaintance of one of the horses when a rather chatty woman approached, asking if I was Emma.

She recognized me from the shrine in the living room of pictures from my childhood; some printed off social media and another from my wedding day on Cocoa Beach. My breath stills when the young girl mentions she owed her life to my mother, who single-handedly crushed the market of sex-trafficking in the Denver area by giving authorities known addresses of local perpetrators.

What I referred to as a tiny-home compound was, in fact, a haven for victims, aptly named *Emma's Safe Haven.* The main house was left intact, occupied by my mother, who was the manager of the housing program. A smaller building sat adjacent to the homes—a community center—where support groups, therapy sessions, and other wellness and self-care programs were held. Reba, I was told, began every morning with prayer and meditation, kept a close eye on the girls, and had zero tolerance for substance abuse.

My eyes water now, as they did when I was told of my mother's change and commitment to the PAHST mission. What we learned from Sadie on the drive back to town was that Reba had confessed to having a raging heroin addiction. She told anyone who would listen how she had sold her only child into a sex-ring to support her drug habit.

The night I fled from the room in Breaux Bridge, she had too. I never looked back, but if I had turned around even once to check for Biscuit, I would've seen my mother trying to keep up with me—I had always been a fast runner. When her lungs gave out Reba limped to the nearest police station and gave a full report. She returned with authorities to the building that had held me, along with other young girls, and some boys captive.

Reba found Biscuit lying in a corner, injured but alive. After seeing to it that Ogre was arrested, she called a local animal shelter to have Biscuit picked up, then she went into a 6-month drug treatment program. It took her a year to fully detox and rehabilitate from her heroin addiction. By the time she left treatment, Biscuit had already been adopted. When she reached out to my father, he filed a restraining order stipulating she could have no contact with him or me...so, my mom returned to her childhood home, caring for her mother until she passed away last year.

Ogre was found guilty and sentenced to thirty years in federal prison. I can't help but wonder what the outcome would have been if Reba had caught up to me that night. Did she turn on Ogre with hopes of bailing herself out of trouble? I can only wonder now.

Sadie mentioned that after she and Reba made peace with their past; acknowledging the love and loss of the same man, they accepted that their daughters were sisters. It was a long time coming, but they were ready to behave like mature adults. She had an interest in my Grandmother's foundation as well, so a meeting was scheduled to discuss ways Sadie could assist at PAHST.

Things I remember hearing...

I write on a blank page. Then I proceed to transcribe every conversation I could remember hearing while in a coma. When the facts have been recorded—as I recall them, I review my journal entry.

I have detailed the full account of my total experience; the kidnapping, escape to Maine, then New York. My alcoholism, the car accident, and then being in the coma. I write of the Corridor and the garden; my talks with the Gentleman, and meeting Suniva. I recall the value of listening to others, and the need to be heard. Only after we've heard all the details of a matter can we begin to understand our role in a situation.

I turn to another blank sheet and write *Twelve Hearings*.

While in a coma, I received twelve remarkable revelations from hearing my loved one's confessions. Because of the hearings, I understand Victoria's confusion, Orion's desperation, and Naomi's faith. I can relate to Tamar's fury, my Uncle Eli's motivation, and my aunt Miranda's sacrifice. I know how my cousins, Amelia and Micah, struggle with family commitment sometimes will collide with their need for independence. I can relate to Sadie's relentless love, and my dad's drive to provide as he competed with his older brother's success. I understood the reason behind my Grandma Rose's mission with PAHST, and even Reba's battle with sobriety.

I should include myself in this list, how my life had become unmanageable as a result of not dealing with trauma, especially from the kidnapping, but even before then. My childhood was troubled from the start, but that journal entry will have to wait until later—after I've sought therapy, and reaffirmed my spiritual beliefs. I had always felt God's love for me—even before He rescued me at the brick wall. I should be dead, but somehow, I'm alive.

After I have written all that was in my heart to capture on paper, I make another attempt to reach Victoria. When there is no answer, my voice message is clear:

"I am back in New York, I expect you to bring my baby to me by tonight."

I must now resign to leave Victoria in the hands of the law, there's nothing more I can do to save her from this trouble.

On Wednesday, Naomi and I meet for lunch in Manhattan. She pulls out a notepad detailing plans for a wedding in February. I try to appear happy; smiling when she smiles, enlarging my eyes for effect. I want to ask about her children and when can we start the search?

"Are you sure this is the right time for a wedding?" I ask. When she wants to know the reason for my question, I shrug my shoulders. "Any good friend would ask," I tell her.

"I've never felt this way before," she blushes, the skin on her cheeks folding into dimples. She didn't expect to fall in love, but was thankful for our friendship that eventually led to meeting what she called her "God-ordained spouse."

"The Bible says, he who finds a wife finds a good thing," I say, wanting her to know I'm back to reading my Bible.

"And obtains favor from the Lord," she completes the verse but then stops talking. She looks me in the eyes as if searching for the dark places of my soul. I am thinking, will she be the same Naomi, after becoming Mrs. Naomi St. Roman? I refuse to shift my gaze, hoping she can read my concerns. She squeezes my hand after hearing my silent question.

• • •

On Thursday morning, Orion leaves early before sunrise. After I've had a cup of coffee and return to our bedroom to shower, I find his handwritten note on the desk.

The name and address to the women's facility where Shelly was serving time for manslaughter is scrawled on a sheet of paper. It doesn't take me long to sit down and write her a letter.

Shelly,

There were many times in the past where I've tried to locate you and Suniva. I am so glad to have found you but saddened to learn what has happened to our baby girl, and you. If you're able, tell me your account of the events, maybe I can be of some help. Please write back. Your dear friend, Emma.

I wonder how she'll respond to my letter knowing Shelly had begged me to stay in Sebec Lake with her and the baby. I wasn't sure if she felt abandoned, or maybe she blamed me somehow for Suniva's untimely death.

By Saturday evening, we have no updates on Victoria's whereabouts, and Orion's mood has become depressing. He blames himself, and there's nothing I can say to convince him otherwise. He shouldn't take responsibility for another person's actions, but he continues to sulk. Naomi and I decide to attend Church on Sunday morning, with Orion and my cousin Micah joining us.

The Pastor receives me with open arms, though I notice he checks out my chopped hair; which now has about four inches of new growth. I'm pleased with my coils that are somewhere between my Grandmother's coarse strands and my Mother's curls, and uniquely my own.

251

After hearing all that I had gone through, the congregation gathers to say a special prayer of protection for Orion and me. When the service was over, Naomi asks to have her wedding ceremony performed at the church. When the pastor gives her his blessing, she smiles…and she is still smiling when we return home.

SITTING UPRIGHT IN bed, I blink my eyes several times while scanning the dimly lit room. Orion is sleeping beside me but stirs when he senses I've awakened. He reaches for me, then pulls me close and kisses along my neck. When his head moves away, I hear his light snoring.

It was a dream that wakes me; Victoria was in my Manhattan apartment, sleeping in my bed, combing through my closets, and eating at my kitchen table.

Why hadn't I thought to go there first?

Had she not been snooping around my hospital room so often the thought would be absurd. It is the only place we haven't looked, and the only place that makes sense…home.

When I am sure Orion is sound asleep, I rise again and then tiptoe to the bathroom.

"I know she's there; I can feel her," I whisper.

My adrenaline is pumping, as my brain almost short-circuits imagining the many outcomes of the day. I know the others will protest, but I must go alone; it must be me, and me alone who finds her. When I return from the bathroom, Orion is up.

"There's a lead," he says before showing me a text message from the private investigator. His lead is in Brooklyn, so I don't mention my suspicion. Orion rushes from one side of the room to the next, snatching undergarments from the dresser drawer, and pants from the closet.

"This is the day we get our baby girl, I can feel it," he says, grinning with wild eyes.

I step in front of his path, slowing him enough so that we can hug first, followed by a tender kiss. Afterward, he tells me not to worry before jogging down the stairs and out to the car. I wait, listen for the engine to start before reaching for my phone to call for a ride. The car arrives within twenty minutes, giving me enough time to throw a comfortable outfit together. When the driver pulls up, I'm already waiting by the curb. Sliding across the rear seat, I lift my head to say, "Good morning."

In the rearview mirror I catch a glimpse of myself. In my rush, I forget to wear the wig, but I find my short curly hair appropriate for the day. When I smile at my reflection, the driver mistakes my gesture and greets me with a head-nod.

The ride shouldn't take long, but the morning traffic is heavy. In between twiddling my thumbs, and rubbing my curly coif, I check my cell phone for messages. No word from Orion means he hasn't reached Victoria before me. Almost forty minutes later, the car stops outside my old residence. I have already prepared myself during the drive for this wave of nostalgia that comes. Standing in front of the glass doors, the limestone building is just as elegant as the day Tamar met me and my father hear for a showing.

When I inhale, a pinch in my chest reminds me of the biting winter air. Stepping inside the doors, I rub my arms for warmth. There is a fireplace burning in the lobby, but I sidestep its temptation hoping to avoid any familiar faces.

For eight years, this building was my home. But like a baby grows into a toddler, I have outgrown my apartment. To live here now would be my cage. I am free, like the emperor butterfly, at liberty to spread my wings and cast-off the old chrysalis. I will miss some things, like Friday night gourmet cooking with Tamar, and the convenience of sprinting around Central Park to relieve anxiety. There's also a deli around the corner that makes the best panini sandwich.

To my delight the lobby is empty. Skirting around a large column, I head for the mailroom first. Giving Orion a copy of my keys last year turns out to be the wise decision. When I open my mailbox, it's empty.

Someone's been in my mailbox says the momma bear.

On the elevator I recheck my reflection in the mirrored paneling. I'm about fifteen pounds thinner, with a short-curly fro, so I doubt anyone would recognize me. Even I must do a double-take in the mornings after washing my face.

It is a short ride to the second floor. When the door opens, I brush past an older woman who is bent over retrieving her Russian blue kitty; she has always been kind, but her kitty and his green eyes scared nine lives out of me one morning when I came home at 3 a.m.

I make quick strides walking the length of the hallway, then slower as I approach the door to my apartment. It could be my imagination, but the doorknob feels warm. When I slide the key into the lock, my stomach churns wondering if the deadbolt is engaged. My heartbeat quickens as the door opens, and I step inside.

Listening for sound or movement, I remain standing at the entrance while making a quick scan of the living room and kitchen area. When it appears that all is clear, I step inside, shutting the door behind me. At first glance, everything looks the way I left it—minus the shattered cup and spilled coffee from the morning of my accident.

Is that where I left the remote? Or maybe I hadn't left the pile of magazines lying on the floor. In the kitchen is where my growing suspicion is confirmed. Cans of baby formula line the countertop, and empty milk bottles drying on a dish rack. The cupboard is well stocked. My health-conscious meals replaced with processed foods I'd never buy.

Someone's been eating in my kitchen says the momma bear.

Stepping further into the apartment, the guest room/dance studio is now a nursery. Naomi and I had spent an entire weekend in spring preparing this room for my baby—this is how Victoria was able to leave the crib with Orion. We had made a game out of stocking the walk-in closet with diapers of every size, hanging the racks with baby clothes of different stages; blankets, and bibs stored in the hand-painted dresser-drawer. The crib bedding is tossed about, and the trash bin filled with soiled diapers.

As I'm leaving the nursery to head for my bedroom, the front door opens and then shuts. I listen as the deadbolt clicks into the lock position. Taking quick steps backward, I slide into the nursery and tuck into the closet.

"Now let's get you cleaned up before nap time," says Victoria in a cutesy tone. She enters the nursery, grabs a few items, and is gone before noticing my keys lying on the dresser. Squeezing further into the closet, I wait in the darkness between two stacks of diapers. My heart melts as I listen to the "ga-ga," and "da-da," babbles from my baby.

Victoria is moving around in my bedroom, speaking baby-talk to my baby girl, and running water in my bathtub. It's now or never—but this game must come to end today. I get to my feet and leave the safety of my hiding place. From the hallway, I hear Victoria's phone call.

"What do you want?" she says, annoyed with the caller. "I told you already, they paid me to take care of the baby!"

Her back is turned as I stand ten feet away in the doorway. Victoria clings tight to my baby in one hand, while struggling to remove her winter coat. When she leans to toss the garment aside, I see my babies plump face and round eyes. Orion was right, she has a lot of his features.

"...and what does any of this have to do with you, Tamar?" says Victoria. She stops fidgeting to listen now.

My baby turns her head and looks me in the eyes; she smiles before letting out a burst of laughter, which I want to believe is because she recognizes her mother.

"I told you already, Orion paid me to do a job that's why I have her keys, so stop calling and don't come here again..." Then there's a pause as she listens to the response. "I gave you my number because you pressured me, but that won't happen again." Another pause and I can hear the wrath of Tamar from where I stand.

"Leave us alone! Oh, and by the way they're married now, so forget about your plans to steal Orion away from my sister," she says before ending the call. Victoria turns to walk into the bathroom, and my knees knock together. How she remains oblivious to my presence is astonishing.

Stepping carefully, I follow behind her and watch as my baby is placed into a tiny bathing tub. I'm aware this puts Lynn in a dangerous situation, so I must retreat for now. Silencing my breaths, my steps are lighter than floating clouds. In the hallway, I remain facing the bedroom, walking backward until reaching the dining table.

Victoria has made herself comfortable here; playing mommy to my baby, carrying on like this situation will last forever. Her justification will be that my father never claimed her; therefore, she was owed the life I had been given. She believes this is what it takes to behave like a St. Roman; twirling around a fancy New York apartment, with cotton for brains and bubbles for thoughts. No, being a St. Roman is a duty, a holy calling to service. It's spreading a message of hope and standing firm for what you believe in.

Twenty minutes pass before I hear the musical-mobile playing in the nursery. Humming to the lullaby of 'Go to Sleep Little Baby,' Victoria speaks softly.

"It's naptime, my sweet girl."

A few moments go by before I hear footsteps in the hallway. I watch her smiling as she walks, her head down carefully gauging her steps. She turns into the living room first, stares out the window as she continues to hum the lullaby. When I stand, she startles from my movement.

"I'm home!" I say, loud enough for Victoria to hear but not to wake my sleeping child.

With steady, purposeful steps, I move closer. Standing within arm's reach of her neck, I see Victoria's fear, not anger. Her face contorts as she clutches at her throat, then struggles for air. I am poised for a fight but watching as she gasps for breath, I change my footing. Grabbing her shoulders, I force her to sit, all the while praying she's not in cardiac arrest. Do I know anything about CPR?

"Breathe, take a slow deep breath—that's it," I say.

Now she's crying, and still struggling for adequate air. I'm sure no one would blame me if she dies like this, but despite her folly, I remain empathic toward Victoria.

"Just breathe," I say hoping to convey my intentions for her wellbeing. When Victoria's breathing settles, her eyes still bulge as she focuses in on me.

"I'm not going to hurt you," I say. Though what I'm thinking is, 'I have every right to!' How do you keep from strangling an enemy who has kidnapped your baby? Placing my hand over hers, I wait for her fear to subside. She flinches when I reach to steady her trembling hands. Victoria shuts her eyes, allowing for tears that dampen her cheeks.

"You scared the life out of me," she whispers. Then her eyes land on my low haircut, she opens her mouth but says nothing.

"Why are you here—how did you get in?" I ask.

After a whimper, Victoria tells the story of how she slipped into my hospital room and made off with my wallet and keys. She almost got caught the day Uncle Eli came to pack a few things for my trip to Florida. She had been sitting on a park bench across the street that day. Watching as my uncle entered the building, she followed, hoping for an opportunity to introduce herself as his other niece. After he and my aunt left the apartment, she stood near the elevator, and decided when he looks at her, she would speak.

"They were in such a rush, neither one of them even noticed me," she says.

As she talks, I am sure of our family resemblance. If my uncle had seen her face, he would know this was his blood relation.

"You were here all that time," I say laughing at our history; past, and present.

"I knew Orion despised me. At first, I was scared he would fire me, and without the baby I didn't know how else to gain your trust. He was going to take you both from me, so I left," she says.

"Why didn't you just tell me you were here. I could've protected you then." I stand and walk away, "Things are out of hand now, there's an amber alert issued for my missing baby."

"You were too sick. Besides, how do you explain a half-maybe sister to a family in turmoil? Your uncle and Orion would've tossed me away so fast. I had nowhere else to go." Victoria tells me how she used my debit card for food and to maintain household bills.

As she confesses, I leave her sitting on the sofa and walk toward the nursery. Baby Lynn has walnut-brown skin and straight thin hair that barely curls. Her face is chunky, round with patchy blotches on both cheeks from the harsh winter air. Now that I've seen her, she doesn't look like a Lynn or Suniva.

"What shall we call you, my precious angel?" I wait for her eyes to open, and then I'll know what her name should be.

"She's such a good baby, which made it harder for me to give her back," says Victoria. I hadn't heard her enter the room, but it doesn't matter, my baby is leaving with me today at any cost.

"I don't like the name—Lynn, I've always hated that name," I say while stroking my baby's hair, continuing to admire her delicate nose and mouth. "Orion thought he was doing me a favor, but what he did was pronounce a curse over our baby. It's an obligation from my great-great-grandmother, every female born off-spring must share her name," I explain.

"It's just a name," she chuckles nervously. Victoria isn't sure how to respond, so she fidgets with the bedding, making sure to keep enough distance between me and her escape.

"There can be no more Lynn's," I say. Under different circumstances I'd go further into what my Grandma Rose had shared with me about the original Lynn.

"She does favor her daddy. Ori—Oriyah, we'll name her Oriyah Stone." I look closer at my baby, remembering the day Orion had teased about how much she resembled him.

"What happens now?" asks Victoria.

I gesture for her to follow me out into the hallway. When we enter the living room, I explain the amber alert and kidnapping charge. "I don't know how to help you without you first turning yourself in."

"I can't go to jail, I won't—I was only trying to help," she says, sobbing and whining. "We're sisters, they should understand."

"Turn yourself in and I'll bail you out by evening. Don't make this any worse, for either of us," I plead with Victoria.

"I don't want to leave, I belong here with you and Lynn—I mean Oriyah," she begs.

"And what about my husband?" I go to her, readying to shake the delusions from her brain. "You can have this apartment, but you must turn yourself in first!"

She stops crying long enough to scan the room. It's almost funny how she's able to turn off her tears so suddenly. When my baby begins to whimper, we both stand, and I grab Victoria's arm to prevent her from going in front of me.

"But what if it's me she wants?" she asks. It's a reasonable question because Victoria has been the only mother-figure my baby has known since her birth, but I'm here now, and it's my baby who needs me.

Leaving Victoria standing in the hallway, I reenter the nursery and shut the door behind me. My baby is a little fussy at first, but once I pick her up, we smile at one another. Walking over to the rocking chair, I sit down and hold my baby close. In a few minutes, she is sleeping again. Pulling my cell phone out of my pocket, I snap a picture of us together and send it to Orion. My phone begins ringing within two seconds.

"Where are you?" he asks. I can hear him mumble to someone, and I know it wouldn't be long before a squad-team comes for Victoria.

"My apartment in Manhattan, my home." I say casually. I place my sleeping baby back in the crib and close the door behind me. I want to warn Victoria, but I am too late. The front door shuts as she leaves.

"WAIT— don't leave like this!" I say, dropping the phone on the floor to chase after her.

"I'll turn myself in, but not here," she answers, as the elevator door opens. I nod my head.

"This is your home!" I call to her when the door shuts.

Victoria mouths the words, "thank you," as the elevator closes. When I'm back inside my apartment, I run to retrieve the phone.

"No need to come with guns blazing, she's gone, and I have our baby!"

WEEK TWENTY-TWO

I HAVE NEVER been an early riser. Between the two of us, Orion should take the morning shifts and leave the bedtime routine for me. Since I insist on taking full responsibility for Oriyah's needs, I am up for the fifth day at 3 a.m., to feed and change a bright-eyed baby.

If this morning is like the past week, Oriyah will feed, burp and then giggle while playing footsies-and-toesies in my arms. I feel like I'm doing this motherhood thing right; her eyes beam, as her cheeks flush when she smiles. She makes the cutest little shapes and sounds with her mouth.

Orion leaves for work later nowadays, always an hour past breakfast. Last night he accused me of being stingy with our baby, claiming he's only allowed to touch her when I'm cooking, cleaning or bathing; so he hangs around after breakfast again this morning to steal time while I clear the table and load the dishwasher.

"Take your shower while I'm still here," he says.

I shoot him a look before deciding to take the offer, and he blows me a kiss when I pretend to frown at him. He's been this way ever since our first night home, and that next morning when I told him my desire to rename our baby after him. Within a day's trip to the vital records office, baby Lynn became Oriyah Rosemary Stone.

When I return from showering, Orion plays a voice message from a detective handling our case; Victoria still hadn't turned herself in as she promised.

"The most important thing is that we're finally together."

"Yes, but until she's caught—"

"Shhh," I say while placing a gentle kiss on his lips.

I know he worries that Victoria will show up on our doorstep, or worse, but I don't share his concerns. After my shower, Orion leaves for work. I check in to see if Oriyah is still sleeping before dialing Victoria's phone number. The call goes straight to voice mail.

"What happened to our deal?" I whisper my message, "You turn yourself in, I bail you out and give you the apartment." Although Orion and my uncle disagree, my intention is clear, this isn't some ploy to catch a thief. As I've told the other's; she's one of us no matter what has happened.

If someone would've told me a year ago that my closest friend would turn on me, and my oldest enemy would become my sister, I would've laughed in their face. Tamar wasn't answering any of my phone calls, and although we weren't speaking, her twins, Dilan and Dalani, deserve to see their Aunt Emma and my new baby.

I try calling her again, and when the call is rejected, I forward a picture of me, Orion and Oriyah. Afterward, I intend to write: Baby Oriyah wants to meet her—her what—cousins…siblings? No, not siblings because thankfully that plan was derailed. I refrain from sending the text message because now I'm questioning my motive; did I send the picture out of spite?

I set the phone aside, still agonizing over my decision, then decide to journal before Oriyah awakes. I'm still working on a lengthy journal entry that seems to be more like the beginnings of a memoir. I call it,

Twelve Hearings; Confessions to a Dying Woman.

In it, I detail the relationships with each of the twelve people I've listed. I try to write until I'm able to come up with a final verdict of love, no matter what the outcome of the relationship has been. When my cell phone chimes, I startle, knocking my pen to the ground.

Uncle Eli wants to know if we're free for dinner. I exhale before sending a response. Sure, I reply. It is hard to shake him these days, with planning a wedding for his son and the business venture with Orion—he's literally everywhere. I still think of my Dad and Grandma Rose, but I must admit those thoughts have lessened now, thanks to my growing family. The dark areas of my past are now colored over in love, even for Reba; I decide to call her soon, and there's no better time than the present.

"I'm so glad to hear from you," she says.

Her voice is calm and sincere. My mind scrambles with the many things I want to say but don't. Breathe, Emma - keep it simple - I tell myself.

"Hi, Reba," is all I can say.

"I don't blame you for keeping your distance from me," she begins. "The things I did to you were unthinkable, no mother would ever place her own child in such a predicament."

"And what predicament was that, Mother?" I say, knowing she prefers to be called by first name.

"Taking you against your will—"

"It's called kidnapping, Mother," I say with an even tone.

"I kidnapped you and forced you into sex-trafficking," she says breathy and defeated. "That was the last horrible thing I'd done to you, and I know there were many other things I failed at throughout the years... I apologize, and I ask for your forgiveness?"

I should tell her that she already has my forgiveness, but it's hard to speak the words. I was comfortable with things the way they were, at a safe distance. That's what I should tell her, we should start with phone calls and see where it takes us.

"I have a daughter now. Her name's Oriyah Rosemary, not Lynn," I say, knowing it was expected of me to brand my female offspring.

"Thank God, the curse will end now. I never wanted it for you—they'll come for any female born named after Lynn, Terra Lynn will see to it," she says.

"But Terra Lynn is dead, she has been for a very long time—that's impossible!" I say.

The idea that my mother believes her dead, grandmother was controlling our destiny is troubling; and what about Suniva's fate? She hadn't been given the name Lynn.

"My first daughter, Suniva, didn't have her name either. She was conceived from that predicament you put me in, mother—but she died."

"I didn't know, I don't know how I'll ever forgive myself. But I'm doing better now, as you know. Sadie told me you came," she says.

As she scrambles to explain herself, I look in on Oriyah who is still sleeping. When she stretches and yawns, I pick her up and hold her in my arms.

"I-was—I was a monster. I didn't appreciate your father, and I didn't know how to be a mother other than what I was taught. There were things I hid to protect you both."

"How did it begin?" I ask, searching for a thread of humanity within my mother. "When did you start using drugs?"

"It began in my early teens, it's what you do to cope when you're raised in a brothel. I must tell you about it, but it'll have to be face-to-face...when you're ready," she says.

After telling her I'd like to speak again, I ask if she was

aware that Victoria was my half-sister. She hadn't known for years and only learned about another child during divorce proceedings. I tell my mother about Victoria's breakdown as a result of not being claimed by our family.

"But we all have choices, Emma. We can't blame others for our bad decisions no matter the root cause," she says.

There's no need to disagree with my mother because it's the same sentiments everyone else has expressed. After I admit that it was nice speaking with her, and we should talk again soon, she tells me how proud she is of the woman I've become. "I love you, Emma. I always have."

I thank her for the words I've waited to hear for years, and after our conversation, I determine to be the mother for Oriyah that I had longed for. When she cries, I'll be the one to wipe her tears. When she's sad, I'll do my best to make her smile, and when she's happy, we'll rejoice together. She may turn out to be a spoiled princess, but she'll never feel unloved by me.

The next day I meet with Naomi in Soho to help her select a wedding dress. When I arrive, she and my cousin Amelia are deliberating over four gowns.

"Sorry I'm late, I'm still trying to get the hang of motherhood," I say, holding up an empty bottle but no baby.

"Where is the baby?" asks Amelia.

"Orion stayed home with her—he insisted," I say, rolling my eyes.

"Well, look who's here. I'm glad to see you are yet still

alive!" A voice proclaims from behind me. When I spin around, Faith grins and holds up a glass of champagne.

"Yes, but no thanks to you or your dude from the Bronx," I remind her.

"WHO OWE'S YOU A FAVOR," we all say together, and our laughter fills the small boutique.

"Hey, I hear when people are near death they see Heaven or Hell. Which one did you see? I was worried about you because of all the partying we used to do," says Faith.

"I'm pleased to announce, I made it into the pearly gates."

"But now you're here, so that means you were rejected," she teases. "Jesus took one sniff of you and said, nope, that's not my blood I smell, that's gin!"

We laugh again, but her words are a sobering reminder of my failure. I had become a born-again Christian a few years ago. Then when my father died, anger turned my world into a tailspin. I was back to my old ways within a few short months.

"Don't worry, God doesn't reject us that way," says Naomi. "It's by grace we are saved," she whispers this, so I'm the only one to hear. Otherwise, we run the risk of another round of jokes from Faith. When the next gown is brought over to us, Naomi's eyes brighten, and her smile widens.

"This is the dress," she announces.

She has become to me more than the peculiar coworker who read Bible passages on her lunch break. I couldn't imagine that my curiosity to befriend someone I had nothing in common with would lead us here; preparing for her wedding that will brand her as a St. Roman, and family.

Amelia seems pleased with her brother's choice in marriage, showing her approval with kind words and offering to assist whenever possible. I worry as they grow to know one another that Amelia's differing beliefs may cause a rift. I remind myself that Naomi was used to dealing with strong-willed personalities, which could explain her relationship with Faith; when I figure out the connection between them, maybe I'll worry less.

When we've finalized our purchase, Faith tells us she has another appointment. Then after giving us each a hug, she is gone. It is chilly outside, but the sun is shining so we decide to walk. With buttoned-up wool coats and gloves, we march along the pavement in search of a restaurant to tuck into for lunch.

It's a little less crowded mid-week in Soho; fewer speedster pedestrians and less honking horns. Still, shopping in New York can be a dizzying experience, evidenced by Amelia's darting eyes and gaps in her conversation; she tries to take it all in, the noise, the crowds, cast-iron buildings, side streets opening to perfect photo-op moments.

Once we find our restaurant of choice and take our seat, Naomi says she has some news to share. "After our wedding, Micah has agreed to help locate my children," she says. They plan to honeymoon in Antigua for eight days, with an extension to their trip in Guatemala, during which time Naomi hopes to locate and reunite with her children. I watch Amelia hoping to measure her reaction, unsure if she knows that her sister-in-law comes as a pre-package of six. Her breathing remains even, she doesn't even blink an eyelid.

"What will you do if they want to live with you? Things have changed since you first came to America," I say.

Naomi nods her head. If anyone knows about the dangers of crossing over into the United States, she does.

"That's the other barrier, but for now I'll be content to hold them in my arms again," she says. Amelia raises a cup to her lips and sips her drink, still saying nothing, listening and observing it all. I don't think her silence is an indicator of distaste. She is here with us, but her thoughts are a hundred miles away. Our shopping excursion ends with lunch. Afterward, I leave in a car for home and Amelia goes with Naomi to her apartment in Morris Park.

When I arrive home, instead of placing Oriyah in my arms, Orion hands me an envelope. Beneath Shelly Duvall's handwritten return address are the words, Inmate Correspondence, stamped in red ink.

"I'll read it after dinner," I say, taking my baby instead.

"Or, I can open it and read it to you now?" he asks.

My mind is spinning with what I imagine to be confessions written in the letter. Noticing my anxiety, Orion suggests that I first unwind, the letter will be on my desk when I'm ready.

Later in the evening, after Oriyah falls asleep, I tell Orion of my wishes to contribute in a more meaningful way. "I've always admired your work ethic, you make a difference in people's lives," I say.

"And you make a difference in our life, our baby is well-cared for, and I'm a happy man," he assures me. When he reads my expression, he understands I mean a contribution to society.

"What do you have in mind?"

"My Grandmother's organization, PAHST," I blurt out almost without thinking it over. "Wouldn't it be nice to open a branch here in New York." The more I talk, the vision seems achievable. "My mother's doing amazing work with the women there at the ranch. We don't need the land, just a small space, maybe at your center?"

"Sounds like you've put a lot of thought into this."

"No, not really, but this is what I've known since I was a young girl," I say. My passion continues to grow with each spoken word.

"Well, then you'll definitely need to pursue this, and you have my full support." Orion sits on the bed where I'm folding a load of clean clothes. Then hands me the envelope containing Shelly's confession. I can read her letter now, but I'm not sure if Orion should hear what she may have written.

"If there's anything I can do—maybe some of my connections at the law firm—I want to help her," he says. When I see how insistent he has become, we open the letter together.

> *Dear Emma, I am sorry for letting you and Suniva down. I deserve to be punished, just like all the other takers in this world. I want you to know, I tried everything to make her well, even traditional medicine and Doctors, but my efforts weren't enough. Maybe I waited too long before taking her into town. I dream of Suniva every night and haven't smiled since she left us. But I want you to know I smiled for the first time when I received your letter, then I cried again. In closing I need you to know, I loved Suniva with all my heart and would've given my life to make her well. Sorry for letting you down, Shelly.*

"What can we do?" I ask. There's no need to hide my emotions, and my tears flow like a levee breach. "I shouldn't have left her, I knew she wasn't fit to be alone with a child."

I know the blame doesn't rest on my having left, or Shelly's inability to parent, neither of us was equipped to handle that situation alone.

"Write her back, and tell her you'll contact a lawyer who can help," he says.

Together, Orion and I compose a letter expressing genuine concern, with an offer to help. I write my apology for leaving, and not coming back to check on them as I had promised. Then after saying that I am now married and have a new baby girl,   seal and address the envelope with a sense of relief, and a sliver of hope.

THIS MORNING I find more time to write in my journal. Today I work on my Father's hearing because of our discussion in the garden; after a conversation with Uncle Eli, I have learned of a long-standing feud between them. My dad, Emanuel, worked hard to win his father's approval, and Uncle Eli believed his drive to build an empire stemmed from a desire to please his mother.

My father had always worked long hours, leaving me alone with my mom, who needed him even more than I did. But he was someone's son before he became my father, and before becoming a workaholic; he wanted his father's approval. Grandpa was hardened by military life, so perhaps he felt Uncle Eli could withstand the pressure of his demands. For whatever reason, he clung to his firstborn more than the second.

After I have finished my entry, I listen for Orion, who is preparing a morning bottle for our baby. When I don't hear them I leave our bedroom and search the house where I find him standing in the kitchen.

"Don't panic, but there's something I need to show you," he says. I brace myself as he brings Oriyah closer and shows me the fluid-like substance pooled in her right ear.

"I'll get her dressed, call her pediatrician," I say.

It's just before 7 a.m. when he makes the call. A nurse answers the after-hours line, and after the tele diagnosis, she suggests it's probably an inner ear infection. Then we are scheduled for an afternoon appointment, but we agree, due to our lack of experience a visit to the emergency room will comfort us both.

During the drive over, I mention how Suniva's death began with a common ailment. I know the comparison is harsh, even before Orion's weary gaze finds me. He accelerates on the gas, maneuvering through traffic as if we're the only people in New York with an emergency this morning.

At the hospital, we are soon triaged, and then after a short wait, led into a room. A little while longer, and the on-staff physician confirms Oriyah's inner ear infection.

"The antibiotics will work," he assures us, seeing the lingering questions between Orion and me. "And you will need to follow up with her pediatrician," the doctor says.

We decide to keep the afternoon appointment for 3:30 with the pediatrics' group familiar with our baby. By the time we leave the hospital, it's 10:30 a.m., which leaves five hours to burn until the scheduled appointment later in the afternoon. To my surprise, Orion suggests that we head into Manhattan and check in at my old apartment.

"Maybe there are a few things there we can take back home for you or Oriyah," he says. I can't help thinking he's still in search of clues or a warm body explaining Victoria's disappearance.

The apartment is empty when we arrive. After a thorough investigation, Orion turns on the television, hoping to watch some of the morning news he's missed earlier. After telling him I would start a pot of coffee, I leave him on the sofa. While the pot brews, I head for my bedroom closet to grab the leather boots I had purchased last year.

Orion wouldn't have seen the sign, but I'm sure the towel lying at the foot of the bed, wasn't there on my last visit. On top of the comforter is an emptied bag, with a receipt for a trench coat, and combat boots. In the bathroom droplets of water on the floor, the bathtub was still damp from recent use.

In the nursery, nothing seems askew, but I recheck the closets and underneath the bed. Victoria had been here today but somehow manages to slip away before our arrival. When I return to the kitchen, I notice a stunning orchid arrangement sitting on the butcher's block. I approach to admire the

278

blooms, and there the note was tucked partially beneath the pot.

> *Emma, I hope you get this letter. I needed some time to clear my head, but now I understand how wrong it was of me to take off with your baby that way. Please forgive me for the fright I've caused you and Orion. By the time you find this letter I will have turned myself in. Thank you for your kindness after all that's happened between us through the years. Maybe someday we can be sisterly, Victoria.*

"I found this note from Victoria, says she went to turn herself in. I'm not sure when it was written, but she was here this morning—the bathtubs still wet," I say, then hand him the note. He reads the letter and then goes for his cell phone.

"We got her," says the voice on the other end. I watch as a smile erases frown lines from Orion's face. He laughs now, maybe to keep from crying. I look to Oriyah who is sleeping in her chair, then kiss her warm forehead before going back into what used to be my bedroom.

"I'll be in the room, going through some of my things," I whisper to Orion who gives me a thumbs up. In the bedroom, I send a group text message to Naomi, my Mother, and Sadie: Victoria turned herself in this morning.

I'm relieved, but I also want us to be okay; Victoria and me, along with Reba, Sadie, Shelly, and Naomi. All of us, daughters of mother's who conceive babies through pain, out

279

of love. If there's one thing I can change with the life I've been given, it is to be intentional about love—because life is hard, and love shouldn't be.

I am holding a bottle of liquor when Orion finds me inside the closet. "I forgot this was here," I say before leaving to pour the contents down the drain. "Don't worry, that part of my life died in the accident," I tell him.

"What do you need from me?" he asks. Oriyah starts crying at the same time my phone rings. "Answer your phone, I'll get the baby," he's quick to say. We still race to see who will get more time with Oriyah. Lately, Orion seems to win.

A call comes through from Reba, and before I can answer, there's another from Naomi. I answer my Mother's call first.

"Hi, mom."

"I know things aren't quite right between us, but I should be there with you," she says.

"I'm ready, please come as soon as you can," I tell her.

After I give her the address, she asks if it's okay for Sadie to come as well. "Of course, Victoria will need her, and there's plenty enough room here for you both."

When I return to the living room, I remind Orion of my decision to help Victoria, with a place to live, and bailing her out of jail.

"I'll look into what I can do about having charges dropped, but the state may pick it up," he says. I nod my head without argument. By the time we leave for Oriyah's appointment, I have gathered piles of items in each room to bring home. Orion will come on another day with a small truck, but later this evening we have dinner plans with his parents.

This will be the first time meeting my in-laws. There was a phone call on our wedding day, another the evening Oriyah was returned, but it's different meeting face-to-face. When we return home, I set to work cleaning my home in Grandma Rose fashion; every corner dusted, window glass streak-free, floors polished, matching dinnerware, plants rearranged, and fresh-cut flowers on tabletops. Afterward, I am ready to wash and change.

My mother-in-law, Mabel, is a modest woman, so I select a beige knit dress with Grandma Rose in mind. When I am pleased with my reflection in the mirror, I eyeball the wig setting on its stand. I want to make a good impression, but I've over-heated twice wearing the hairpiece; I couldn't risk making a spectacle of myself tonight. Besides, my hair continues to grow, like the strength in my arms and legs.

My mother-in-law is a thick, heavy-handed woman who walks with her back straight and head held high. She smells of fresh herbs and spices, and talks with an accent—I wasn't expecting the accent. She smiles when greeting me, chatting about her trip and the gifts she's brought, all the while she continues to smile. Even as Orion tell our story, how we met, the accident and Oriyah's miracle birth—she is still smiling.

My father-in-law, Jackson, is a silver-headed, jovial man.

He speaks in a low tenor voice, also with an accent. Jackson likes to tell jokes he's learned from the indigenous people of his travels. He laughs at us when we fail to understand one of his riddles, a squeaky noise, that causes Oriyah to flinch and search for the unfamiliar sound.

The only way my mother-in-law can settle her husband is by turning on the sports channel. He immediately makes himself right at home, taking off his shoes and asking for something to drink. Orion tells him that dinner is ready, and he hops right up as if he hadn't sat down. Their grief over losing a child is long gone, at least not evident on the surface.

"I like that it smells fresh in here. It's very good, yes," says Mabel. She remarks on the housekeeping, and then on the blackened fish. "The right amount of peppa, and you used ginger— I love ginger," she says, smiling.

After dinner, they ask to stay with us for a few days, rather than traveling back-and-forth to their home in South Jersey.

"Of course," I answer, without checking with Orion to see how he feels about our houseguests. "Perfect! That'll give us more time to know one another, and more time with my adorable grandbaby," she says.

When I mention that my mother was traveling to visit us, Jackson suggests that Reba stay here too, instead of Manhattan. When I tell them that a friend of the family is also coming, I'm grateful for the excuse.

"My mother and I are working through some things," I

282

admit, hoping to drop the subject.

Oriyah is like most babies who enjoy being the center of attention, and she is happiest when being held. So naturally, having the extra sets of hands fills our home with more of her squeals and babble. I feel a little jealous when she doesn't notice I've left the room several times. Orion is more vocal about his feelings.

"I'm ready for my baby now," and when Mabel fails to hand her over, "We have a bedtime routine I don't want to break," he insists.

"You two go right ahead, we'll bring her when she's tired of us," says Jackson.

Orion looks to me, but I refuse to back him on this one. When we ascend the steps to our bedroom, we are both pouting, though we dare not let them see our expressions.

The next morning, I awake to an empty bed. I know Orion has been here because his tossing and turning awakens me several times through the night. I'm sure at some point he left with intentions to bring our baby to bed, but now he's missing too.

I find Orion in the living room with his father. They stop talking when I approach, and each takes a sip from their coffee cup.

"Good morning, my love. You were sleeping when I got up, so I left you alone," says Orion.

In the kitchen, I hear Oriyah's baby talk and a constant thumping.

"Good morning, I hope you don't mind me starting breakfast, and your sweet-one has been fed," says Mabel in a sing-song way. I can still hear the accent that Orion tells me they've both had since his childhood, on account of the many years living in Ghana. The thumping noise comes from Oriyah, who sits strapped in her highchair, beating a wooden spoon on the Rubbermaid tray. Upon seeing me, she drops the spoon and then whines until I come to her rescue.

"Mommy misses you too," I say after she is in my arms. I kiss her sticky fingers and nuzzle around her neck, which smells fruity, like ripe pears or plums.

"I gave your sweet-one some home-made baby food. It's very, very good—yes. I've made this very recipe for over thirty years, learned in the village even before raising my own children." she smiles.

I shake my head, "No, I don't mind." I can't take my eyes off Oriyah, as we continue nuzzling.

"She has been fed, bathed, and dressed—all before 6 a.m. I'm afraid you'll spoil us, and we won't want you to leave," I say to my smiling mother-in-law as she nods her head and blushes a little.

"We can stay the week through, but by next Sunday we'll be needed at church," she says.

After breakfast, Orion and I plot on how to ask if Oriyah can stay with his parents while we drive to the airport.

"Tell her you're worried she'll catch a cold in the snow," he whispers.

"You tell her, she's your mother," I whisper back.

Why the need for secrecy, I don't know. We're in the privacy of our bedroom closet. After we have rehearsed our respective lines, we leave our room.

"We're leaving now, headed out in all this snow," Orion says, and then nudges me for my line. When I swat his hand away, my mother-in-law spies our behavior.

"I want to meet your Mother. Please bring her here."

"Yes, of course, we'll do just that," Orion answers. Then he clears his throat before saying, "We're headed out in the snow now," and waits for my line again.

I refuse to ask my mother-in-law to do another thing, she's already done so much this morning. When I mouth the words to him, "I can't ask," he rolls his eyes.

"Oh, leave the baby with us, it's cold and snowing out," says his father, shooing us away. When my mother-in-law waves, we make a quick shuffle through the backdoor. Once we are in the car, I break my silence with laughter.

"Why wouldn't you say your line, honey," Orion asks.

I shrug my shoulders. "I don't know, maybe it's because she's been up since before dawn. I couldn't ask," I say.

It's a good, hearty laugh we share together, before leaving the garage and heading towards the freeway. When the traffic slows on the interstate, my mood changes.

"I haven't seen my mom in about ten years," I admit.

By now, Orion is all too aware of the reason for our estranged relationship.

285

"You think you're ready for this? I can go by myself and drop her off?" he offers.

"I'm ready. I'm in a good space now, and thanks to you I have plenty of support."

"You think we should wait, and have your uncle there when you face her, or Naomi?"

"NO, please not my uncle. He'll be over-protective which may do more harm than good, bless his heart." If his treatment of Reba turns out to be anything like he monitored the hospital staff things could get out of hand.

Seeing my Mother standing on the platform gives me mixed feelings. She seems less of a threat now with thinning hair and round wire glasses on her face. When I exit the car, I can feel Orion's watchful eyes over me. After our embrace, he sticks his hand between us, and with a grin, introduces himself as my husband.

"Your hair," Reba exclaims. "I like it, you look happy," she says.

I notice the lines on her forehead, and the twitch of her face, a side-effect from her years of substance abuse. But she fidgets less with her hands and arms.

"A new look for you also," I say, pointing to her glasses and casual attire.

"There are a lot of things different in my life." She was going to say more but stops when Sadie exits the building.

Orion leaves my side to put their luggage in the trunk, and after our greeting, we enter the car. When I turn to let them know we would be stopping so they could meet Orion's parents, my mother says, "Thank you."

Thank you for what? I can't help myself from thinking when I turn around in my seat. Thank you for not having me arrested? Thank you for giving me a second chance? Thank you for your forgiveness? When the traffic stalls on the interstate, Reba becomes chatty.

"My first time in the big city," she says. "I've seen hundreds of streets and towns, but this is a first for me." She gushes at the buildings, observing the many facets of each city-block. When we turn down a side road, a woman stands on a corner with a blank stare, scratching at her arms and neck.

"Your daddy died while I was in the streets battling a heroin addiction," she says.

I turn my head in time to see Sadie reach over and pat her arm. "I wasn't there for my daughter, either. It's a miracle she's turned out so well—I owe that to her Grandmother Rosemary," she says.

"I'm sure you played a part in some way," says Orion.

Not sure if every root of bitterness has left me, I opt to keep my mouth shut. The Gentleman's words come back to me now, "The hearing will bring healing... listen to understand." We all have a need to be heard.

"I always wanted her to be strong, not weak. It was something I drilled in her from a small child—be strong, don't show weakness. It was the best tool I could give her.

287

It's what my Ma had always told me." Her face is hard-set but softly edged with regret.

"Yes, you did teach me to be strong," I say, and then I thank her for instilling in me the kind of strength that has helped in many tough situations. I nod my head at her, as I finger the seam of my jacket searching for material to wring. I hadn't felt the urge to self-soothe like this since my car accident.

"I was a weak, nervous child. When I was ten years old, I was diagnosed with Tourette Syndrome," she confesses.

I flinch at hearing this, and my response is obvious. "What are you saying?" I ask her. Orion remains silent, and Sadie looks at my Mother as if she has become her advocate, encouraging her to continue.

"Yes, it's true. Your daddy knew it, and so did your Grandma Rose—I have the tics! Mostly just my eye twitches now, but it was worse when I was a kid," she says.

I continue staring until my disbelief turns to confusion. Where were the clues? What memories from my childhood are marred by her disease?

"Having this disability actually changed my fate. I was of no use to my granny; I'd laugh in client's faces and said the worst things imaginable." She looks away, shrugs her shoulders, and smirks. I wonder if this, along with other behaviors, is an adaptive way of masking her tics.

"Terra-Lynn thought I was possessed. When my twitches started, she came to me with her bag of bones. I won't get into the rituals, but after one of my twitching fits sent her flying across the room, she left me alone for good saying my inherited powers were somehow stronger than hers..." she pauses to take a sip from her water bottle.

"That ole' bone lady," she snickers. "She was an Afro-Cuban woman…had the scariest, veiny hands and her red-eyes seemed to glow in the dark—she never liked me because I could see the darkness in her. Oh, the superstitious," Reba laughs. "She instilled fear all throughout Louisiana, but it took a nervous, twitching child like me to rattle the satchel of bones she wore around her neck."

"My great-grandmother was a witch?" I say in a small voice. My imagination runs wild with images of a cloth pouch filled with chicken bones, rattling around the neck of a busty older woman with long grey hair, and thin crow-like claws for fingers. "It's ridiculous," I say, shaking off an eerie feeling lingering at the base of my neck.

"That's some kind of woman who can leave a mark of terror long after her demise," says Orion. When he looks at me, I know he feels the same chilling sensation.

"But look how blessed you two are now!" Sadie exclaims. She doesn't seem to share the same uneasiness as the rest of us. If so, she hides her fear. "Both of you are saved by God's grace. Whatever your great-grandmother practiced has been destroyed by the works of Christ—you're no longer bound."

"Yes, so long as there are no more Lynn's—you did tell me her name isn't Lynn?" says Reba.

"I named her when Emma—" Orion begins.

"I changed her name after...it was done while I was—I was in a coma." I manage to spit the words out and then turn around in my seat to avoid her gaze.

She wants to blame herself for my accident, but I won't let her do that. I tell my Mother of my drunk driving incident, and how Oriyah was born while I was in a coma. This was the reason for my shaved head. When Reba begins weeping Sadie steps in on cue, rubbing her shoulders and whispering words of comfort. Sadie has become to my Mother what Naomi is for me; a friend who sticks closer than a brother. After she manages to pull herself together, Reba asks Orion about his parents. What do they do for a living?

Upon learning they are missionaries working in Ghana, she looks at her outfit and gushes. "I shouldn't have worn this dashiki, they'll think I'm trying too hard to make an impression," she says. When Orion pulls the car into our driveway, Reba exits and looks herself over, tugging, pulling and readjusting her outfit.

Oriyah is still in her Grandmother's arms when I return. I'm relieved when she whimpers upon seeing me and doesn't stop until I go to her. After Orion introduces his parents to my mother, and Sadie, he grabs his father and retreats to the kitchen.

When we are alone, Sadie apologizes for any pain her daughter may have caused us. As my mother-in-law and Sadie discuss the woes of parenting, my mother asks to hold her granddaughter. I test Oriyah to see if she'll cry when she doesn't my mother takes her from my arms and sits away from us in a corner.

"She's tough already," my Mother says when Oriyah grabs hold of her fingers. "But I don't want her to feel like she has to be—it's okay not to be okay," she reaffirms.

IT HAS BEEN two days since the reunion with my Mother. After our first night together, despite my in-law's request, Orion and I finally dropped my Mother and Sadie off at the Manhattan apartment yesterday. I understand my mother-in-law's perspective; if we're all here together, everyone could avoid having to go out into the biting winter air. However, wisdom tells me to take things slow.

Reba has Tourette syndrome? If this is true, it does explain my biggest complaint of her; pull me close and push me away—she never could tolerate touching or closeness for too long. Now I'm sure this disease is the reason for my mom's unexplainable behaviors.

Standing in the mirror, I search my features for our similarities; same oval-shaped face, and brown eyes. My nose and lips are like my father's—and Victoria's. There was a time admiring myself in a mirror would provoke the verbal assaults from the ugly voice. I shudder to think my troubles may have stemmed from my great grandma's dark side. Had her spirit been reaching from the grave, or hell, trying to reclaim a birthright?

When I ask Orion this question, he tells me it's a silly thought. "We believe in Jesus, nothing else matters," he says. Yes, I tell him, but even Jesus spoke of demons, so they do exist.

"We are saved by God's grace. That's all that matters," he tells me what the others' have already reiterated. I know he's right because the Gentleman and my encounter in Heaven bear witness to this fact, but still, the idea lingers. Orion shares a story of how some of the villagers in his birth country believed in different rituals, performed to ancestors and gods.

"I remember something to do with bones," he says, pointing out the similarity in Reba's story to his own experience. When my cell phone vibrates on the nightstand, we both startle a bit. After reading the text, I hand the phone to Orion.

"Don't respond, she doesn't mean us any good," he says after reading Tamar's message.

I remind him that she and I were close once, like sisters. Orion says he understands but also reminds me that her happiness is not my responsibility.

"You can't save everyone, especially someone who doesn't believe they need to change," he urges. But a part of me wants this argument, with him, and with Tamar. It's because of their betrayal I have one less friend. He follows me to the closet as I search for an outfit. I refuse to look at him. My lips are tight, and my movement is sharp.

"Are you kidding me, you can't possibly be mad. She's poison, you said so yourself. She wants the old Emma, the one that drinks and gets wild with her," he says.

I turn to face him, and before I speak, wave him into the closet to buffer our voice from his parents. "Our friendship was so much more than that. You know it, but you're choosing to forget," I say, deciding this is the nicest way to remind him of his poor decision. Plus, he's partly right, but I don't want to give him the satisfaction just yet.

"Is this our first fight," I say, leaning against the closet door, and then lowering myself to the floor for dramatic effect.

"I'm not telling you what to do, but think of us before you agree to meet with her is all I ask," he says.

I do consider him, and Oriyah, before sending my response: Meet us in the park, the entrance closest to my apartment, at 1 o'clock.

It was difficult convincing my mother-in-law that we had to take Oriyah out in the cold weather, but she finally agrees.

"I won't have this time with her always, and it's so cold outside," she reasons. Orion agrees with her but says there's an appointment that can't be rescheduled.

It's just before noon when we reach Central Park. With time to spare, Orion suggests we drop in on my Mom and Sadie. This time when I enter the building several of my old neighbors notice me, remarking on my new hairdo and congratulate me on my marriage. I'm sure they're aware of my accident, though no one dares mention.

Once we arrive outside my apartment, I ring the doorbell rather than use my key. When Sadie opens the door, a whiff of cinnamon and brown sugar trails into the hallway.

"Come in, your Mother has been up cleaning all morning, and I'm baking treats," she says.

Inside, the dining table is lined with bags filled with groceries and other household items. In the living room the window sheers have been changed from black to taupe, and several four-wick soy candles flicker on the mantle, sending their sunset-fields aroma throughout the apartment.

My mother gives us a tour of the changes; the furniture my Dad and I had purchased years ago remain, but everything else is new. Bed linen, curtains, bath towels, even the oriental rug has been replaced. The nursery is now converted back into a second bedroom, although the floor-length mirror still lines the walls. Both Reba and Sadie have concerns about Victoria living alone in an elegant New York apartment. Then they ask how I managed by myself in such a fancy neighborhood.

"Daddy took care of everything, all I had to do was stay

out of trouble, and keep the apartment clean," I tell them. Sensing the conversation is getting heavy, Orion takes the baby from my hands, and returns to the living room.

Sadie says she'd feel more comfortable if we referred to this apartment as "our home." That way we'd each have a key; Victoria, Reba, Sadie and me. Then we could hold Victoria accountable without her knowing.

"It doesn't matter to me, so long as she's happy here. That's all I hope for," I say.

When the time draws closer to meeting with Tamar, I pull Orion aside to ask how he feels about me meeting her alone? He doesn't give his answer quickly, but after staring out the window for some time, he finally agrees. "But leave Oriyah," he says.

I want to protest, but it has been a short while since we've gotten her back, so I agree to do things his way.

"You see that bench right there," he taps a finger on the window. "That's where I want you to sit. That way, I can keep an eye on you the whole time." We talk low to avoid my mother and Sadie overhearing.

When the time approaches, Orion walks me to the elevator. There's only one flight of stairs, but I made a promise to my dad that I'd use the elevator, just in case someone with bad intentions lurked in the stairwell.

"I'll be watching the whole time. Wave your hand if you need me, and I'll come running like the Flash," he says. I lift on my toes to give him a kiss, hoping it'll calm him, but he holds me back. "What will you do if she gets violent?"

"I'm not that fragile," I say while reaching a hand to stop him from entering the elevator. "Go get more acquainted with your mother-in-law…and stop worrying. We were close friends for years, she wants to talk," I assure him as the elevator door closes.

During my short elevator ride, Orion's concerns linger with me. Tamar was career-driven, fierce, and bursting with confidence, but never violent. She wouldn't—she couldn't. If she has forgotten, I'll remind her of the bond we once had before husbands and babies…and betrayal.

Despite the freezing temperatures, the sun is shining, melting the snow piled into street gutters by snowplows and other vehicles. The air fills with exhaust fumes, as a passing city bus splatters slush inches from where I stand. When the traffic clears, I spot Tamar sitting on a bench just outside the 96th Street park entrance. She looks like a snow-angel, dressed in all white; ankle boots, wool slacks, and coat with white faux-fur around the collar.

"You cut your hair," she says, after our embrace. Then she takes hold of my left hand. "Only 2 carats," she sucks her teeth, before letting go of my hand. I almost defend my ring, but seeing Orion's shadow in the window calms me. I look away before Tamar notices him.

"I can't believe you married him, you do know I'm getting divorced because of what he did?"

Tamar stares at me with a hard, unblinking glare. Then

she proceeds to tell a different story of how Orion approached her for money, and when he learned of her problem, offered to help—for a fee.

I tell her Orion's version of the story. He was struggling with debt and considered being a sperm donor. When the two of them end up at the same clinic, it was Tamar who made the offer. After learning Orion never gave his specimen, she became furious—and rightfully so.

"It's manipulation anyway you dissect the story, Emma!" she raises her voice, proceeding to advise me of how my husband was a thief and an opportunist.

"Did he repay your money?" I ask when she finishes her tirade. But Tamar insists that the money is beside the point. It's the intention behind his actions she wishes for me to understand.

"Where are you living at now, and why is that crazy girl staying at your place?" she demands.

Watching her throw fit after fit, I now understand Orion's concern. He is still watching from the window, waiting for me to wave a hand in the air, and he'll come running. But Tamar is so angry, I can't imagine how things will turn out if he shows up.

"Victoria is my sister—" I try to explain, but Tamar cuts me off, yelling profanities about how my trusting an enemy's story is asinine. For a moment, I think to match her emotion, but history reminds me that this is what Tamar does when things don't go her way.

"You don't understand the whole story. My mom and her Mother are here at my apartment now—Victoria is my sister!" I manage to say calmly. Tamar settles down, but I see her biting her lip, thinking of what to say next. This argument won't end until she has an answer for each question.

"I think it's about time you get a reality check, just because you come from money doesn't mean you get a happy ending!" says Tamar. She stops speaking after seeing the confused look on my face.

It's not her fault she has this perfect picture of my life. All those years we spent together as friends, I never told her how I ended up in New York. When we met, I had recently turned 18 years old, and my Dad had flown in from Denver. She received a nice commission as our real estate agent.

"I was on the run when I came here," I say.

When she questions my statement, I tell Tamar about the night of my high school graduation and the events that led to our meeting. Her facial expression changes from anger, to shock, then empathy, and finally disgust. When I finish my confession, Tamar says I'm not the person she thought I was.

"I won't deny it, you've been through a lot, but you carry on like a spoiled brat," she seethes through gritted teeth. "Look around Emma, there are victims everywhere in this city." When she waves her hand for effect, I remember Orion in the window.

Without thinking, I snap my head in his direction, and Tamar follows my gaze. My building had to be over 100 feet from where we sat, and two stories up, but it felt like Orion had been there with us on the bench the whole time.

Tamar swears loudly when she spots him. After we both get to our feet, I look back at the window and Reba is holding my baby in her arms. I know it will take Orion less than ten minutes to reach us.

"Let's not end it like this. We were like sisters, I'm your children's godmother," I say when Tamar starts to walk away.

"We were like sisters, but you have one now—remember?" She yells back at me when the streetlight turns green. By the time she crosses the road, Orion reaches me on the bench.

"This isn't over, you'll both pay for ruining my marriage!" she says from the opposite street corner. Then she turns and walks away with hard, determined steps.

"I'm okay, you didn't have to come," I tell Orion as we leave the park bench. He puts his arms around my shoulders and escorts me across the street.

"I know, but your mother's the one you'll have to convince," he says.

During the elevator ride, Orion tells me how Reba had been watching him the whole time, as he spied on me. If he didn't do something quickly, she was prepared to go and get me. When I enter the apartment, Reba hands Oriyah over to Sadie and comes near.

"I couldn't live if anything else happened to you," she says before pulling me into her arms.

"I'm okay, mom – nothing happened."

But she continues holding me and won't let go until Orion suggests that we sit down for comfort.

"I like when you call me Mom," she says, and this is how I know my mother has changed.

We sit alone on the sofa, apologizing to one another, for the many flaws of our personality. I admit to misunderstanding her, it must've been hard to parent with a disability. Time has softened my mom in ways she never wished for either of us, but it's these delicate areas that bring us back together.

• • •

My Mom leaves on Friday morning. Several times we change our minds; should she depart on schedule, or stay longer? It has been a delight having her around. My mother-in-law was fascinated by her life and makes her promise to finish the story of Terra-Lynn the next time they meet.

In the end, it's decided the tenants at the ranch—*Emma's Safe Haven*, have a greater need for her now. I know it brings her joy to be useful. At the airport, we remind my Mother of our planned visit next month. Then we will further discuss a strategy to implant PAHST here in New York.

We all agree, for this idea to work, we'll need Uncle Eli's approval. My mom doesn't mind, saying how he's been very generous toward her. Orion is left with the charge of presenting the proposal to my uncle. After the business talk is over, we embrace.

"Until next time," I say.

We are both smiling, happy with the idea of more days together.

SADE HAS USED her time wisely in New York. After her
visit to the county jail, she began her search for a therapist
who specialized in childhood abandonment issues. Victoria is
desperate, so the argument in favor of professional help is an
easy sell—for the time being.

Victoria and Sadie call soon as she's made bail this
morning. She wants me and Orion to know how sorry she is
for taking off with Oriyah. Then she expresses her intentions
to do whatever it takes to fix this; even mental health support.

When she asks to meet with us, neither me nor Orion
thinks it's a good idea; mostly because we are all scheduled to
be in court tomorrow morning. Then we will find out if our
plea to have the charges dropped to a misdemeanor, with
probation and court-ordered psychiatric treatment has been
granted.

When I tell her it's better to wait until tomorrow afternoon, she tries to convince us that she understands. "I would like that," her voice cracks. Allowing space for unspoken questions, the silence between us grows. Together, our stories would take a lifetime to tell, and even more time than that to heal; so, where do we begin?

"I hope you like the changes to the apartment," I say.

"It's more than I deserve. I just want to start over from the day I found out we were sisters and do things the right way," she says.

"I'm hoping for the same outcome, It feels like this huge force has been working behind the scenes to bring us together since childhood, only we didn't understand the attraction, so we fought," I tell her.

Victoria agrees, except her interpretation is the opposite; it's a secret conspiracy that has kept us apart. "Maybe our Mothers are to blame, but definitely something wicked," says Victoria.

Sadie clears her throat, reminding us both that she is listening. Our laughter marks the conversation as an attempt to move toward the future; not as enemies, nor a frenemy, but as blood-bond sisters. After the phone call, Orion holds me close.

"With my parents gone, we'll have to take Oriyah with us in the morning," he says. "How do you think she'll react?"

"It may be emotional for all of us," I say, thinking of the weeks they were alone.

304

If tomorrow goes as we hope, Victoria will be free, and it will take many occasions before she earns our full trust. For now, our attention must shift to another issue. Uncle Eli has phoned to give us the news he intends on meeting us at court. He uses the excuse of wanting to mesh out details for the New York PAHST branch, but I know better. I decide against warning Victoria; I have had no buffer with our uncle, so she will get her initiation into the St. Roman clan by fire.

When morning comes, both Orion and I are quiet. There are many outcomes for this court appearance, and we have considered them all. I believe we are short with one another, because he's afraid to say what his hopes are for today, and I'm tired of expressing mine.

The court hearing turns out to be mediation. I'm sure my husbands' legal connections, along with my uncle's backing, has influenced this change. Victoria is given a stipulation to have a mental health assessment, with 30-day inpatient, and 60-day outpatient treatment after that. She is crying when the terms are outlined. I'm unsure if her emotions are a result of the objection, or if she understands the treatment is necessary. Victoria wipes her eyes, and after looking at Oriyah in my arms, and Orion at my side, she nods her head.

"This never should've happened; I know I need help," she admits.

Uncle Eli clasps his hands together and opens his mouth. I wait for the lecture, but his words don't come; instead, he softens. When I look to him, his damp face greets me. If I had to put myself in his shoes, I'd think it'd be hard to side with one niece over the other; the one you love versus the other you're anxious to meet. Not wanting him to feel there's a side to choose, I take the liberty to speak.

"Victoria, allow me to officially introduce you to our Dad's brother—your Uncle Eli," I say. He shows his approval by reaching over and kissing me on the cheek.

Seeing how Victoria gushes over our display, Uncle Eli raises from his seat and goes to her. Wrapping her in his arms, he warns, "let's get this out of the way now, because by tonight you'll be pretty annoyed with me," he says, and his laughter barrels against the walls.

Victoria is smiling, not knowing this isn't a joke. Orion and I laugh together because of our first-hand dealings with him these past months. As we walk the hallway toward the exit, I spot a woman with silver hair entering the court building. When the crowd before us thins, I see the woman is Violet, the Empress, staring back at me. I smile to acknowledge her, and she waves me in her direction.

"Give me a moment, I want to use the restroom before we leave," I tell Orion and the others, and with Oriyah in my arms, I follow Violet into the restroom.

"Miss San Romun, it's so good to see you again; and look at this gift the Lord done gave you!" she exclaims, touching Oriyah's tiny fingers and rubbing the fine hairs on her head. She stops to ask permission before lifting her from my arms.

"I feel blessed," I say, "things are finally falling into place...I hope it's a friendly visit that brings you here today?" I question.

"Yes, it is. I'm here several days a week, hoping to be a light wherever possible." Her voice and hair are the same, but her hands seem stronger than before. The lines in her face are smoother, as if she's younger somehow.

"We never finished our conversation, when was it that you visited the garden?"

"Hmm, are you sure we haven't?" she says, scratching her head with a free hand. "I remember being there with you."

As she speaks, her eyes shine as the Gentleman's had in the Corridor, her laughter is lively as Suniva's were; the scent of her is brassy like the worn-door knob, but there's a hint of every cherished scent from my childhood—the orange blossoms, lavender, and jasmine. To me, the mixture of sweet and citrusy fragrance is like the smell of bergamot.

"The Gentleman was there, and—wait, are you—"

"People don't usually remember us messengers. It's the big J they can't forget. I want you to know we're real proud of you, and your Mother, for carrying out your Grandmother's mission. After all, it was Reba's story that gave Rosemary the vision for PAHST," she says.

Violet chuckles, seeing my mouth gaping open. When she places Oriyah back in my arms, I'm reminded to take a breath.

"After hearing your Mother's story, your Grandmother had a burden to fight against human and sex trafficking. It was her dream to run the organization with Reba—you like to write about hearings, wait until you hear the rest of that story," she shudders and then turns to wash her hands as if rinsing away the filth from the knowledge. When the bathroom door opens, I jump, causing Oriyah to whine.

"Are you okay in here," asks Sadie. She holds the door open, giving me a glance of Uncle Eli talking as Victoria listens.

"Yes, I was just speaking with—where did she go?" I peep under the three bathroom stalls and double-check again. "Yes, I'm ready," I say. Sadie smiles, holding the door open for me.

During their conversation, Uncle Eli decides on a catered lunch, at what has now become Victoria's apartment. As he struts out of the court building, his cell phone is up against his ear. With a loud voice, he places a food order, and with the same tone instructs Sadie and Victoria to keep up.

Orion and I stroll off in the opposite direction, holding hands and grinning at each other. "She'll wish for the jail time after spending the evening with your uncle," Orion teases.

After buckling our sleeping baby into her seat, we sit in the car for a moment to discuss the outcome. Because we are recounting the day, I feel it appropriate to share my bathroom encounter with him. Before I can speak, the cell phone in my handbag vibrates. I pause to check the message. "It's from my Mom, listen to this," I read the text aloud.

Mom: I just woke from a nap with an urgency to tell you of how your great-grandma, Leneta Machado, became known as the terror, Lynn Machete (Terra Lynn). It'll all make sense when you hear her reason for keeping the bones.

Orion is in such a good mood he makes fun of the text, which I find quite eerie.

"Wooooh!" he says in his most ominous impression, and when Oriyah whimpers in the backseat, I swat at him.

"We better get going before my uncle comes searching for us," I tell him. Then to my Mother, I reply:

Emma: I'll be in town a few days before Naomi's wedding. Can it wait until then?
Mom: Yes.

By the time we arrive at the apartment, the aroma reminds me of the Thanksgiving dinner I missed while recovering from my injuries; roasted turkey and dressing, macaroni and cheese, collard greens with ham hocks, candied yams, and apple pie. Christmas is next week, but for now, we celebrate reconciliation and forgiveness. I rub the top of my head when Uncle Eli mentions how much has changed, and the expectations he has for the future St. Roman generation.

"Look around this table, this is but a mere portion of the increase this family is about to experience!" he declares.

I pass a hand over my head again, and can't help but smile. It's not only my hair that experiences this exponential growth during these last few months. My limbs are stronger, and my mind is renewed. I attribute this miraculous healing to my time with the Gentleman in the garden.

"In hearing you will be healed," the Gentleman's words return to me. He was right, I smile, remembering his charge that gave me the courage to return and to live again.

Victoria and her mother, Sadie. Orion, Naomi, and even Tamar. Uncle Eli and his wife, Miranda. My cousins, Amelia and Micah. My mother, Reba. My father, Emanuel and Grandma Rose's legacy. Their stories revived me and gave me hope, a newfound purpose in life.

I am home.

ABOUT THE AUTHOR

Laura Gaisie was born in High Point, North Carolina in 1971. At the age of 5, her family moved to Atlantic City, New Jersey, where she and her siblings alternated between city life and rural living on her grandparent's small farm in McKee City, New Jersey. After graduating from high school, she relocated to Covina, California.

Laura returned to North Carolina in 1995, after giving birth to her first child. In 1997, she married her first husband and soon had her second child. In 2000 she enrolled in High Point University and went on to graduate with a Bachelor of Science degree in Psychology with an emphasis in mental health. After her first marriage ended she relocated to Austin, Texas to work for the State. She returned to California in 2006 to marry her current husband.

She has participated in National Novel Writing Month (NaNoWriMo) writing contest for the past five years and has won the last four years. She coaches aspiring writers in, The Writing Room (a book coaching program). She is the owner of, Purple Pearls Publishing (an independent publishing company). She is co-founder and Executive Director of a nonprofit, Authors Inside, an organization that provides writing resources and publishing services to incarcerated authors.

For further information visit her website at:

Website: https://www.lauragaisie.com

ACKNOWLEDGEMENTS

My mom, Juanita Bridges, my biggest cheerleader. My husband, Emmanuel, your support means everything to me.

Ellie, my rock-star beta-reader; thank you for your keen eye and dedication to this process. I truly appreciate you. Linda Q, you are an amazing woman. Thank you for your support and encouragement, and for the many discussions on Latin culture. Brenda, for sharing Guatemala with me, Heather, for Castle Rock, and Penny for Breaux Bridge. And for my readers, for your patience.

Twelve Days of La Clairiere ...

1

Haiti, 1901

THE DAY THE youngest child chose to never speak again was just as unbearable as any other day. Standing before her open bedroom window, four-year-old Zuellie waited for *Papa Legba*, the guardian of crossroads, to grant the supernatural request. If not permitted to converse with the ancestors, she had a backup plan in mind. Paralysis…maybe that would evoke the attention of her deceased grandpapa's soul. Investigating the midnight sky, she marveled at how the fireflies below seemed to mimic the twinkling stars above.

"Shoo, hurry and carry my message," she whispered to the closest firefly. Its light dimmed, blending it into the shadowy night. If she did not receive an answer soon, next she would pray to *Erzulie Mansur*, protector of children. Perhaps she would gain more sympathy from him. With one ear she listened to the sea roaring in the far distance, and with the other, she listened for her sister's voice.

"Zuellie!" She heard a voice whisper from the dancing flicker of darkness.

Straining to hear, she pressed her tiny body against the bare windowsill, leaning far enough to see the front of her home one way and *Tante* Dorinda's backyard in the opposite direction. Her papa's elder brother, Uncle Leonide, sat with a tin can at his feet. Occasionally, he and the others would take a sip of the rum in their cups and spray the contents into the air. The drum player wore a straw hat and smoked on his pipe. Sitting cross-legged, he began to beat the skin of the drum. This was how her papa said the spirits, or *loas*, responded to their prayers. If the drummer kept playing his djembe drum, and her uncles continued to sip rum from their tin cans, *papa legba* would surely answer this night.

"Zuellie," the voice came closer.

She turned just as a firefly illuminated from out of the darkness and nearly touched the tip of her nose. Losing her grip on the windowsill, Zuellie fell against the wooden frame. She let out a small moan when her tummy hit the track that should have held a screen in place. After pulling herself back upright, she fell to the floor and kicked at the wall.

"Wait a minute," she said, before standing on her feet. "That must have been my sign."

She wiggled all of her stubby toes, then bent at the knees to see if they were still flexible. Zuellie pouted when her limbs continued to bend and move as normal. That is why she needed the *loas* help. If she had not learned to walk, losing her speech would be easier to explain away. But for a healthy four-year-old to suddenly stop talking for no reason would bring more outside attention than necessary. If her hand was not played carefully she could end up in the hospital, or worse, on the other side of the trail where her papa secretly ventured for remedies from the *mambo*. Zuellie needed time to revert or freeze so her family could stay together, just as they had before the walls in the front room grew wings and carried them off in different directions. Mostly what she needed was for her papa to look at her *manman* as he had done before.

"Baby Li, don't you hear me calling you?" Said Karlina. She stood before her sister with hands on her hips.

THANKS FOR READING!

Reviews are extremely important for Authors.

Please add your review on Amazon and/or Goodreads!

Don't forget to share your review on social media.

I truly appreciate your support!

Made in the USA
Las Vegas, NV
24 March 2022

46268782R00192